"*The Body Reader* earned its five stars, a rarity for me, even for books I like. Kudos to Anne Frasier."

—The Wyrdd and the Bazaar

"A must read for mystery suspense fans."

—Babbling About Books

"I've long been a fan of Anne Frasier, but this book elevates her work to a whole new level, in my mind."

—Tale of a Shooting Star

PRAISE FOR *PLAY DEAD*

"This is a truly creepy and thrilling book. Frasier's skill at exposing the dark emotions and motivations of individuals gives it a gripping edge."

—RT Book Reviews

"*Play Dead* is a compelling and memorable police procedural, made even better by the way the characters interact with one another. Anne Frasier will be appreciated by fans who like Kay Hooper, Iris Johansen and Lisa Gardner."

—Blether: The Book Review Site

"A nicely constructed combination of mystery and thriller. Frasier is a talented writer whose forte is probing into the psyches of her characters, and she produces a fast-paced novel with a finale containing many surprises."

—I Love a Mystery

"Has all the essentials of an edge-of-your-seat story. There is suspense, believable characters, an interesting setting, and just the right amount of details to keep the reader's eyes always moving forward ... I recommend *Play Dead* as a great addition to any mystery library."

—Roundtable Reviews

PRAISE FOR *PRETTY DEAD*

"Besides being beautifully written and tightly plotted, this book was that sort of great read you need on a regular basis to restore your faith in a genre."

—Lynn Viehl, Paperback Writer (Book of the Month)

"By far the best of the three books. I couldn't put my kindle down till I'd read every last page."

—NetGalley

PRAISE FOR *HUSH*

"This is by far and away the best serial killer story I've read in a long time ... strong characters, with a truly twisted bad guy."

—Jayne Ann Krentz

"I couldn't put it down. Engrossing ... scary ... I loved it."

—Linda Howard

"A deeply engrossing read, *Hush* delivers a creepy villain, a chilling plot, and two remarkable investigators whose personal struggles are only equaled by their compelling need to stop a madman before he kills again. Warning: don't read this book if you are home alone."

—Lisa Gardner

"A wealth of procedural detail, a heart-thumping finale, and two scarred but indelible protagonists make this a first-rate read."

—Publishers Weekly

"Anne Frasier has crafted a taut and suspenseful thriller."

—Kay Hooper

"Well-realized characters and taut, suspenseful plotting."

—Minneapolis Star Tribune

PRAISE FOR *SLEEP TIGHT*

"Guaranteed to keep you awake at night."

—Lisa Jackson

"There'll be no sleeping after reading this one. Laced with forensic detail and psychological twists."

—Andrea Kane

"Gripping and intense . . . Along with a fine plot, Frasier delivers her characters as whole people, each trying to cope in the face of violence and jealousies."

—Minneapolis Star Tribune

"Enthralling. There's a lot more to this clever intrigue than graphic police procedures. Indeed, one of Frasier's many strengths is her ability to create characters and relationships that are as compelling as the mystery itself. Will linger with the reader after the killer is caught."

—Publishers Weekly

PRAISE FOR *THE ORCHARD*

"Eerie and atmospheric, this is an indie movie in print. You'll read and read to see where it is going, although it's clear early on that the future is not going to be kind to anyone involved. Weir's story is more proof that only love can break your heart."

—*Library Journal*

"A gripping account of divided loyalties, the real cost of farming and the shattered people on the front lines. Not since Jane Smiley's *A Thousand Acres* has there been so enrapturing a family drama percolating out from the back forty."

—*Maclean's*

"This poignant memoir of love, labor, and dangerous pesticides reveals the terrible true price."

—*Oprah Magazine* (Fall Book Pick)

"Equal parts moving love story and environmental warning."

—*Entertainment Weekly* (B+)

"This is one of the loveliest books I have ever read, it reaches into the very heart of the word love and exemplifies its meaning with an unbelievable depth of understanding."

—Cover Me

"While reading this extraordinarily moving memoir, I kept remembering the last two lines of Muriel Rukeyser's poem 'Kathe Kollwitz' ('What would happen if one woman told the truth about her life? / The world would split open'), for Weir proffers a worldview that is at once eloquent, sincere, and searing."

—*Library Journal* (Librarians' Best Books of 2001)

"An unforgettable story . . . This story of hardship and suffering, and love and hope pretty much stole my heart."

—Rhapsody in Books

"She tells her story with grace, unflinching honesty and compassion all the while establishing a sense of place and time with a master story teller's perspective so engaging you forget it is a memoir."

—Calvin Crosby, Books Inc. (Berkeley, CA)

"One of my favorite reads of 2011, *The Orchard* is easily mistakable as a novel for its engaging, page-turning flow and its seemingly imaginative plot."

—Susan McBeth, founder and owner of Adventures by the Book, San Diego, CA

"Moving and surprising."

—The Next Chapter (Fall 2011 Top 20 Best Books)

"Searing . . . the past is artfully juxtaposed with the present in this finely wrought work. Its haunting passages will linger long after the last page is turned."

—*Boston Globe* (Pick of the Week)

"If a writing instructor wanted an excellent example of voice in a piece of writing, this would be a five-star choice!"

—*San Diego Union Tribune* (Recommended Read)

"The truths she lays bare about the life of a farm and the farmers who work it are both simple and, dare I say it, profound."

—Madison Public Library (Madison, WI)

"This book produced a string of emotions that had my hand flying up to my mouth time and again, and not only made me realize, 'This woman can write!' but also made me appreciate the importance of this book, and how it reaches far beyond Weir's own story."

—Linda Grana, Diesel, a Bookstore

"*The Orchard* is a lovely book in all the ways that really matter, one of those rare and wonderful memoirs in which people you've never met become your friends."

—Nicholas Sparks

"A hypnotic tale of place, people, and of Midwestern family roots that run deep, stubbornly hidden, and equally menacing."

—Jamie Ford, *New York Times* bestselling author of
Hotel on the Corner of Bitter and Sweet

THE BODY COUNTER

ALSO BY ANNE FRASIER

Hush
Sleep Tight
Before I Wake
Pale Immortal
Garden of Darkness

The Jude Fontaine Series

The Body Reader

The Elise Sandburg Series

Play Dead
Stay Dead
Pretty Dead
Truly Dead

Nonfiction (as Theresa Weir)

The Orchard: A Memoir
The Man Who Left

THE BODY
COUNTER

ANNE FRASIER

Text copyright © 2018 by Theresa Weir

Published by Thomas & Mercer, Seattle

www.apub.com

Amazon, the Amazon logo, and Thomas & Mercer are trademarks of Amazon.com, Inc., or its affiliates.

ISBN-13: 9781503900981
ISBN-10: 1503900983

Cover design by PEPE *nymi*

Printed in the United States of America

THE BODY COUNTER

CHAPTER 1

The woman in the apartment upstairs was screaming again.

These weren't your normal screams, if any scream could be considered normal. They weren't screams of sexual delight or screams of surprise. These were sounds of terror, pain, fear, so bloodcurdling that the first time Elliot heard them he'd called 911.

Cops had arrived with sirens and flashing lights and boots on the stairs. Shouts, then quiet conversation from above. Once it was over, an officer had knocked on Elliot's door. "Everything's fine," one of them had said.

"Is someone hurt?" Elliot had asked. Or worse: "Dead?"

"Just a bad dream."

Bad dream. That had been a helluva bad dream.

One of many, it seemed, because the screams became so frequent he started keeping a broom next to his bed. When the screaming started, he'd knock the wooden handle against the ceiling. The sounds of terror would stop and he'd go back to sleep.

The woman's name was Jude Fontaine, and she was a detective. Whenever Elliot ran into her in the lobby, she'd give him a slight smile and sometimes even say hello. But that hello didn't welcome more. That hello didn't welcome scrutiny or an invitation to stop by for coffee. In fact, Elliot couldn't imagine Detective Fontaine sitting at his kitchen counter eating cookies and talking about books or movies or music.

And yet . . .

Elliot understood some of what she was going through. Like everybody in Minneapolis and beyond, he knew her history. Knew about the three captive years of rape and torture, and her subsequent escape. If she'd seemed the least bit willing to talk, Elliot might have shared a little of his own unusual childhood. Instead, he watched the detective from a distance and wondered if she'd be okay, at the same time doubting she would.

Now, with resignation and a conditioned reaction, he reached for the broom and banged it against the ceiling. A couple minutes later he heard a ringing phone, followed by footsteps, a softly closing door, and the sound of someone in the stairwell. He drifted off, but was jolted awake again by the roar of a motorcycle exiting the parking garage.

Jude Fontaine had left the building.

CHAPTER 2

An hour earlier

The final credits rolled in the dark indie theater. Mitchell stood near the exit and moved his flashlight beam back and forth between the three remaining moviegoers, all men, who were spread evenly throughout the cavernous space, the narrow ray of light illuminating the backs of their heads. Mitchell's main job was to make sure people weren't kissing or even having sex during the screening, but he was also responsible for kicking out the ones who fell asleep. His mom called the place a dive, but the owner didn't have the money to fix it up.

He cleared his throat. "Show's over. Please exit the theater."

None of them responded.

He hated this part. He was barely old enough to drive, and here he was kicking out adults, often adults who were either too wasted to walk or so wasted they wanted to fight.

He gave his red usher vest a tug and moved down the aisle, clicking the flashlight to high and shining it in the face of the nearest guy. He was slumped forward, the front of his pale-green T-shirt soaked with something dark and red. Mitchell's heart pounded, then settled down. His initial alarm made him feel stupid. Performance art, right? Fake blood, right? There was some locally famous artist who was always doing that crazy shit. Mitchell didn't know much about the guy, because he seemed to like to create mystery about himself, but girls Mitchell's age were apparently really into him.

He redirected the beam across the width of the theater, shining it on the other two moviegoers. Unmoving, chins down.

Heavy sigh. "I don't want to call the cops," he told the man a couple of feet from him, "but I will. Come on, buddy." He shook the man's shoulder, easily at first, then harder. The jostling made the guy's head flip back like a Pez dispenser.

An ocean roared between Mitchell's ears, and his legs went weak. The man's throat had been sliced. He swore he could see arteries—and what looked like a spine. And now he realized he could actually smell blood.

The flashlight dropped from his hand and rolled slowly under the seats, the handle hitting chair legs every so often on the way down. Mitchell shouted over his shoulder, hoping the projectionist or the other usher would hear. "Turn on the overheads!"

Someone flipped the switch and the room went dull-bright, revealing the shabby seats and the concession cups littering the floor. The other usher must've heard Mitchell's shout, because he appeared in the back of the theater with a bored look on his face, candy bar in his hand.

The flashlight finally stopped rolling.

"Call the cops." Mitchell's voice was tight and weird, and an acidic taste filled his mouth. He'd call the cops himself but he was afraid he was going to throw up.

Not getting that this was serious, the coworker said, "Just make 'em leave."

Mitchell's eyes latched on to a popcorn bucket on the floor as he looked for comfort in the mundane. "They can't!"

The hysteria in his voice must have finally given the other usher a clue, because he pulled out his phone, suddenly sounding nervous. "What should I tell them?"

"Tell them three guys are dead!" Mitchell thought about all the people who'd trailed past him in the dark on their way out of the theater. One of them had done this. One of them had committed murder while the lights were off. Mitchell himself had maybe even torn the person's ticket. And then he wondered if *he* was in danger. The cops would ask if he'd noticed anybody suspicious and he'd say no, but the killer might think he could identify him.

While the coworker made the call, Mitchell grabbed the empty popcorn container from the floor and threw up in it. Then he took a photo of the nearest body.

CHAPTER 3

It was after midnight as Jude leaned low over the motorcycle, roaring down I-94 in the direction of the homicide. It wasn't like her to ride without a helmet, but she couldn't wear a full face mask tonight, not with the claustrophobia of her dream lingering in the corners of her brain. Strange to welcome murder, but she'd been relieved to hear Uriah's voice on the phone, telling her she was needed. Just minutes before her partner's call, the person in the apartment below had banged against his ceiling and Jude had come awake sweating, heart pounding. Over the past weeks, that same neighbor had made a few feeble attempts to strike up a conversation in the hallway, but Jude had effectively shut him down. What could she say? *Sorry my screams wake you?*

Two months had passed since the shoot-out on the interstate. Two months since Jude killed her estranged father and brother to save her partner and a kidnapping victim named Octavia. And even though there was solid proof of their guilt in several murders, including the murder of Jude's own mother, many in the area refused to believe that the governor—Jude's father—had been behind such atrocities. After all, the man had posed for photos with their babies and comforted them in times of personal tragedy.

The governor's death had polarized the state, turning Jude into a hero or villain, depending on one's perspective. She'd seen the negative press about her, and she would've liked to say it didn't bother her, but that would be a lie. It was hard enough to take a life, but to take the lives of people you'd grown up with, at one time even loved? No matter that she'd saved lives in the process.

The department psychologist had suggested she take a year off, but a year off would mean a year of looking at herself more closely than she wanted to. Instead, she'd stayed in Homicide, dutifully gone to therapy, and privately obsessed over certain things in ways that might be considered unhealthy. Along with that, she carried an emptiness inside that had nothing to do with the loss of her old self. That would make too much sense.

Minnehaha Creek Theater was located in Longfellow, a Minneapolis neighborhood of small bungalows built in the thirties, now occupied by singles or young couples. It was an area of town Jude had visited a few times, but not recently, not in this new rendition of herself.

Arriving at the theater, she adjusted her bike on its stand and strode down the sidewalk, past flashing emergency vehicles, a coroner van, and police cars. At the intersection near the theater, she glanced up, reassured by a surveillance camera. Hopefully they'd have footage. The marquee advertised two action movies from several years back.

A young cop stood near the entrance, positioned to keep out the uninvited. He gave her a nod of recognition as the scent of popcorn, along with a sense of horror, wafted through the open door. "Screening room two."

"Who was the first responder?" Jude asked.

"Not sure, but one of the ushers discovered the bodies after the show ended."

A member of the crime-scene team squeezed past them, a processing kit in her hand. Jude thanked the officer at the door and stepped into the controlled chaos of the lobby.

Cops with tablets and pens took statements from young people in red vests. With a surreptitious glance, Jude read their stances and expressions, noting whether anyone was sweating or fidgeting—all signs of possible involvement or guilt. She spotted no tells.

As she cut through the throng, she checked high along walls and ceiling, looking for security cameras, seeing none. Plastic numbered cards trailed down the center of the red-carpeted hallway, marking a path of dark smudges leading from screening room two. Blood tracked by shoes. It could have been picked up by anybody exiting the theater. Regardless, she crouched and examined the prints, snapping photos with her camera.

Just inside the heavy door, Jude stepped back to give herself a few minutes to take in the scene. The theater needed a serious update. Paint was peeling, and some of the red-velvet seats were tilted at odd angles and worn bare in places. Like most small businesses in Minneapolis, the movie house was struggling, more so in the aftermath of the blackouts and fires that had brought higher crime and vandalism to an already-volatile city. The blackouts were over, but the violence spurred by the darkness still lingered. Some of their best cops had transferred out, consigning the force to a high percentage of newbies, the nervous, and the inexperienced.

Yellow tape had been strung around three areas of the screening room. Unusual to use tape inside, but the layout presented a unique problem and the scene had to be contained. Three clusters of crime-scene personnel. From her location, she couldn't see a body.

Her partner and head homicide detective Uriah Ashby spotted her and crossed the theater. He'd thrown himself together, the goal to reach the scene as quickly as possible, not dress for success. Like her, he wore jeans, the differences being his black hoodie and her leather jacket. His curly brown hair was a mess, his expression alert, considering the hour and his love of sleep.

Homicides woke you up fast, but even this new horror wasn't enough to chase away the dark mood of Jude's dream. She never remembered the nightmare, yet she couldn't shake the cloud of ineffable sorrow and fear it left in her heart, along with a despair that made this scene, this killing, feel less real than that place in her mind she couldn't even remember.

With a jerk of his head, Uriah motioned for Jude to join him in a private corner, away from the nearest people. As she passed them, she saw Caroline McIntosh among the detectives. The woman's obvious attraction to Uriah, not to mention her penchant for inappropriate comments, was a source of amusement in the department. Jude had once tried to advise her against being so transparent, but that hadn't gone over well.

"Not everybody wants to be an unemotional robot," Detective McIntosh had said. Jude now kept her distance.

"Sliced throats." Uriah's whispered words were delivered with grim expectation.

That was interesting—it was an MO they'd seen before, and recently. "Witnesses?"

"Not yet."

Three dead bodies, evenly spaced, no witnesses. It seemed like an impossible feat to pull off. And the sliced throats . . . Everybody in the room was probably thinking about the two murders barely three weeks old, unsolved, each involving a victim whose throat had been sliced—one of the slayings having taken place in a restroom, another in a city park. Something like that was especially hard to get away with today because of numerous security cameras throughout the city. These weren't crimes of passion. They'd taken planning.

"It feels like another possible thrill kill to me," Uriah said.

She nodded. And killings of strangers were the hardest to solve.

"The seats and slanted floor are making it hard to process the scene," he added. "Too many people, too little space, so we're rotating in and out. We can get a good look at the bodies once the crime-scene team has done a preliminary."

"Victims?"

"All male." The earlier victims had been too, but that didn't necessarily mean anything.

"IDs?"

He rattled off names that at this point meant nothing. "One has a DUI on his record, one a few parking tickets. From here, it seems they were pretty average citizens."

Anybody could look average on paper. "We'll have to dig a little deeper, see if they might have known one another." Unlikely, though.

Uriah pointed out the first responder and Jude excused herself to talk to her. "No witnesses?" she asked for the second time.

The cop rested her hand on her belt and shook her head.

"In a theater full of people, nobody saw the murders or even noticed these guys were dead?"

"It wasn't a full house."

Someone sitting alone, near the center of a row, might go unnoticed if no one had to step past or around him. "Has a weapon been found?"

"We have people checking trash containers and canvassing inside and out, but nothing yet."

"What about the usher who discovered the bodies?"

"He's pretty shaken up and didn't give me much information. I was hoping you could get more out of him. Tall, skinny, red hair, name is Mitchell Davidson. Last time I saw him he was in the lobby."

That was where Jude found him.

The poor kid was a mess. Face was pale, eyes bloodshot, and he gave off a suspicious whiff of vomit as he clutched a popcorn bucket to his chest.

"Mitchell Davidson?" Jude asked, even though she knew this was her guy. Upon closer inspection, she noted he was sweating profusely. She knew an oncoming faint when she saw one. She urged him into a chair and he dropped like his legs had been kicked out from under him.

"Down." She removed the bucket from his hands and gave the back of his head a gentle shove forward. "Between your knees."

While he recovered, she slipped behind the concession stand and grabbed a bottle of water from the small glass-doored refrigerator. She doubted the theater owner would care, all things considered. Back at Mitchell's side, she uncapped the bottle and offered it to him, helping him sit up straight again. "Small sips." While he nursed the water, she pulled a chair near and sat quietly beside him. When his color began to look a little better, she started asking questions.

He told her about the moment he realized the man in the theater was really dead. "I've never seen a dead body before." He glanced at her but didn't hold eye contact. "You're probably used to it."

"You never get used to it," she told him.

She got to what she really wanted to know, and what she wanted him to try to remember before his evening had been overrun by the horror of the past hour. "Did you see anybody suspicious? Somebody who gave you a feeling you couldn't explain? That can happen. People call it a sixth sense, but I just think it's a throwback to survival instinct. Anybody and everybody has it, if they pay attention."

She knew about survival instinct. Surviving had fine-tuned her senses when it came to reading other people. But lately, especially after a dream-filled night, she caught herself trying to dull those senses.

"That's half the people in here," Mitchell said, "especially at a late-night screening. I mean, my job is to make sure people aren't making out or . . . you know." He squirmed.

"Masturbating?"

Faint color rushed back to his face. "I don't get it. It's not like we show porn, but they do it anyway."

"I think it's something to do with being in a public space," she told him. "With people nearby. The risk and thrill of possibly getting caught. The rush."

"They should jaywalk instead."

She smiled slightly, appreciating his attempt at humor, then got back to the questions. "Did you see anybody who raised any suspicion above and beyond your normal red flags?"

He considered for a moment before shaking his head. "I don't think so."

"Maybe something will come to you later." She said that while wondering if *he* could possibly have committed the crimes. This boy, this hardly-more-than-a-child, appeared innocent, but sociopaths were difficult and often impossible to read because they didn't have the tells people with a conscience revealed.

"I doubt it, but I'll try."

"Don't force it." That could result in false memories. "You're going to have to go downtown so we can take your statement officially. An officer will give you a ride."

"Am I a suspect?" He didn't seem alarmed. Shock did that. People never reacted in the way regular citizens expected them to; often odd and unconcerned behavior was mistaken for guilt.

"It's standard procedure to officially document an interview," she explained.

"Who'll do it? You?"

"I can, but if you'd rather have someone else, a male detective, that's fine."

"I'd like it to be you." He looked down, flustered and a little embarrassed by his next words. "I know who you are. That was some pretty badass stuff you did in the middle of the highway. It was like a movie. I saw it on the news." He zeroed in on the part of the story he could most relate to. "Rescuing that girl and all."

It was hard for Jude to go unnoticed in Minneapolis. Her short white hair stood out, but she refused to dye it. She'd fought too hard to get back to this world. She wasn't going to pretend she was someone else now that she was here.

"Do you think I'm in danger?" Mitchell asked.

She could break it down for him. Tell him there was a small risk, but that wasn't the answer he was looking for. Some people wanted the truth and some people wanted lies. She wasn't willing to lie for him, but she softened her reply. "I doubt it, but it wouldn't hurt to keep your eyes open." She reached inside her leather jacket. With two fingers, she pulled out a business card and handed it to him. "If you see anything suspicious, call my cell, day or night."

That at least gave him some of the reassurance he was looking for.

A minute later she introduced him to the officer who'd take him downtown, and then she returned to the heart of the theater. The clusters around the bodies had shrunk and she approached, ready to take her turn. Crime-scene techs from the BCA—the Bureau of Criminal Apprehension—moved aside so Uriah, Jude, and Caroline McIntosh could examine the first body while Medical Examiner Ingrid Stevenson waited, arms crossed.

Male. Probably in his late thirties.

Jude leaned closer, and someone handed her a flashlight so she could get a better visual in the less than adequate theater lighting. She clicked it on and passed the beam across the man's face. Leathery, suntanned skin. Hands that were also dark and weathered. Construction worker, possibly. Worn jeans and severely scuffed boots backed up that theory. It wasn't until she was done getting a sense of the man that she brought the beam to his neck to scrutinize the gaping wound.

"That took some serious strength," Uriah said.

"Or possibly serious adrenaline." She'd recently met a repeat burglar whose MO was to climb a rope to escape the buildings he was robbing, but he couldn't climb one under any other conditions.

Adrenaline was powerful.

"Weapon?" Jude asked Ingrid.

The woman was brusque, about fifty, one of those Minnesota Swedish blonds who were a real thing. She was also one of the state's best medical examiners. "I'll be able to tell you more once I do the autopsies." Ingrid didn't care to speculate, especially on-scene.

Jude clicked off the flashlight, handed it to Uriah, and stepped back.

"Hey, got something for you," McIntosh said. She produced a heavy sheet of paper, unfolded it, and passed it over. Jude expected something to do with the crime, but no.

The already-slanted floor shifted more, and she braced her legs as she stared at the auction flyer in her hand. A picture of a house. Just a house. Just bricks and stucco and broken glass. And inside would be a basement. The basement where she'd been kept for three years.

"What the hell, McIntosh?" Uriah asked angrily.

With a stiff and jerky movement, Jude pulled her gaze from the sheet of paper to take vague note of her partner's glare.

Color bloomed in McIntosh's face, but she managed a nonchalant shrug. "Just thought she should know." She'd obviously been carrying the flyer around, waiting for an opportune moment to deliver it. This was not opportune; this seemed like a moment specifically designed to get back at Jude and humiliate her in front of her colleagues.

Uriah wasn't falling for the woman's innocent act. "I don't know what you're up to, but stop it."

"It's no secret." McIntosh lifted her chin, defensive. "Everybody's wondering who would even buy it."

One of the cops chimed in. "I could see someone exploiting it. Like making it a house of horrors or something."

"We should bid on it and burn it down," another cop said.

Someone let out a faint murmur at the inappropriate conversation. Others nodded. Mesmerized, Jude went back to staring at the flyer in her hand.

Ingrid straightened and snapped off her gloves. "Could we have a little more professionalism here?"

"Just making conversation," McIntosh said. "It helps sometimes."

"The only thing you should be talking about is the crime," Uriah said. "*This* crime."

Jude pulled her gaze from the photo again. McIntosh looked near tears. Reprimanded by both the ME and Uriah. At a crime scene.

"It's okay," Jude said, trying to soften McIntosh's public flogging because she didn't like seeing anybody in pain. "I'm glad to get the information."

She folded the paper and tucked it inside her leather jacket. Once the image was stashed close to her skin, she could feel its vibration and promise. Truth was, she already knew about the upcoming sale. And she had plans of her own.

CHAPTER 4

"Could you please, for the record, state your name and address?" Jude sat across from Mitchell Davidson at a small desk in one of the interrogation rooms of the Minneapolis Police Department. The ceiling camera's green light was on, along with the digital recorder Jude had placed on the table between them.

Eight hours had passed since the call to 911 had come in, and neither Jude nor Uriah had slept. The murder victims were scheduled for autopsy. Video footage from surveillance cameras had been uploaded to the department's virtual private network. Mitchell was still nervous, but most people sitting in his seat typically were. Like when a cop stopped you even though you were doing nothing wrong. Most people got flustered. And the ones who didn't often had something to hide.

He gave her his name and address. "I live with my parents." Then he answered her question about his typical day with "I'm in high school." That pretty much said it all.

"Can you tell me what happened in the early-morning hours of September fifteenth?"

With halting words, he explained it all again. About how he'd walked down the aisle to tell the person to leave. How he shook the guy's shoulder and saw his head flip back. The lights were turned on and 911 was called.

She dug deeper.

"What about before the movie started? What was that like?"

Nothing to add. He tried, but she didn't want him making things up just to have a response.

"You took tickets." It might be better to focus on small things. "Did anything or anybody make you feel uneasy? A feeling. A face. An expression. Hands. Calloused hands, soft hands. Odors you might recall?"

He squirmed. "I don't usually make eye contact when I'm taking tickets. I just don't." He didn't look up. "People call me shy, but I don't know if that's right. I'm just not that social. And I'm focusing on the next hand and the next ticket, not the face or person."

"Sometimes shy people are the most observant."

"Like you?"

She smiled. "I don't think I'm shy either. I'm just . . . reserved." She got to her feet. "I'm going to grab some water. Would you like something? Soda? Coffee?"

"Coke."

She deliberately gave him time alone to reflect without the distraction of her presence. A few minutes later, she returned with a can of soda and slid it across the desk. She removed the cap on her water bottle.

He popped the metal top and took a swig, swallowed, made eye contact, then broke away. "While you were gone, I was thinking and I remembered something."

She nodded, not in an intense or excited way, just casually. The kind of nod you might give a friend who was bitching about the weather.

"I remember this girl . . . She was pretty. Long blond hair. About my age. And she smelled good. Like cookies or something."

That surprised yet didn't surprise her. "A boy's going to notice a pretty girl."

His pale cheeks grew pink.

"Why did you notice her? Was she acting odd? Nervous? Did her hands shake when you tore her ticket? Was her breathing noticeable?"

"She was alone."

"Alone?"

"You ever hear of a teenage girl going to a movie by herself? Girls can't even go to the bathroom alone."

"That's an astute observation."

"I shouldn't have said anything about her." He took another drink of soda. "I don't want to get her in trouble. A girl wouldn't do something like that."

She didn't bother to remind him of the females involved in the brutal 1969 Tate-LaBianca murders. He was way too young to be familiar with those anyway.

"How do you know she was alone?"

"She wasn't talking to anybody, and when she walked down the hall she was by herself."

"So you do look at some people."

"I guess." He shifted in his seat and jammed his hands between his thighs. "I didn't mean to lie." Nervous again.

"I know," she said, settling deeper into her chair and considering her next words. "I'm telling you this in confidence, so please don't mention it outside this room." It was good to let him know she was trusting him with pertinent information about the case. "There might have been more than one perpetrator. If so, those people might or might not have gone in together. If they went in together, they most likely split up."

She opened her laptop and logged on to the VPN, then pulled her chair around and sat next to him so they could both see the screen as she clicked keys and started the video feed of people entering the theater.

Unfortunately, the sidewalk was dark. Broken bulbs weren't a priority in the city, and it was entirely possible they'd been replaced and rebroken. Maybe even more than once, because vandals had decided they liked it dark. The department's audio-visual specialist was trying to lighten up the footage, but Jude didn't feel very hopeful. On top of it being dark, the night had been cold and windy. People were wearing knit caps, heads bent, faces down, in a signature Minnesota pose developed from years of living in a cold climate.

Mitchell had nothing more to add, so Jude told him she'd be in touch. "You have my card and phone number. Call if you think of anything else."

Her next witness was another usher. He lacked any kind of observational skills, and the interview was over in a couple of minutes. That was followed by the projectionist. Neither was able to add anything of significance.

She got a text from Uriah.

Meet me upstairs. Ortega wants to talk to us before we head to the morgue.

CHAPTER 5

I know death when I see it," Uriah said five minutes later when Jude caught up with him in Homicide. "There's no sign of life there. I'm sorry."

She stared at the limp Chinese evergreen on her desk. She'd had such high hopes for it. In some weird way, it represented more than a plant. It represented her ability to nurture something, anything, and keep it alive.

The Homicide Department amounted to a scattering of desks throughout a massive room on the third floor of the Minneapolis Police Department. Open, no cubicles. On a sunny day, light poured in from a row of windows overlooking the city street below. If a person had a green thumb, plants could do well. A couple of officers even grew herbs alongside the typical array of framed photos. Jude didn't have any framed photos, but she'd been into the idea of a plant.

"Maybe it needs more light," she mused. She'd chosen this particular plant because the woman at the nursery told her it was unkillable. Jude had liked the sound of that. Unkillable.

"It has plenty of light," Uriah said. "It's the water. You've watered it almost every day."

Eyes still on the drooping plant, Jude said, "I think it's alive."

"It's dead." He emphasized *dead* as if the word should have been in all caps.

She opened her water bottle and poured a third of the contents on the plant, resaturating the soil and roots.

"That's what I'm talking about," Uriah said. "Over–cared for. Killed with kindness. I grew up in farm country, and I know what yellow leaves mean. Too much water."

She was overreacting, and she knew she was projecting. She must have looked upset, because Uriah continued to reassure her. "You can get another plant. And you can kill that one too. And when that happens, you can try again with another one. The nursery will love you."

"I don't want another plant," Jude said. "I want *this* plant."

"Sorry. Just trying to help." Uriah was getting better at reading her. Or maybe she was losing some of the blank expression she'd worked hard to perfect in captivity. During that time, it hadn't taken long to learn that a lack of response or visible reaction often resulted in being left alone. Torture was no fun if the victim didn't react.

"You've done okay with your cat, and that's more important than a plant."

"He's not my cat." Uriah was right, but she didn't want anything to die, not even a plant. She was tired of death.

They heard knuckles rapping on glass and looked up to see Chief Ortega motioning them into her office. There was something that made Jude uneasy about a room separated from everyone else by a wall of glass. It felt more like a stage. She would hate to work in there.

Inside the glass fishbowl, Jude and Uriah briefed the chief on the case. "I just officially interviewed the main witness," Jude told her. "A kid named Mitchell Davidson. So far he hasn't provided us with much information."

"What about cameras?" Rather than taking a seat, Chief Ortega perched on one corner of her desk and swung a long leg. She was a beautiful woman with shiny dark hair and a different shade of lipstick every day. Today it was pink, yesterday red. Too pretty for the job, some might have said. There were whispers (which she'd surely heard) that she ought to dress more professionally, but she ignored them. Jude had always admired that about her and tried to emulate it in her own reactions to public opinion.

"We've gone through footage a few times," Uriah said. "But the crowd made it easy for the perpetrator to hide in plain sight, and heavy coats and hats made it easier for any blood to go unnoticed."

"Doesn't take a specialist to know these probably aren't drug deals gone bad or revenge killings," Ortega said. "Randomly deliberate is what I'm calling them. I'm hoping they're not connected to the previous slashings, but if they are, we've got something big on our hands." She crossed her arms, her expression so worried that anybody beyond the glass would be able to see it. Not her typical behavior, positive no matter the situation. Even given the severity of what they were dealing with, she seemed unusually agitated.

"We've checked all the databases, including CISA and CODIS, looking for similar MOs over the past few years," Jude told her. "Nothing."

"One of the victims from last night's killing was a friend of a friend," Chief Ortega admitted, sharing his name and exposing the reason for her out-of-character behavior. "Nice guy. Recently divorced, having a hard time of it."

The death of an acquaintance had a way of changing everything. The separation of work and home had been breached, at least a little. For someone with children and a husband, having that false sense of safety violated would have to be especially unsettling.

Jude understood that love and fear went hand in hand; she'd witnessed that combination of emotions in the faces of parents who'd lost their children. And now she sensed that same fear in Chief Ortega. Just a shadow of it. Just a hint. Just a sprinkle, a bit of flavor. But it was there, working its way into the woman's subconscious.

"We'll keep you in the loop," Uriah said.

"I want to be more than in the loop," the chief said. "I want to be immediately informed of any new development. Send me a text, give me a call, but stay connected." She slid off her desk, a sure sign the conversation was winding down. "I want you both to live and breathe this case and the previous ones until they're solved. I know that goes against my philosophy of maintaining our sanity in this job, but this is going to require more from everyone."

"We've got an event tonight," Uriah reminded her.

"Cancel it."

"We can't," Jude said. "Crisis Center fund-raiser." This was the second one of three, the hope being to raise enough cash to bring the crisis hotline back after a budget cut had ended the program. The third and final fund-raiser would involve a live interview with Uriah, who the center considered to have star power because he'd lost his wife to suicide. The program's main focus was suicide prevention, and with Uriah as its poster child, its organizers hoped sympathetic viewers would open their wallets. To put even more pressure on him, Uriah had agreed to spend the interview talking about his own loss. It wouldn't be easy.

"I understand," Chief Ortega said. Suicide prevention wasn't some-thing any of them took lightly. "Of course you have to go."

Poor Uriah. Manning a phone at the telethon had been hard on him the first time. The truth was, he was probably the one who needed a hotline. Survivors needed support too.

As the partners turned to leave, Uriah checked his watch, probably calculating how many hours he had left before tonight's event.

"I plan to view it from home," Ortega said with sympathy. "And I plan to donate. It's a good cause." As an afterthought, she said, "Don't forget the yoga class."

Uriah and Jude screeched to a halt.

"I'm not a yoga person," Jude said.

"You just said to live and breathe these homicides," Uriah reminded the chief.

"Didn't you get my email?" Ortega asked. "It will take very little of your time, and it could help with the investigation. Relax your mind in order to tap into your subconscious."

Ortega had recently attended a mental-health conference, and she was now pushing activities Jude would just as soon avoid.

"Ever since the blackouts and riots, we've had more PTSD and compassion fatigue within the department," Ortega was saying. "And we've lost good men and women to smaller, safer towns. We've got officers making poor decisions under stress. I'm trying to find a way to remedy that."

Jude didn't like the way she was looking at her.

"It's just a few times a month, that's all. I'm hoping officers will even be able to use calming techniques in the field."

Most detectives would envy having a chief who insisted her detectives have a home life and not live for their jobs. It was different for Jude. She had no one at home, and that was fine and that was good. It made things easier, made her job easier. The same could be said for Uriah. They were both loners. But sometimes Jude looked at Ortega's life—a husband, two tolerable children, and two charming Labs—and she wondered if anything like that could exist for her.

"Can you really make us do this?" Jude asked. That seemed like a misuse of power.

Ortega rolled her eyes and didn't try to hide her annoyance. "No, and I have little influence beyond Homicide, but I hope you'll participate." Her face softened. "If you both attend, officers from every department will be less likely to balk. And the mental health of everybody here is something we need to make a priority."

Uriah nodded. "I'll give it a shot, but it won't be pretty."

As far as Jude knew, Uriah spent most of his spare time visiting antiquarian-book sales and listening to obscure music. She wasn't sure if he *exercised* exercised, but his downtown apartment building was one of the tallest in the city, and she knew he rarely took the elevator, always challenging himself to beat his previous record. He'd even announce it upon arrival in the office, as if the typical time it might take someone to scale sixteen flights of stairs was common knowledge. His current time was two minutes and nineteen seconds. He wanted to shave it to an even two.

Jude's and Uriah's phones buzzed simultaneously. They pulled them out and checked their screens: summoned to the office of the Hennepin County Medical Examiner.

CHAPTER 6

At the ME's office on Chicago Avenue, they followed Ingrid Stevenson into an autopsy suite. The medical examiner was known for her efficiency, so it was no surprise to see that the three bodies from the theater had already been autopsied, although they were still taking up residence on separate workstations under large round lights. Jude and Uriah didn't attend every autopsy, but it wasn't unusual for Ingrid to call them down to her world to share her findings. She was pragmatic, didn't overanalyze, but was excellent when it came to detecting things some people might miss.

"I know there's a lot of speculation about these murders possibly being connected to the two previous ones," she said, "but I've noted a discrepancy."

As Ingrid spoke, Jude moved among the stainless-steel gurneys, giving Ingrid's assistant a nod as he stepped aside to offer full access to the nearest body. She challenged herself to find the clues before Ingrid launched into an explanation of her discovery.

All three victims' expressions hinted at the surprise and horror sometimes seen in the faces of the dead. Uriah and Ingrid might not have picked up on it, but Jude could see the suggestion of a reaction, a moment of awareness before death. Oddly enough, that reflection of surprise and horror was often mixed with embarrassment. *This is how I'm dying. This is the humiliation of my end.* The expression of knowing you were suddenly and unwillingly involved in an odd and ritualistic act of public mortification, yet could do nothing about it as your blood drained and major arteries went flat.

It would not have been a silent death, but the sound systems in movie theaters could be deafening. If all three kills happened during moments when chaos on the screen occupied all eyes, even the eyes of the almost dead, then the gasps and gurgles of the victims would have been drowned out by the other noise.

"An action-adventure was showing," Jude said. "Explosions, gun-fire, special effects—no shortage of scenes that would have been loud." And even the type of movie felt like part of the finely tuned murder scene. "Did the killer or killers watch the movie at home first to figure out the optimum time to kill? When the noise was the loudest and longest?"

She moved from one body to the next, leaning close, then finally glanced up, first at Uriah, then at Ingrid, thinking she'd spotted the discrepancy the ME was talking about. "The wounds aren't quite the same. One is shallower."

Ingrid looked pleased. "I suspect the differences we're seeing are due to a variation in the strength of the perpetrators." She nodded to the body in front of her. "But even though the wounds aren't the same, I'd say they were produced by similar knives."

She walked to her laptop. With a few key clicks, she pulled up the autopsy reports on a large monitor, complete with images of the two previous victims. "As you can see, these bodies have similar wounds." She drew small circles with the mouse. "Visually they all look very much alike, and measurements of depth and length are similar. Accomplished with an extremely sharp blade, maybe a hunting knife, carried out from behind by a right-handed person. Left hand is placed on the victim's forehead, neck exposed. But while it's true the body with the shallower cut reveals evidence of a weaker individual, that particular slice is also

from a left-handed person. Throats sliced from behind always begin
with a deep cut, then taper off."

"Female?" Jude asked, wondering about the girl Mitchell Davidson
had mentioned.

"Possibly, but not necessarily. Could be hesitation, although I don't
see any signs of struggle. More than one slice to the throat would be
indicative of struggle."

Standing behind her, looking at the screen, Uriah said, "So that
pretty much confirms our theory of more than one killer."

"You've got at least two perpetrators," Ingrid said.

Jude looked up. "And possibly three."

Uriah untied his gown. "We need to check out local shops. See if
anybody is buying duplicate knives, especially hunting knives."

"They could be making those purchases online," Jude said. "That's
what I'd do." But smart criminals could be surprisingly stupid. Many
were caught due to things like rope fibers and other items purchased
nearby and used for their kill.

"Possibly," Uriah said. "I'm going to call the chief and update her.
She'll want to schedule a press conference soon. We all know how cru-
cial the first forty-eight hours are."

"Do you think it's wise to go public with this?" Ingrid asked. "It
could set off a panic."

"I agree we need to get this information out as quickly as possible,"
Jude said. "We'll keep some details to ourselves, like the left-handed
kill." A press conference was the most direct way to reach the public. Community members with pertinent information often played an
essential role in the capture of criminals.

Uriah pulled out his phone. "And there's a good chance people are
already in a panic." He scrolled, then turned the screen around to reveal
a close-up of a theater victim. Jude winced. It was the chief's friend of
a friend. Someone, possibly Mitchell, had posted the photo to social
media.

CHAPTER 7

"Got a caller who specifically requested you." The young man pushed a cream-colored desk phone toward Jude while other operators conversed with pledge-drive supporters. The press conference had gone smoothly, and the tip-line number would be scrolling across the bottoms of television screens during every newscast. Jude and Uriah were now at the Twin Cities Public Television station on Fourth Street in downtown Saint Paul, working telethon lines.

With his phone to his ear, Uriah shot Jude a look of curiosity, his expression a nice break from the pained one that had made her wonder how much longer he was going to last. On the light-rail ride from Minneapolis, it hadn't been hard to see that Uriah had been on the verge of a meltdown. As shops on University Avenue flashed past their window, she'd tried to talk him out of working the phone bank again. "You've done enough." But he'd insisted. Tonight they were selling gala tickets for one hundred dollars a plate, the event to be held the same night as Uriah's upcoming on-air interview. This fund-raiser was important.

"I'm committed to seeing this through," he'd said.

But now, thirty minutes later, she noted the strain on his face and the stiffness of his shoulders. And there was no way to miss those surreptitious glances at the clock on the wall, the raised eyebrow of surprise at the slow passage of time, the wondering if he'd been there long enough to excuse himself. To maybe go to the restroom and never come back. That's what she'd do. It was hard not to feel Uriah was being exploited, and that he'd been guilted into doing something mentally unhealthy. As far as she knew, he didn't drink himself into oblivion anymore, but this could be a trigger.

Ever since her abduction, she'd had enough of reporters in her face. She normally went out of her way to avoid them except for the required press conferences, but she'd agreed to answer phones so she could keep an eye on Uriah. If things got too bad, she'd force him to leave while politely making some excuse. They were detectives. They always had a reason to be elsewhere.

Standing up, Jude inched past volunteers to swap seats with the young man who'd told her about the personal request. A dozen humans packed into a tiny room almost had *her* running. It wasn't just her ability to read people that had become more acute in her basement prison, where she'd learned to decipher every nuance of her captor's face and body; her sense of smell still hadn't adjusted to the onslaught of odors in the world. The alchemy of shampoos and deodorants, lotions and hair products, combined with the odor of tech equipment and the buzz and flickering of the overhead lights, was unnerving. Homicide detectives sometimes had to wash the stench of death out of their hair and clothing. Her return home would require the same kind of purging.

She sat down in the vacated chair and picked up the receiver, trying to ignore the strong smell of coffee from the cup the young man had forgotten. She answered with the prepped response they'd all been given. "Crisis Center telethon. Thanks in advance for your generous donation."

At first it seemed the caller might have hung up or been accidently disconnected, but finally someone spoke. A girl who sounded like she could be anywhere from fourteen to eighteen, speaking in a breathy, nervous whisper. "Are you Jude Fontaine?"

Just those few hesitant words told Jude this wasn't a donation call. She pressed the receiver closer to her ear. "Yes. Who's this?"

"My name's Clementine. At least, that's what people call me today."

So, not her birth name. Jude understood the desire to revamp your name and life and become someone else. "What can I do for you, Clementine? Why did you want to speak with me?"

"I thought you might understand."

This was not a suicide hotline. Few in the room had been trained to handle a crisis call, but Jude quickly assessed the situation, mentally logging it as a possible plea for help. "I think maybe you should talk to a specialist," she told the girl. "Someone more qualified."

"I want to talk to you."

Jude fell back on training she'd received years ago. "Are you thinking of harming yourself?"

Heads in the room swiveled. Jude adjusted her hips in the plastic chair, turning her back to the camera, elbow on the table and arm shielding her face.

"Not right now, but I think about it," the girl said. "Sometimes. And I was flipping through channels and saw you. I thought you might understand."

"Have you been abused? Is someone harming you?"

The girl hesitated before saying, "He makes me do things I don't like."

Jude fumbled for a pen. "Why don't you give me your phone number in case we get cut off."

"No!"

"Is he in the room with you?"

The voice dropped. "Yeah." A pause, then louder and with indifference she said, "We want a large pineapple and mushroom pizza."

"Smart," Jude said. Pretending to order pizza. "Why don't I give you my cell number so you can call me when he's not around. Pretend you're writing down an order number."

"Okay."

Jude shared her number and heard the scratch of a pen across paper.

"Tell me where you are," Jude said. "I can come for you. Just me. Nobody else."

"No, thanks. All I need is the pizza."

"Also, please consider calling the national crisis hotline. They can help."

The girl's voice faded as she spoke to someone in the room. "I'm just ordering pizza." She hung up.

The telethon room came back into focus. The ringing phones. The drone of scripted conversations. The odors. The face of a concerned Uriah from the other end of the table. Jude stood up, told the young man thanks, and moved back to her seat.

"What was that about?" Uriah asked.

"I'm not quite sure." She related what the girl had said.

His eyes lost focus and she knew he was thinking of his young wife, who, as far as they knew, had never reached out for help before her death. "Maybe you'll hear from her again," he managed to say.

"You should leave," Jude said, noting the tension in his face. "We'll be fine here without you."

He nodded. "Meet me in the bar around the corner when you're done and we can ride back to Minneapolis together."

Relieved that he was getting away from the source of his anxiety, she nonetheless gave him a distracted nod, her thoughts still on the girl named Clementine.

CHAPTER 8

Sitting cross-legged, Clementine watched Jude Fontaine on the motel-room television screen. She was talking to a good-looking guy in a suit and tie. He was a detective too. Uriah Ashby was his name. He was watching Fontaine with concern.

"How was that?" Clementine asked the man standing beside her. "Was it what you wanted?"

"That was great, babe." Leo settled himself on his knees behind her, the bed dipping.

"I'm surprised she believed me, but I think she did. Pretty sure she did."

"That's because *you* believed what you were saying. Right? Like I told you. That's how you fool people. Even someone like Fontaine can be fooled if you believe. People pass lie-detector tests because they believe their own lies."

He wouldn't tell Clementine how old he was. Older than her by several years. Wavy, shoulder-length hair that was almost black. He might have been thirty. Or fifty. Hands with long fingers that were strong when he used them to cut a throat or hurt her when she was bad. She'd never been invited to his apartment, but she'd imagined herself there, cooking his meals and doing his laundry. Maybe they'd have a cat or a dog. Or a snake. She'd stood on the street, trying to see him through the window, but he was never more than a shadow behind a curtain.

"We can't be seen together," he'd explained.

It made sense, but she wanted to be a bigger part of his life.

What he'd said about her being convincing was true. When she was talking to the detective, she'd felt her own fragility. And yes, it was probably true that a part of her wondered if things would be better if she'd never met Leo, but being without him was unthinkable now. He understood what it meant to be alive, and he understood *her*. He'd *chosen* her.

"Life is performance art," he always liked to tell her.

"Are we going out tonight?" she asked now, half hopefully, half with dread.

"We have to practice." He smoothed her hair, leaned close, inhaled the way he had the first time they'd met, in the shelter, where he'd come to teach a class. He'd rescued her and her boyfriend, along with some other homeless people, brought them to a motel, bought them clean clothes, fed them. Their savior. It hadn't taken long for Clementine to become his favorite, so much his favorite that he sometimes invited her to motel rooms to spend time alone with him. Tonight they'd turned on the TV to the telethon, and there was Jude Fontaine. She wondered if it had been his plan all along. For Clementine to call the detective while he watched.

Performance art.

"We'll stay here at the motel," he said, "then go home in the morning."

"A shelter isn't a home. I wish I could stay with you. All the time."

"You can't. Not yet."

"When?"

"Someday." And then he told her how they'd move to New Mexico and he'd buy a parcel of land where they could roam naked all day. She was beginning to wonder if it was true and if it would really happen.

"You always say that."

"Don't you believe me?" The hand on her head moved to grip her blond ponytail. He tugged so hard her eyes watered, but she didn't make a sound.

"I do. I'm sorry." She hated it when he was mad at her.

He relaxed his grip and she tried to blink away the tears. On the TV screen, she noted that the guy was gone, but Jude Fontaine was still there, a receiver in her hand.

"Are you going to kill her?" Clementine asked.

"What?"

"That's what you want to do, right?" She twisted around to look up at him, hoping he would say yes.

"Fontaine's just part of the show."

She didn't like his face when he talked about the detective. It seemed like he had a crush on her. And Clementine was supposed to be his crush. But then, half the world was fascinated by Fontaine. For a while, you couldn't turn on the television, or go through the checkout at the grocery store without seeing her face looking back at you from a magazine.

She wasn't that special. She wasn't even pretty. And so what if she'd been held captive for three years? That could have happened to anybody. *Anybody.* And so what if she'd escaped? Other people who weren't cops had escaped from captivity. If Fontaine was so special, she should have been able to get away a lot sooner. Three years. It took her three years. Not special.

People called the detective haunting, ethereal, otherworldly. *A tragic beauty.* That was stupid. She'd chopped off her hair and people started comparing her to Joan of Arc. Anybody could chop off her hair. Clementine could chop off her hair if she wanted to, if she was mental enough. That's all Fontaine's hair said. *Crazy on board.*

Leo gave her hair another tug, harder this time, pulling back her head. His leather bracelet rubbed her cheek, and she felt cold steel against her throat. She smiled up at him, swallowed a whimper, and hoped he wouldn't kill her.

CHAPTER 9

Early the next morning, before heading downtown, Jude pulled to a stop on a familiar residential street. Straddling her bike, she turned off the engine and secured the vehicle on its stand before dismounting.

She removed her helmet and strode toward the house, taking in details as she walked: cracks in the sidewalk, tree limbs cut by the power company, rust on the chain-link fence, street trash trapped in corners against the crumbling foundation.

The house was typical of Midtown Phillips, a neighborhood located north of Powderhorn and east of Whittier. Red trim, cream stucco, one and a half stories. In need of repair. Rotten wood, chipped paint, broken window in the attic, a yard that had been mowed by the city. She could tell because of the weeds in the fence and the pale, thick grass stems, indicating the lawn had gotten out of control at some point. But the property didn't stand out as being much worse than any other on the block.

Hopefully she'd acted surprised when Detective McIntosh had handed her the flyer, but she'd known the day the auction announcement showed up on the house's front door, because she stopped here a lot. That day, she'd approached with caution until she was close enough to read the details, close enough to commit the auction's web address to memory. Once back in her apartment, she investigated more thoroughly, and then she began to plan.

She'd assumed nobody else would know about the sale, at least no one in the department. Now she could see that assumption had been foolish. Everybody was watching her. Some out of curiosity. Others, like McIntosh, were waiting for her to crack. Even Uriah, as supportive as he was, worried. No missing that. And that subconscious input, the awareness of being watched, had a hand in shaping her new persona, the person she'd turned into after her escape. It drove her to become closed off and secretive in everything she did and everything she thought. Sometimes she wondered how different she was from the killers she chased. They all had their private lives and their public personas. And their secret obsessions.

A homeless woman shuffled toward Jude on the sidewalk, her gait slow, her attention on the ground as she leaned into a small shopping cart packed with everything she owned. A few feet away, the woman stopped. "A murderer lived there," she said. "He tortured some girl. I walked past here every day and I never knew. I never knew there was someone in there who needed help. Because I would've helped. I would've busted in and told that man to leave her alone."

Jude pulled out her wallet, extracted a twenty-dollar bill. "I like to think any of us would've helped." She spoke as if she herself felt sympathy for the victim in the house.

For years she'd been kept in a box in the basement, naked, in the dark. Now that she was free, she marveled at how she'd lived through it, but people adapted. People were resilient. They became who they needed to be in order to survive. That was the takeaway. That was what she'd learned. That was what she knew.

"I'm not a beggar." The woman's bloodshot eyes flared at the money.

"I just want you to have it." Jude didn't drop her extended arm. "A meal on me."

The woman relented. "Who would buy that place?" she asked, tucking the money somewhere inside her clothing. "What kind of crazy person would buy that place?"

"Do you have somewhere to stay tonight?" Jude asked, ignoring the question. "A shelter?" Fall in Minnesota was breathtakingly perfect, but it could snow in late September, and come November temps could drop below zero.

"I have a place. How 'bout you? Ever since the blackouts, you never know. Shelters are full of people who don't look like they should be there, but they lost their homes in the street riots and arson fires. We find places where we can."

She was right about the shelters being full. And not just the shelters. The Twin Cities were divided by lakes and a river, and many areas were dense woodland. River camps had always existed, but there were many more people now living in tents in those undeveloped areas.

"*You* got a place to sleep?" the woman asked.

"I do." Jude smiled. "Thanks for your concern."

"If things take a turn, I'm at the shelter downtown, on Washington Avenue. Look me up. Ruthie Logan. I might be able to help you."

The name sounded familiar. "Did you have a home before the blackouts?" Jude asked.

"I've lived on the streets for ten years, long before the blackouts. I like it."

Jude was being nosy, but the detective in her couldn't help but ask, "What did you do before?"

"I was in real estate." The woman laughed, probably because of the idea that she used to buy and sell homes, places for people to live, and now she was homeless. No wonder the name had seemed familiar. Jude recalled seeing her ads on bus-stop benches. She pulled a business card from her leather jacket and passed it to Ruthie. "I'm Detective Jude Fontaine, the person who was held captive here."

She'd managed to surprise the woman, probably something not easily done. "Oh, you poor dear."

"Don't feel sorry for me. I just want you to have my contact information in case you need anything. If you ever want to get back into real estate, maybe I can help."

"To hell with that, honey. I'm enjoying my freedom."

Jude didn't point out that she was getting older and wouldn't always be able to live on the street. She could connect Ruthie with the right people. "We have to look out for one another," she told the woman, then said good-bye and headed downtown to the police station.

CHAPTER 10

"They should make a trail mix that only contains good stuff," Jude said.

She and Uriah were in one of the smaller break rooms. Uriah was lying on his back across a row of padded chairs, knees bent, one arm slung across his eyes. Jude sat at a round table, a gaping bag of trail mix in front of her, and a tea bag in a cup that said *Hennepin County Coroner*.

"That would be called M&M's," Uriah said without moving his arm.

It was early afternoon, and the day had already been grueling, with another press conference along with several interviews, one with the theater owner and many with family members of the three theater victims. Two tips had resulted in arrests and very quick releases when both suspects' alibis were confirmed. No wonder Uriah had a headache. Then it was a meeting with the task force set up by Ortega and headed by a new hire from Chicago, a guy named Dominique Valentine. Now they were taking a break before returning to the crime scene in hopes of spotting something they'd missed the first time through.

Jude slipped out of her chair and cut the overhead lights until the room was dim shadows. At the sink, she wet a paper towel with cold water, squeezed out the excess, and carried the towel to Uriah. "For your head." He fumbled blindly and found the towel.

She didn't like the number of migraines he was getting. "Have you slept at all the past few days?" she asked.

"A little." He draped the cloth over his eyes.

That probably meant not at all. "You should go home for at least a couple of hours."

"I'll be okay," he mumbled. "We need to give the theater one last pass before the crime-scene status is lifted. I'll be ready to go soon."

Five minutes later, Jude put her empty cup in the sink, Uriah tossed the wet paper towel in the trash, and they headed for the elevators and the parking garage and Minnehaha Creek Theater. Jude drove the unmarked car, Uriah looking deceptively casual in the reclined passenger seat, dark sunglasses covering his eyes.

Once in the Longfellow neighborhood, Jude cruised slowly up and down streets, looking for anything odd or out of place. Along the way, at various points, she stopped the car and they both got out to talk to people, flashing badges, passing out business cards. If anyone had the slightest bit of something to share, Jude wrote down names and numbers, which would be entered into the case's database when they were back downtown. Some people were cautious and reserved, but most couldn't wait to share what they knew or often didn't know. Sorting through the people who just wanted to feel like a part of the investigation was tedious and time consuming, but it had to be done.

"This neighborhood's gone downhill fast," said a woman with a stroller, standing in front of a coffee shop with the peculiar name of Dark Soul. "People are always wantin' to blame the blackouts, but that's not what's happening here. It was going on before that. We need more cops who care. More cops on foot and not in their cars. What about horses? I know they have horses downtown. We should get horses too."

"I'll pass on your concerns," Jude said without trying to explain that those things cost money they didn't have. She turned to let Uriah know it was time to go, and was surprised to see him squatting in front of the stroller, glasses on top of his head, entertaining the baby with a toy.

The sight was jarring. Maybe it was the collision of two worlds, the normal and the world they lived in—the world of evil beasts who killed for pleasure. But it was also the knowledge that if his wife had lived, he might have a baby of his own now. Death, no matter how it came, changed the course of a life.

A baby . . . She remembered a time when she'd wanted a child, or at least thought she'd eventually have one. Uriah could still go down that road, but she couldn't fathom anything like that for herself anymore.

He straightened, dropped his glasses over his eyes, and waved good-bye to the little girl.

Outside the theater, they excused themselves to slip through a mob of bystanders and reporters several bodies deep. The perimeter had been narrowed, and the street and sidewalk were no longer blocked. Memorial photos leaned against a decorative wall, along with bouquets, burned and unburned candles, and signs, some written to the killer. *Get ready for a life sentence.* And: *You won't get away with this.*

Their certainty of a quick arrest made Jude uneasy. She wasn't feeling that confident.

A cop unlocked the door, and Jude and Uriah ducked under the yellow tape to slip inside the building, the deadbolt falling into place behind them. Just the two of them this time. Decorative wall sconces threw light toward an ornate ceiling. The scent of popcorn still lingered.

"Is this as strange as I think it is?" Uriah asked, eyeing the string of plastic evidence cards still on the floor.

She knew what he meant. "The smell of popcorn signals entertainment, however inaccurate that might be right now."

"We have to rule out someone connected to the theater," Uriah said.

"I'll have Detective McIntosh get a list of employees dating back several years," Jude told him. "But I don't think we'll find anything."

"Just something to eliminate."

"Agreed. Let's say there's no connection to the other two murders," Jude said. "Is it possible this was supposed to be a massacre and the plan went awry?"

"Unfortunately, people being killed in public places is on a sharp increase, but I'd tend to throw out your theory simply due to the method."

They pulled out their phones and took photos.

The theater could screen two movies at one time. They searched the adjoining room, finishing with the projection booth. Tomorrow a crime-scene-cleanup company called After the Fact would come in and remove all traces of blood and death. The seats the victims had died in would probably be replaced, but maybe not. A few days later the theater would reopen and the morbidly curious would buy tickets, some just wanting to see the room where horrendous things had happened, others hoping to sit in the actual spot of a murder. It could be good business.

"How's your head?" she asked once they were back in the car. Somehow it had gotten dark while they were inside.

"Not good."

"You need to pace yourself." She eased the car away from the curb. "Let's both go home, get some sleep, start in again tomorrow."

He didn't argue, which meant he must have felt worse than he let on.

His phone rang. He pulled it out, looked at the screen, and answered in a deceptively strong voice. Then he lied to the caller and said he was feeling fine. Jude glanced over. He was talking with his head back, eyes closed, elbow high. "I'm in the car," he said. "I'll call you back a little later." His next words explained the fake-out. "Give my love to Mom." He disconnected. To Jude he said in a whisper of explanation, "My dad."

"You're a little old to be lying to your parents."

"He doesn't have a lot to do now that he's retired, so he worries about weird things."

She wondered if Uriah was trying to keep her from worrying too.

CHAPTER 11

After returning downtown to drop Uriah off at his car and swap the unmarked vehicle for her bike, Jude headed for her apartment to feed the cat and take a shower. The Powderhorn neighborhood where she lived was continuing to improve now that the blackouts were practically ancient history. Fewer windows were covered with plywood and graffiti, and days ago she'd actually seen a couple pushing a baby in a stroller. While she'd experienced a brief pang of fear for their safety, she'd also been thankful for their bravery. It took guts to move into a high-crime area.

Inside the foyer of her brick apartment building, she unlocked her mailbox and opened the small ornate door, pulling out two envelopes. One was a card from the girl whose life she'd saved. Both Octavia and her mother, Ana, kept in touch, and they'd all gotten together at a café a few times since the rescue. Jude needed that contact to reassure herself that she'd done the right thing.

The card was handmade, cute, with an orange cat on the front and a note inside.

Let's meet for lunch soon.

The other piece of mail was from the attorney handling her father's estate. She'd already told him she didn't want a dime, but the law had to be adhered to, no matter her wishes.

With one finger, she tore open the envelope and unfolded a letter typed on heavy paper. She scanned the legal jargon, all polite, all archaic. The attorney was letting her know several people had come forward claiming to be legal heirs to her father's estate. DNA tests were being conducted, and she'd be informed if any produced positive results.

No surprise there. People crawled out of the woodwork when a large amount of money was involved. She had no idea what her father's estate was worth, but it very well could have been millions.

She refolded the paper and tucked it back into the now-ragged envelope. It was entirely possible her father had other children. Part of her hoped they found someone so she could be excluded from the whole business, over and done with. No court appearances, no lawyers—because the killing of her father and brother, though justified, had complicated everything and invoked what the court system referred to as "the slayer rule." Normally, a killer couldn't benefit financially from the person he or she killed. But Jude's case was different because it could be proven that she'd killed them to save lives, even though those deaths left her in line for the full inheritance.

She didn't want it. Not any of it.

"Hi."

Jude slammed her box closed and turned to see her downstairs neighbor standing a few feet away. She'd allowed herself to be distracted by the letter, and she hadn't heard him. That didn't happen very often. He could have attacked her, grabbed her, dragged her off. She had to be more vigilant.

"Didn't mean to startle you," he said.

For all her intuition, she was having trouble figuring him out. Not that she gave him much thought, but she tried to be aware of the people around her, especially the person living below her, pounding on the ceiling in the middle of the night.

She knew his name was Elliot. She'd checked the mailbox shortly after he moved in. First name only. He gave the impression of someone who might be a student, older, nontraditional, someone who'd gone back to school a little later in life, although he had to be several years younger than she was, and seemed more like a kid than an adult. Maybe she guessed student because she found it hard to imagine what kind of job he might have, so she stuck him in a school.

"That's okay." She gave him the smile she always gave him, the one that didn't reach her eyes. The one that didn't invite conversation, and didn't invite scrutiny. In the past, her friendly chill had worked. But today he seemed a little more determined.

"I'm thinking about adopting a cat," he said, "and was wondering if you could recommend a rescue shelter."

"No idea." With her back to him, she headed up the stairs. He lived on the third floor, so he jogged up the steps beside her. She tried to ignore him.

"You have a cat. I've seen you carrying litter," he rushed to explain. "I thought maybe you got him somewhere nearby."

"I didn't." She paused on the landing of his floor. "Well, actually, I did. He was feral and I fed him. It just kind of happened."

He smiled, and she felt a basic human response she didn't want to feel. Because she understood what he was doing. Trying to get to know her, maybe for romance or sex, but the odds of that being the reason seemed remote. She no longer thought of herself as attractive, and he'd have a much better chance with pretty much anybody else.

Her eyes narrowed. "Are you a journalist?" That would make sense. Someone like him, someone who wasn't downtrodden, wasn't seeking darkness, who looked almost too normal, moving in, asking questions. She could *feel* his secrets.

"I'm not a journalist. And what if I was?" He pulled out a set of keys and paused in front of his apartment door.

Playing it cool. Most people in Minneapolis knew who she was and what had happened to her. For him to pretend there was no reason a journalist would find her interesting revealed a lot about him. He might have as many secrets as she had.

"Okay, a writer." Now *she* followed *him*, stopping a few feet away, face to face. "Better not write a story about me." Her voice was like a finger poke to his chest, and he recoiled slightly, taken aback.

He was nice looking. It wasn't fair, but she was especially suspicious of nice-looking guys; her father and brother had used their looks to get what they wanted, no matter how twisted their desires. Shoulder-length dark hair, sometimes secured in a ponytail at the back of his neck. Well-worn leather bracelet that might or might not have significance. Maybe purchased on a trip to another country, or given to him by a girlfriend or family member who was dead now. Or picked up at Electric Fetus just because he liked it. His irises were almost as dark as his pupils, and his skin tone hinted of mixed race. Jeans, untucked flannel shirt, close shaven. He looked like someone who showered every day, and he always seemed to be wearing clean clothes. That in itself made him stand out in this neighborhood. And made her more suspicious.

"I'm not a writer." He shrugged. "I'm just a guy who wants to adopt a cat."

"What do you do for a living?" Her tone was meant to be intimidating.

"Forget it." He spun around.

As he was inserting the key, she slammed an open palm against his door. He lived right below her. Their beds were probably just yards apart; she needed him to know he shouldn't mess with her. "What do you do for a living?"

"I can tell you what I don't do." He looked at her over his shoulder, all friendliness gone from his face. She suddenly regretted her aggressive response, because she missed the friendliness already. But his next words solidified her earlier suspicions: she couldn't trust anyone. "I don't scream in the middle of the night," he said. "And I didn't kill my father and brother. Yeah, I know who you are. Everybody in this building knows who you are. I'm just a guy who thought you might need a friend or even just a neighbor to lend a hand now and then. I'm just a guy who's interested in getting a cat." The key engaged, and he stepped inside his apartment and slammed the door in her face.

She thought the unpleasant altercation was over until he shouted at her through the door. "I'm a photography major at the University of Minnesota, if you really want to know. But if I were a writer, I could sure write some shit about you."

Well, hell. How had this happened? How had she allowed paranoia to take over? He was just the guy who lived downstairs. Nothing more. A student. Her first guess had been right.

Upstairs, Jude found a note from the building manager taped to her door, telling her he'd be coming inside soon to attend to a problem with her shower that was causing a leak in Elliot's kitchen. She removed the note and tossed it and the lawyer's letter on the kitchen counter, propped Octavia's card on the shelf above the couch, fed the cat, showered, and heard a knock on the door. Dressed in a T-shirt and underpants, towel on her head, she checked the peephole. Nobody there. She unlocked the deadbolt and chain.

On the floor in front of her apartment door was a plate with foil over it. On top of the foil was a Post-it note that said *Sorry*. It was signed *Elliot*.

A plate of anything left in front of a person's door was suspicious. She couldn't help but feel freshly annoyed. If he meant it as a peace offering while knowing her history, he should have also known it was a bad idea. Food of the homemade variety in front of a door immediately signaled a trap. But then again, maybe it wasn't food at all. She bent over and peeled one corner of the foil back enough to see several Oreos.

Oreos. Now that was funny.

She carried the cookies inside, kicking the door shut behind her. Sitting down on the orange couch that had come with the apartment, she tossed the towel on the floor, opened her laptop, and logged in to her bank account, like she'd been doing every day for the past week. Without looking, she grabbed a cookie and took a bite, thinking, *What the hell? The most it can do is kill me.*

The money she'd been waiting for was finally in her account, all $20,000 from her 401(k). Talk about arriving at the eleventh hour.

The young man at the financial institute had tried to dissuade her from cashing in her retirement funds, citing the penalty and loss, but she'd been adamant. She needed money and she needed it fast.

She had a house to buy.

CHAPTER 12

J ude tugged a black knit cap over her white hair, slipped on a pair of dark glasses, and walked two blocks to the nearest bus stop. No motorcycle today. She didn't want to draw unnecessary attention to herself.

The bus ride took thirty minutes.

Her last-minute disguise worked. Nobody paid attention to her, which was new. She'd gotten accustomed to people shooting her furtive looks. Some didn't even try to hide their curiosity and would simply stare. A few would come right out and ask if she was Jude Fontaine. If she said yes, they'd press for details of her imprisonment. Some even asked how it felt to kill her own father. "That's some cold shit, man. Blood is blood."

She disembarked at a corner not far from her destination, approaching the rest of the way on foot. As she got closer, she noted the reporters and protesters at the auction site. She'd expected press, but not protesters. Some were carrying signs that said the house should be razed, the lot left empty. *Interesting.*

Vendors were set up along the sidewalk, and people stood in line to buy hot dogs, soda, popcorn, and cotton candy. The grass was already packed down, and flattened snow-cone holders seemed to be the signature litter of the day.

A typical Minnesota fall consisted of one beautiful day after the next, the perfect weather lulling residents into denial of the brutal winter just around the corner. Today was one of those beautiful days. The sky was clear and deep blue, the air crisp but not too cool, and the rich and heady scent of leaves underfoot made the scene almost inviting.

She would have preferred to bid online, but Hennepin County required interested buyers to come in person. At the sign-up desk, located next to a gray van parked under brilliant orange leaves that didn't look real, Jude was given a bidding paddle—a small piece of cardboard stapled to a wooden handle. Her number was seven, which meant there were at least six others bidding on the house. She hadn't expected to be the only one, but six was a surprising number. Her chances of getting the property dwindled.

There were maybe a few hundred people there, and the size of the crowd made it easier to blend. Her strategy was to hang back, watch the bidding, and enter at the last moment, after most of the others had dropped out.

The price escalated quickly; she joined in, and with each new bid her heart sank a little. Finally, there were only two bidders left.

She didn't relent, and her competition finally gave up.

She won, with money left over. What a strange way to put it. Like winning a bad dream. Like winning your own private monster.

She could feel eyes on her, feel the media moving in to question the motives of the woman in the black knit cap and dark glasses. Some probably recognized her.

She had twenty-four hours to get a cashier's check to the bank.

She ducked away, vanished into the crowd, and managed to catch a bus seconds before it pulled from the curb. Dropping into the nearest vacant seat, she looked out the window, heart pounding as she wondered what she was going to do with the house now that she had it.

Thirty minutes later, she was downtown at the Minneapolis Police Department, knit cap and glasses stashed in her bag. News of the sale had beaten her to the office.

"I hear the house sold," McIntosh told her. "Whoever bought it has to be crazy."

Jude might have mumbled in agreement.

CHAPTER 13

J ude was a proud homeowner.

The next day, with the key in her pocket and the paperwork for the sale in the messenger bag strapped across her chest, the property deed to follow, she eased her bike up the driveway of weeds and broken concrete that flanked the house where she'd been tortured. Straddling the machine, she cut the engine and secured it on the stand.

It was impossible for her to comprehend her compulsion to buy the house. She imagined putting her feelings in a jar and holding that jar up to the light in hopes of finally understanding herself. Truth was, she didn't know why she'd made the purchase. Was it to keep others from exploiting it? Maybe, but that seemed unlikely. Her story had been paraded across the globe so many times she'd begun to think of the main character as someone separate from herself. It was an interesting tale, but the public narrative was not even a snapshot of what had really taken place. The story had been tweaked and embellished and edited so many times there was little left of pure truth. And even pure truth was always shifting, depending upon the perspective and the moments and years that had passed.

Maybe if she'd agreed to in-depth interviews after her escape, it would have been different, but she'd been through enough. She didn't care to share more of herself with the world. She didn't owe anybody anything. And if the public got a sanitized or sensationalized version of what had happened, and if they enjoyed it, that was fine. It was all entertainment masquerading as news anyway.

She removed her helmet and hung it on the handlebar of her Honda, then dismounted to hike the crumbling steps to the door. Inside the kitchen, the smell of death still lingered. She'd killed her captor too. Most people left that out of her story when they brought up her father and brother. She was a killing machine.

The odor of death inside wasn't the overpowering stench that was typically so pervasive early on. This was the other one, the one that came after a body had rotted, after the fat had melted into a greasy puddle that never went away. Along with the remnants of death, there were other odors. Nicotine and fried food, mildew and urine. She'd never forget that alchemy. If she didn't smell it again for thirty years, she'd recognize it.

Home sweet home.

Months after her escape, the kitchen sink was still piled high with dishes. A layer of dust and grime covered everything. But there was also evidence of squatters: the kitchen table was strewn with clear-plastic food containers, empty now, and a black insulated mug with the First Ave logo. The mug, from the downtown music venue made famous by Prince, told her the squatters might be young.

Just past the kitchen was a short hall that led to a bedroom and a filthy mattress littered with more food wrappers. On the floor was shattered glass from a broken window—evidence of the entry point. She hated to lock someone out, but she'd have to make arrangements for plywood to be put over the windows.

Life on the street was hard for anybody, but it was especially brutal for young people. They were attacked and raped, and a high percentage became drug addicts and prostitutes. She saw no signs of drug use here, and no condoms on the floor that might indicate prostitution, but the fact that someone would even consider staying here spoke of desperation.

She tested a couple of switches, not surprised to find the power off. The house was small, hardly more than six hundred square feet. Back in the kitchen, she eyed the basement steps, heart racing. She pulled out her iPhone and turned on the flashlight, giving the beam a pass across the blood-spattered walls of the stairwell, stains left from that night when she'd killed her captor and escaped into the blackout. Hand on the railing, she descended, shifting the phone to illuminate a tiny room not big enough to lie down in, built in the center of the basement, ceiling to floor, the walls thick. Hanging from the ceiling was a single bare lightbulb. The image had been used in many a horror movie, and for good reason. It was a chilling visual. At the bottom of the steps was the grease spot left by her captor's body as he'd decomposed. She completed her descent, sidestepping the stain on the floor.

The cell door was ajar. Inside were the soundproof walls she'd written on with her fingernails. Scratching and scraping until she bled, trying to document her story. *I was here. This happened to me.* But she'd written in the dark, and the scratches weren't legible. They never had been. Years and layers of words, one on top of the other. Even if a person could peel the layers off one at a time, would it make any sense? She doubted it.

She felt an unsettling urge to go inside and pull the door shut behind her. Curl into a ball. Deep down in some dark corner of her soul, she could admit the emptiness she'd been feeling lately was due to a different and disturbing and surprising kind of loss. Her darkness of soul came from missing this place, the place she'd called home for three years.

And there it was. The reason behind her purchase.

Shocked by that realization, she turned and ran up the stairs. Outside, heart slamming, a cold sweat on her body, she locked the door, pocketed the key. Before getting on her bike, she searched online for a repairman, called a guy named Joe the Handyman, and told him she needed the house secured.

"Sure," he said. "I'll send you a bill when I'm done."

She hung up, wondering if it would really happen. Repairmen didn't have a reputation for showing up. Then she put on her helmet, strapping it under her chin, turned the key to her motorcycle, and headed for the police department.

CHAPTER 14

An hour later, Jude sat in lotus position in a meeting room at the Minneapolis Police Department. Chairs had been pushed aside, lights dimmed.

Even though she'd balked when Ortega brought up meditation, Jude had nothing against it. She might have been more open if not for having to do it with other people at an inconvenient time. Apparently, the idea was to have a shared experience. Being home by herself, following along on YouTube, was her preference.

The instructor, a woman with gray hair and a well-toned body, exuded calm confidence. Even her voice was soothing.

"Close your eyes and cleanse your mind. Push away all of those unwelcome thoughts. Imagine balloons that you bat away. Go away, thoughts. Go away. Once those bad thoughts are gone, I want you to concentrate on the space between your breaths . . ."

It was all about a rest for the troubled mind and stressed soul. A few minutes of respite from disturbing cases. But the moment Jude let herself go, let herself drift, she felt a nervous flutter in her chest, along with a deep thud of terror.

Dark memories lived in the spaces between those breaths, and the more she tried to give in to the meditation, the worse those memories and thoughts became. As if the act of extreme relaxation was a conduit for the dark things she normally kept at bay.

She'd fought him at first. Her abductor. She didn't know for how long, because time in the cell had been skewed. Sometimes it seemed she'd been there weeks, not months and years. Other times it had felt like most of her life.

But she *had* fought him. That's why he'd started wearing the Taser on his hip. He'd zap her and rape her. So it made sense that she finally quit fighting him, right? She hoped she'd fought him for weeks, even months, but she didn't know. It might have only been days. She hoped it was longer.

She'd started playing a game of pretend. Pretending he was someone else, pretending he wasn't loathsome. It made it easier. Less painful. And if the cell was the rest of her life, what did it matter if she turned him into someone she could care about? And a worse thought: maybe she missed the unwelcome touch of the man who'd tortured her.

"Breathe in . . . breathe out. In. Out."

The instructor's voice pulled her back to the room and the feel of the floor beneath her. Soft music played as the woman continued to guide their journey. Jude heard a ticking clock—which sounded ominous—and nearby breathing, probably Uriah's. Along with all that, she continued to feel the deep panic of her heart. Hands that were supposed to be resting on her knees were curled into fists so tight her nails dug into her palms. She swiped a sleeve against the sweat on her face.

"You should give it a chance."

She jerked a little and opened her eyes. Uriah beside her, legs crossed, eyes closed, lotus pose. "If we have to do this anyway."

"I'm trying." She unclenched her fists, then quickly closed them again to hide the crescents of blood.

"Your breathing's uneven," he whispered. "You're going to hyperventilate. Do it like this." He inhaled slowly and deeply, then exhaled just as slowly. In the background, the instructor's voice was saying something about letting go of the past, that today was the very first day of the rest of your life.

Finally it was over, and people began to shift in preparation to leave. "Just ten minutes a day," the instructor said.

Uriah jumped to his feet, rolling his shoulders. "That wasn't bad." His tie was undone and he was barefoot. Hair a mess. "I actually liked it." Earlier, she'd caught him eyeing her with a mix of curiosity and concern. He was probably picking up on her unease about her new purchase. Soon she was going to have to tell him, before he heard it from someone else—McIntosh, for instance. Jude had requested anonymity from the auction house, but that kind of thing had a way of getting out. Salacious news was hard to contain.

Her cell phone rang.

"You left your phone on?" Uriah asked.

"I'm a rebel." She answered. It was a security officer from the front desk.

"There's someone down here who claims to have important information. Says he needs to talk to Detective Fontaine. Nobody but you. I can send him on his way, but I wanted to double-check with you first. Pretty sure you're too busy."

Right now Jude welcomed any diversion. And there was something in the guard's voice that hinted of things he didn't want to say with the person standing in front of him.

"No," Jude said. She'd been in the same position not long ago, standing at the security checkpoint, trying to convince the officer she was Jude Fontaine, the detective who'd gone missing three years earlier. She often wondered what would have happened if Uriah hadn't been on duty that night. Would she have turned around and wandered back into the cold with no clothes and nowhere to go? "Have someone escort him up."

CHAPTER 15

He wore a dark suit and a wide burgundy tie that was out of date by about twenty years. Not that Jude knew much about men's fashion anymore, but it was easy to tell the clothes were old—and might not have been cleaned much in that twenty years. They gave off an odor of sweat baked into the fibers by body heat, along with a mustiness and a hint of mothballs. His age was probably around fifty. He had light brown hair, thin on top, hand-smoothed to one side, the strands having a suspicious shine that added to the overall impression of *unwashed* and *lack of awareness*.

She told him to sit down in the chair next to her desk. He did, thin fingers fiddling, groping at the air almost as if he were playing a piano. Now she understood the guard's reluctance to send him up. This would go nowhere, but nonetheless she was interested in his personal story— who he was, who was caring for him, and if she could help in any way.

She pulled a tablet closer. Pen poised, she asked, "How do you spell your name?"

"M-A-S-U-C-C-I. Professor Masucci. Everybody always spells it wrong. First name Albert."

"It is an unusual name. Why exactly are you here, Professor Masucci?"

"I've solved your case." The sentence was spoken with assurance.

Solved the case. It wasn't the direction she'd expected this to go so quickly. "Could you excuse me one moment?" She shifted slightly in her chair. From where he sat, he couldn't see her monitor screen. She typed his name in the search engine and pulled up pages of articles about him, going back . . . yep, twenty years. He'd been a math professor at the University of Minnesota. Jude glanced at the clock on the wall, painfully aware of how precious their time was and wishing she'd taken the guard's advice.

Uriah appeared and dropped a stack of files in front of his chair, shot her a questioning face, glanced at the guy, then finished up with a look of sympathy.

Uriah's station was near hers, but not close enough for him to easily overhear the conversation. The position of her desk had been Uriah's deliberate statement of her unworthiness, back when she'd first returned to work and he'd been unhappy about having her assigned as his partner. Since then, he'd suggested she move closer, but she'd declined. She was used to her spot, and it provided more sunlight for her plant.

Jude turned back to Professor Masucci. "Tell me what you know."

"It's all about numbers." He blinked several times, as if trying to hide behind his eyelids.

"We think the killings are somewhat opportunistic," she told him, without going into the planning that must have been involved in the latest event. Not for him to know.

He shook his head in agitation. "The killer is using the Fibonacci sequence." He went on to talk about spirals and harmonics and asymmetry and something called Benford's law.

She held up one hand. "I'm not that great at math."

Despite the distance, Uriah had managed to listen in, and now he rolled his chair closer. "It's the sequence of ever-increasing numbers found in nature. You know. Sunflowers, shells, leaves, dragonfly wings. The Fibonacci sequence can even be found in fingerprints."

"Yes." Professor Masucci leaned forward, relaxing a little, eager to explain more. "The beginning numbers are 0, 1, 1, 2, 3. And you've had four crime scenes with body counts that follow that sequence." He leaned back. "Fibonacci."

"I'm sorry," Jude said, "but we've had *three* murder scenes with the same MO."

"That's what I thought at first, but I realized this morning that you've had four. And if I'm right, the next time you'll have five bodies."

Jude glanced at Uriah, giving him a small and frustrated shake of her head. She gathered up her tablet, clutching it to her chest. "I'm going to have to go. Thank you for taking the time to talk to us. Someone can escort you back downstairs."

"What about the campers in Wisconsin?" he asked.

Jude hesitated. She'd heard about them, but with the MPD's own cases keeping her busy, she hadn't had time to follow up on crimes in a bordering state. And if she recalled correctly, it had been reported as a crime of passion.

"The prime suspect is an ex-husband," the professor said.

"That's all very interesting," she told the man. "We'll look into it. Leave your contact information in case we want to reach you. Do you need transportation? I could call a cab for you, my treat."

"That's okay. I'll catch the light rail. It goes to campus."

The article had said he no longer taught there. Maybe he'd been rehired, or maybe he was a substitute.

Once he was gone, Uriah and Jude looked at each other. "It's the request for public input," Uriah said with a resigned shrug. "These people go with the territory." But they also knew that the public was their greatest ally.

Jude searched for articles about the Wisconsin murders. It was like Professor Masucci had said: an ex-husband was the prime suspect. But the killings hadn't garnered much media coverage, and states didn't share information. Counties didn't even share information. Minnesota was working on changing that with systems like CISA (Criminal Information Sharing and Analysis) and MRIC (Metro Regional Information Collaboration). But even at that, reports often went out as a weekly bulletin. Not daily. Not hourly.

"We really don't have much in the way of leads right now," Jude said. They'd found no personal connections between the three theater victims, and none of the prints lifted from the crime scene matched any criminals in their databases. She clicked a few keys, found the number she was looking for, and picked up her desk phone. In response to Uriah's raised eyebrows, she said, "I'm going to get in touch with the person handling the Wisconsin case."

"Thinking of a field trip?"

"Yep." She made the call, tracked down the sheriff in charge of the investigation, and arranged to meet him in his office that afternoon.

CHAPTER 16

J ude drove.

Minneapolis to Saint Croix Falls, Wisconsin, was a little over an hour if the traffic wasn't heavy. They took Interstate 35 North, exiting at Highway 8. From there, it was a straight stretch of narrow two-lane. Their uninterrupted time in the car was well spent. They tossed theories back and forth and discussed a strategy for the following twenty-four hours. Sixty minutes into their trip, they hit the Saint Croix River valley, where the speed limit dropped to thirty-five and the road began to wind and descend—water in the distance, giant slabs of black basalt-lava rock erupting from a backdrop of orange and red trees. It was an area popular with city dwellers because of the proximity to the Twin Cities.

The little town of Taylors Falls was perched on a low bluff overlooking the river. As they drew nearer, Uriah grew noticeably silent, possibly taking in the breathtaking beauty.

Luckily today wasn't a weekend, and the typical fall congestion wasn't bad. After a quick stop for caffeine at a place called Coffee Talk, they drove across the river into Wisconsin and the town of Saint Croix Falls, where the county sheriff's office was located steps away from the dam and hydropower plant.

Jude parked on a street with no center line, in front of a low brick structure flanked by American and Wisconsin flags. On the way to the double doors they crunched through leaves, and a woman walking a dog told them hello.

The building didn't look as if it had been updated since the sixties. Dark wood paneling from the floor to the acoustic ceiling tile. Green linoleum that might have been there for decades. And yet it wasn't that unusual to see such interiors. Places in both Minnesota and Wisconsin were known to pay homage to the north shore of Lake Superior. You never knew if this kind of thing was deliberate or due to lack of funds. In this case, Jude guessed lack of funds. She found the space cozy and unsettling at the same time.

A young woman behind a desk announced their arrival. Within seconds, Sheriff Todd Craig appeared at his office door and motioned them inside with an air of annoyance.

He was about forty, white in the way some small-town cops were white, and Jude immediately felt an unwelcome chill coming from him as he took a seat behind his desk and invited them to settle into the two other chairs in the room.

"I was surprised to get your call." The sun backlit him through the window. He was dressed in a crisp tan shirt, a metal badge above one pocket, American flag above the other, stars on his collar, and a *Sheriff* patch on one short sleeve. His suspicion wasn't a surprise. It happened quite a bit.

"I'm not sure why you want to talk to me about something so out of your jurisdiction." He leaned back, elbows on the arms of his chair, fingers clasped.

Uriah appeared to be willing to let Jude direct the conversation, playing it cool, taking in the room while he sipped coffee from his disposable cup. Jude had left her drink in the car, and she envied his ability to use his as a prop in this scene.

She was forced to point out the obvious to the sheriff, something she was sure wouldn't buy her any more points. "We were hoping we could see the case files on the recent murders at Interstate State Park," she said.

"That's an odd request. You realize that, don't you?"

The request might have gotten better traction if Uriah had posed it. "I do." She attempted another tactic. "You might know we had some disturbing homicides at a theater in Minneapolis recently. Today we're following an unlikely lead. It might be helpful if we could look at your files to see if there are any similarities in the cases."

"I hate to have wasted your time, but after you called I talked to a few of my colleagues and we decided it wouldn't be prudent to share information at this time. We're still working to gather enough evidence to convict the ex-husband. You understand."

She did, but she wasn't sure if this was about his wanting to keep their evidence close, or not wanting outsiders involved. Or was he just another person who thought she'd gotten away with the murder of her father and brother? His instant dislike of them, especially her, was a cliché, but it was real.

Jude was out of arguments, and was about to tell Uriah they should leave, when he put his coffee on the corner of the sheriff's desk and finally spoke. "How's the fishing around here?"

The sheriff laughed. Ice broken? "I know what you're doing, but that won't work with me. You people come from the city and think we're all a bunch of idiots."

"I don't think anything of the kind," Uriah said. "I grew up in a small town in southern Minnesota. My dad was a cop there. Recently retired." His words were the truth, but his smile was crooked, sheepish. "I guess the fishing thing was a little much," he admitted. "I'm more of a canoe person. I've canoed from here to Stillwater a few times."

The casual conversation worked. The sheriff warmed to them. Jude took the opportunity to pull a manila envelope from her messenger bag. "I respect your desire to keep the case files to yourself." But *she* was going to share information with *him*. Hopefully it would soften him up a little more. The envelope contained eight-by-ten color photos, which she spread across his desk. "Could you please tell me if anything in your scene was at all similar?"

With a hint of petulance, he pulled the photos closer and shuffled through them, pausing and staring every so often until he'd looked at them all. Some of the photos were of dead bodies, but she'd also included images of the bloody footprints. Possibly noteworthy—the deaths had been quick, the bodies undisturbed once the deed was done.

His words were reluctant. "The wounds look almost identical to ours."

She gave him a nod. "Thank you. And what about the bodies themselves? Can you share anything about them?"

Uriah joined in, and this time he asked about the case. "Were they nude? Were they defiled or mutilated in any way?" All things that might point to the suspected acquaintance murder.

The sheriff stacked Jude's photos and passed them back. Then he reached into a desk drawer and pulled out a brown folder, opened it, and slid several photos across the desk. She and Uriah leaned close. Two bodies, male and female. He was right. The wounds to both necks did look similar. Both victims were fully dressed, and the bodies didn't appear to have been repositioned. There were no drag marks in the dirt, and no blood beyond the immediate area. Not your typical crime of passion.

"What about the autopsy?" she asked. "Do you have a description of the possible murder weapon?"

Still unwilling to share everything, he riffled through papers and tossed the autopsy report down. "A very sharp knife, maybe something used for hunting. I'm telling you, this is straightforward. We just need evidence or a witness's testimony."

He pulled out a blurry photo of a man dressed in jeans and a T-shirt. "Our suspect, Dwayne Hanson." He tapped a finger on the image. "As you can see, he's a big guy. Lifts weights."

She wouldn't go into her adrenaline theory.

"And he's been known to drink and get into fights at the bar where he works. His ex-wife had a restraining order on him. Not only that, neighbors reported an argument in the front yard the day she was killed. They actually heard him threaten to kill her boyfriend. He's also prone to alcohol-induced blackouts, so there's a chance he might not even remember what he did. But I can tell you we're closing in on him. It all fit. It still fits. Your crime? It's a coincidence or a copycat."

"Maybe," Uriah said. Jude was surprised he wasn't so eager to give up on the lead.

"Is the crime scene still a crime scene?" she asked.

"The status was lifted a week ago."

"We want to look at it."

His delivery became a little more enthused now that they would soon be out of his hair. "Right off Highway Eight. Take the main road all the way to the river. Maybe two miles in. There are photos and stuffed animals and flowers there. You can't miss it."

"We'd also like to talk to your suspect," Uriah said.

That didn't make him happy. "There's no reason for you to speak to him."

Jude and Uriah got to their feet. "I was just extending the courtesy of letting you know," Uriah said.

They both pulled out business cards and placed them on the desk, thanked him for his time, and left.

Back in the car, Jude's coffee was lukewarm. She took a drink anyway, put it aside, and drove in the direction of the park.

Homicides sometimes occurred in ugly locations like littered and fetid alleys or abandoned buildings. But more often, they took place in homes that were supposed to be safe havens. Or, like this, in nature, in a secluded area where there was little chance of the killer being seen or heard.

Deep in the park, they left the car on a remote bit of gravel and hiked to cliffs overlooking the river valley, slabs of black rock twenty stories tall or more, with pine trees somehow growing crookedly from craggy cracks, and a sky so blue it didn't look real. She heard shouts in the distance. Across the river, on the Minnesota side, rock climbers could be seen rappelling.

The camping spot was located under a cluster of trees, in an area few people probably went. It was a strange reaction, but whenever Jude visited a crime scene that took place in a beautiful area, she felt a small bit of heaviness lift from her heart, almost like visiting a cemetery. She loved cemeteries. Loved the tranquil sense of peace they evoked. She felt that same sense of peace now as she and Uriah stood staring at the flowers and photos, the candles and words of love so many people had left at the scene. It was easy to see that two families and groups of friends were in mourning.

"It's entirely possible the killer knew the victims and knew they were going camping." Uriah stood with hands in his pockets, wind blowing his curly hair. His observation, especially considering the remoteness of the campsite, made sense. "The method of a knife to the throat isn't rare or unusual. And, like the sheriff said, our killer could be a copycat. The coverage of the events here could have given our killer the idea. We see it all the time with mass shootings."

She shouldn't have allowed herself to be swayed by Professor Masucci's theory. What Uriah said was true. "I'd still like more details." But whatever was going on, this was not their case. The sheriff had been right about that.

Uriah looked across the shining water. "I really *have* gone canoeing here," he said.

"Me too."

"How long ago?"

"When I was a kid."

"My first visit was with my wife."

"Oh. I'm sorry." She felt a sharp pang. "Does it hurt to be here?"

"It's strange." A line furrowed the space between his brows, and his eyes narrowed. "It made my stomach drop earlier when I saw the river, but I'm becoming desensitized now. My heart isn't pounding."

That explained why he'd gone so quiet when they were driving into Taylors Falls. "Let's see if we can find the ex-husband," she said.

They tracked the suspect down at his place of employment on Main Street. A bar called, of all things, Main Street Tap. Upon sliding into a booth, they were offered a lunch menu by the man himself, Dwayne Hanson.

Since it was past noon and neither of them had eaten, they ordered lunch and waited until the food came to pull out their badges. "We'd like to ask you a few questions," Jude said.

Hanson tucked the serving tray under his arm and glanced nervously over his shoulder. "I can't talk here. I'm lucky to still have a job."

"Just five minutes," Uriah told him.

He had another plan. "Go ahead and eat. I'll meet you in the alley."

"I think we should talk now," Jude said, figuring his plan was to bolt.

"Your food'll get cold."

"We eat cold food all the time," Uriah told him. "Goes with the job."

Hanson gave up, his shoulders slumping. "Come on." He nodded his head toward a hallway with a restroom sign above it. Down the hall, he pushed the metal bar and shoved the door open with a crash. Jude shot Uriah a glance. The man had a temper that he wasn't attempting to control. He'd known his ex had a new boyfriend, heard about the plans to camp, gone there, maybe to confront them, but things got out of hand and he ended up killing the boyfriend and silencing his ex-wife so there would be no witnesses. Open and shut. From Uriah's grim expression, she saw he was thinking the same thing.

As if by unspoken agreement, Uriah did most of the questioning while Jude watched for signs of a tell. The guy was full of them, but his barely suppressed anger and nervousness could have had other causes.

And then he surprised them both by bursting into tears. "I loved her," he sobbed. "That guy was no good."

"Were you trying to protect her?" Jude asked softly.

"Well, yeah." Then he realized what he said, and backtracked. "Not that night."

"Sheriff Craig told us your wife had a restraining order out on you, and that you broke it. Neighbors reported an argument in the front yard. And they said you were drunk and threatened to kill her boyfriend."

"I did go over there. That's true. And I told her the guy was bad for her. But I didn't kill her."

"Is it possible," Jude asked, "that you don't remember?"

"No."

"Do you ever have blackouts?" Uriah asked.

"I know there's a record of that somewhere, so yeah. I do. I drink too much sometimes, but a lot of people around here do. It's not a crime. I didn't kill them. Either one of them. I loved her!"

Jude broke in with softer questions. "Tell us a little about her."

"She was an angel. A beautiful angel who shouldn't have died like that." He wiped the back of his hand against his nose. He was no longer crying, but his eyes were red and his hand shook. "She liked to help people. She was always helping somebody. Strangers, friends, anybody. That's why she was with me. I know that. She saw me as somebody she could help, but she couldn't. I wasn't good enough for her, that's for sure. And she left."

Back inside the bar, they asked for their meal to be put in carryout containers, paid, and left.

"What do you think now?" Uriah asked five minutes later, when they were sitting at a picnic table overlooking the river, eating the food from the bar.

"I think this is a false trail," Jude said. "And we don't have the luxury of wasting time." She couldn't get the mustard packet open. Where the hell was the little notch?

Uriah put out his hand. She passed him the packet. He opened it and gave it back. "At least we got out of the city. A mental-health lunch isn't a bad thing."

He held up his sandwich. She tapped hers to his. *Cheers.*

Jude took a bite, then said, "I have to tell you something."

Uriah watched her, elbows on the table, waiting with expectation.

"About the house."

He frowned. She could see him struggling, his mind probably still on the case. "What house?"

"You know."

"No, I don't."

She was surprised he didn't immediately get it. She waited for him to catch up, saw the light come into his eyes as he recalled McIntosh's announcement in the office. He put his sandwich aside. "*That* house."

She looked away, looked back, afraid of his reaction, but it was a secret she didn't want to keep from him. "I bought it."

To his credit, he barely blinked. But then, he was a detective who was used to masking his reactions. "I kind of understand," he said after giving it time to sink in. "You want control of what happens to it."

"I don't know." No, that was a lie. Deep down, she did know. She wanted it for herself.

"I wish you'd told me beforehand," he said.

"So you could have stopped me?"

"I would have helped. Buying a house, even that house, couldn't have been cheap. Maybe we could have found a way around the public sale. Maybe the bank would've sold it to you for a dollar."

"It's done now."

"I know, but . . ." That frown again. He was wondering about her mental state. She'd certainly seen that look before.

"It's okay. I'm okay." She was beginning to wish she hadn't told him, but people would eventually find out. "I know it's weird," she added.

"It's not *that* weird." He was adjusting to the news. "You might be keeping someone from turning it into a public attraction. A freak show. I get that. I might have done the same thing. So, what now? Tear it down?"

"I'm boarding it up for the time being."

He nodded. "You don't have to make any big decisions right away. Or ever." He gave it more thought. "You could always turn it into green space or a public garden."

"I'll think about it."

They finished eating and put their empty containers in the recycling bin, then headed back to Minneapolis, hitting the city at rush hour. Downtown, the traffic was bad, especially near the light rail, but nobody honked. That was something visitors to Minnesota often commented on. No honking cars. And if a driver was pressed to finally try to get someone's attention, it was typically a quick and apologetic beep.

Back at Headquarters, even though Jude had told Uriah it had been a waste of time, she couldn't get her mind off the Wisconsin murders. At her computer, she looked up the boyfriend who'd been killed. Social media made such research easy. Then she checked the Facebook pages of all seven victims, Minneapolis and Wisconsin ones alike, to see if there were any friends in common.

None of the five in Minneapolis had acquaintances in common with the Wisconsin pair. She also explored Dwayne Hanson's Facebook page. Under "Relationship," he still had his ex listed, along with images of them together. The happy couple. She downloaded and printed out a few photos, then exited the site. In the task-force room, she added the state-park murders to the wall containing details of the other possibly connected crimes, tacking photos to the crime board where Wisconsin would be if the map included more than their county. She was careful to include a Post-it note to team members, explaining that a connection was unlikely.

Back at her desk, she went through hard-copy images, looking for possible clues, then she logged in to the database to see if more autopsy results from the theater murders had been posted. A couple of blood tests that seemed insignificant.

She was hesitant to document the Wisconsin trip for fear of underscoring a bad lead. Nonetheless, for the sake of transparency and thoroughness, she typed a report and added it to the file.

At one point, she looked up at the clock and was surprised to see it was after nine. Sometime in the past hour, Uriah had returned to his desk, the glow of the monitor illuminating his face. They weren't alone, but the night staff was reduced. Computer keys were clicking and officers came and went, sometimes dropping files on Uriah's desk. He was probably going over reports from the day. She knew from a recent department bulletin that a shooting had occurred at a downtown bar, and a hit-and-run had taken place on Lake Street, both resulting in death. Homicides continued even as they focused on the theater murders.

The overhead lights dimmed. It was a new policy to save on electricity, and a method of simulating day and night in hopes of keeping everyone's circadian rhythms in better balance—another idea of Chief Ortega's. So far only a couple of people had complained. Jude liked the dim lights.

She stretched her spine and rolled her shoulders. "I need to go home and feed the cat."

"Me too. Go home, that is, not feed a cat." Uriah squinted at something on the monitor, jotting down notes on a pad of paper. Without glancing up, he added, "See you back here tomorrow." He probably wasn't going anywhere. He would sleep on the couch in the break room.

At home, Roof Cat circled Jude's legs like a fish. She bent down to pet him very lightly on his head. Touching was something he allowed only before she fed him canned cat food. Since her schedule was so erratic, especially now, she also left out dry kibbles for him, but he wasn't crazy about them.

She spooned cat food into his dish, took a shower, ate some raspberry yogurt, and drank a cup of herbal tea that was supposed to help a person sleep. So far, all it seemed to do was taste nasty. Her phone rang. It was Uriah. He had either a lead or bad news. She answered with dread.

"Another homicide with a familiar MO," he said.

"Details?"

"All I know is Detective Valentine said he hoped we had strong stomachs."

"Are you still at Headquarters?" she asked.

"Yep."

Figured. "I'll be there in fifteen minutes."

She got dressed and grabbed her bag and helmet. She hurried down the stairs, her hair still wet, resisting the urge to silently retreat when she spotted Elliot with a key in his door.

"Hi." Without making eye contact, she hurried past him, hand on the banister as she turned the corner to take the next flight of stairs to the basement and her motorcycle.

"I got a cat!" he shouted after her.

CHAPTER 17

The crime had taken place in a sprawling mansion overlooking Lake of the Isles, in what used to be one of the most upscale of upscale areas of Minneapolis.

For financial reasons or stubbornness, some owners were in the process of rebuilding after the destruction the blackouts had triggered. Others were trying to sell. The ground itself, due to the location—on a lake, within walking and biking distance of downtown—still retained value according to real estate agents, with the lots and crumbling structures supposedly worth close to a million each. But nobody was buying, and the *For Sale* signs had become a welcome mat for the uninvited. Police were called every few days to address the issues of squatters, vandalism, and drugs. But as far as Jude knew, this was the first homicide to take place in one of the homes.

Something had to be done to keep people out, and yet Jude sympathized with the homeless. They needed a place to go, and, like the woman she'd met the other day had said, shelters were overflowing.

The street was clogged with patrol cars, many parked at angles to deliberately hinder traffic. Uriah pulled the unmarked car to the curb a block away. He turned the engine off, and they grabbed Maglites from the glove box.

Jude didn't mind walking. It meant they could approach the house in the darkness, unnoticed, just two people in a mix of bystanders. The stealth mode also provided an opportunity to watch the crowd, which was small due to the hour. By tomorrow, the streets would be impassable, even on foot.

As expected, their path was dark, barely illuminated by a few porch lights from occupied houses, either lit to keep the criminals away or turned on by occupants in an attempt to figure out what was going on outside. Jude and Uriah had been called to the scene early in the processing, and the low conversation she managed to catch along the way was mostly whispered questions, people wondering what was happening, nothing about a murder. The word wasn't out yet.

"They should tear that place down," someone said.

"They should tear the whole neighborhood down," came a reply.

The house was what Jude expected. Charred wood a person could smell if the wind was out of the right direction. A roof that seemed to have been broken off by a giant.

Burnt wood wasn't the only odor.

"Wow." Uriah put a fist to his face.

Excrement. With no water or electricity, squatters were known to use areas of abandoned houses as toilets.

"More than one coroner van," Jude noted. Which meant more than one body. BCA—Bureau of Criminal Apprehension—was already on site. Cops were everywhere, some standing with hands on hips, watching the growing crowd, some moving through that crowd with pen and paper in hand, taking names, phone numbers, and statements. Yellow crime-scene tape had been strung, and there were already plastic evidence cards littering the yard and sidewalk leading to the door.

Jude was impressed by the rapid response and containment of the area, especially considering the late hour, when crime-scene personnel were at a minimum. Portable generators hummed and electrical cords wound through glassless windows, some of those windows bright with light and others faint, hinting of activity deeper within the structure.

There was no need to pull out their badges. One of the cops watching the perimeter nodded grimly, giving them silent permission to enter. He seemed about to say something, glanced toward the crowd, then pressed his lips together, not willing to risk being overheard. From somewhere within the throng of bystanders, a camera phone flashed, capturing their arrival. Tomorrow, or maybe later that night, the cop's grim expression would hit social media.

Jude and Uriah ducked under the tape, both thumbing on their flashlights, and moved slowly up the sidewalk, careful of their steps.

Even with the warning Uriah had been given over the phone, Jude wasn't prepared for what served as a greeting to all who entered the structure. Intestines strung across the open doorway.

"I guess we found at least one source of the odor," Uriah said in a low voice.

"Human?" Jude asked, knowing they probably were.

"What the hell is going on in this damn city?" he asked.

Had the loss of their governor under such horrible circumstances had a ripple effect? He'd been replaced, the gubernatorial vacancy filled by the lieutenant governor, but both Saint Paul and Minneapolis were still reeling from the events that led to his death. Had his dark deception and sick crimes against young women created a tipping point that gave residents the sense that nobody was in charge and chaos was the rule? If a governor could kill and murder, why couldn't everybody else? But maybe Jude was giving her father too much credit. Maybe she was making this too personal.

"Over here." The shout came from Dominique Valentine, head of the recently established task force. Unlike Jude and Uriah, who wore jeans, Valentine was dressed in a suit and tie, along with a long dark coat and shiny black shoes. Old-school detective attire. A couple of women who ran a crime podcast (did everybody have a podcast today?) claimed all male detectives were handsome. He would probably set their hearts racing, with his dark skin and brown eyes and easy smile. He'd been hired to replace Grant Vang, Jude's former partner, now in prison. Valentine was a welcome addition and had come highly recommended. She suspected the Chicago PD had hated losing him.

"How many victims?" Uriah asked.

"So far, five."

She and Uriah looked at each other. Professor Masucci had said the next victims would number five. They followed Valentine inside.

"It's a maze." He kept his flashlight aimed at the floor and out of their eyes.

"Who called it in?" Uriah asked.

"One of the squatters who's been living here off and on. Just a kid, probably not old enough to be on her own. I took her statement, but she was too shaken up for me to get much info." He glanced at Jude. "Maybe you'd have more luck."

"I can try."

"I'll show you the scene. Like I warned you over the phone, it's bad." It was too dark to read his expression, but there was no need. His words laid it out. "I left Chicago to get away from the violence, but this is the worst thing I've ever seen." They stepped over a pile of trash. "The victims were living in the basement. Probably been squatting there a long time."

"Drug related?" Jude asked, unable to keep a little bit of hope from her voice. There was always relief, from citizens and cops alike, when kills were drug related. Not that those deaths didn't carry as much sorrow and distress, but there was a reason behind them, as unsavory as that reason was. Bad people doing bad things, including killing one another.

"You have to see it." Valentine turned and continued leading the way. "Watch your step."

Some areas of the floor were scorched, and the occasional board shifted and bounced, indicative of a structural problem.

"This place should have been condemned," Uriah said.

The odor detected near the front door was stronger now. More than once, their progress was interrupted by men and women in uniform, subtly fleeing the scene, hands to mouths, jostling their way through in a panic to exit the building.

"Don't throw up in here," Valentine warned an officer as she paused long enough to gag. With watering eyes and a hand pressed to her mouth, she continued down the hall.

Jude sensed they were nearing their goal when Valentine stopped at a basement door and stepped aside. From somewhere in the bowels of the building, a generator was struggling, the plodding, uneven engine creating a visual confusion of flickering lights on the stairwell. Keeping her flashlight trained at her feet, Jude went down the steps first, with Uriah and Valentine behind her.

It didn't really look like a basement, certainly not the kind of basement she'd spent too much time in. This was large and finished, with drywall, a hardwood floor, big-screen TV, bar to one side, leather couches. A lot of sports had probably been viewed here. Along with the seating were two bedrooms and what had once been a spalike bathroom with a Jacuzzi, now someone's bed, with a pillow and blanket. It was the kind of space you might expect to find in an upscale house in this part of town. And the perfect place for squatters. Home sweet home, without the water and electricity.

It looked like the current occupants had brought in items scavenged from the rest of the house, making the area cozy with oriental rugs, candles, stacks of books. One section off to the side had been set up as a kitchen, with a dining table and pots and pans. Cans of Sterno and a camping stove told the rest of that story.

It had been pretty nice, all things considered. It was still pretty nice. Except for the blood, the gore, the violence of the scene, and the words painted in blood on one wall:

All I seek is already within me.

A common affirmation. In a situation such as this, the innocent words became a sinister and narcissistic statement of self-worth and self-adulation. *This is my right.*

Three women and two men, four of them with lamp cords around their necks, three with their hands bound behind them. The women were nude, their bodies covered in blood and stab wounds. It wasn't hard to see where the intestines had come from.

"They were tortured," Jude said softly. "This is not the same MO."

A few crime-scene techs were present to collect evidence, but Jude guessed that, like the cops, others hadn't been able to take it. The lack of windows made it even worse. There was no way to let in air.

As if reading her mind, Valentine said, "We're supposed to get purifiers down here soon. Right now, nobody can last long. For more than one reason, but the smell . . ." He pressed the back of his hand to his face. He still stood near the bottom of the stairs, seeming unwilling to step into the heart of the scene.

She felt bad that he'd left the Windy City for this. Not a good trade.

Someone in a respirator jumped to his feet, turned, and hurried past them. Near a wall, a young female officer stood with her face in her hands, silently sobbing. She was young. Maybe fairly new.

They just needed time to adjust to the horror. People were adaptable. Their brains could shift and change and tolerate the situation. It would be okay. They would be okay.

Life and death.

This was what they dealt with. It was their job. But evil . . . The evil should never be accepted. "We'll find the people who did this," she said. "That's what we need to focus on right now."

Her words had some impact, and seemed to shore up the remaining officers, detectives, and specialists on the scene. *Remove yourself from your own misery, lest it consume you.* That was what she'd learned during those years in darkness.

Uriah inched forward, responding to Jude's words as if she were the head of Homicide and not him.

"The body, in any state, is a thing of beauty," Jude whispered, crouching beside one of the dead women. "Even now." Someone handed her a pair of latex gloves. Without taking her eyes off the victim, she said, "Even in such deep repose." She snapped on the gloves. "Nothing can touch them anymore. Nothing can cause them any more pain. We are here to honor them, serve them, help them."

She felt Uriah's presence beside her. "Throat sliced," she whispered in words meant only for him. "You see that, don't you?" She glanced around, then back to the woman in front of her. "All of them." Otherwise, as previously noted, not the same MO. None of the past victims had been violated like this. But five bodies. They couldn't ignore that number.

"I do." He didn't join her, but instead whispered in a voice laced with despair, "What kind of monsters are we dealing with? These people are hardly more than kids."

She pulled herself away from the body to stand next to Uriah. Right now, he needed her more than the woman on the floor did. "It's okay."

"It's sure as hell not okay."

"The violence, *this* violence, is over. The pain is over for them."

"I don't know how you can find that reassuring. They're dead." He looked at her with angry eyes. "Are you saying we're all better off dead?"

"That's not what I meant."

"I know what you meant. Death is better than life." He scanned the room. "You might be right."

"That's not what I meant," she repeated.

"Really?"

"No."

"Some honesty would be welcome."

"I'm always honest."

"I'm not sure about that." His eyes narrowed; he'd contemplated her mental state many times before. "I think you're doing what you have to do to survive," he said. "And if that means thinking dead bodies are lovely, then . . ."

As others came and went from the scene, unable to stomach it for long, Jude and Uriah remained. When the medical examiner arrived, they pointed out various clues, from size and depth of wounds to the force behind many of those wounds.

"Spree killing," Jude said. "Done for fun."

"The sliced throats look the same as the theater murders," Uriah said. "That's all I know."

His words and dismissive attitude hurt, but she also understood he was dealing with his own pain. He felt responsible for this, and he felt responsible for his wife's death. It was a lot for him to carry.

Uriah remained in the basement while Valentine led Jude upstairs to talk to the girl who'd found the bodies. In a room set up as the command center, the young woman sat in a chair, a blanket around her shoulders, trying to drink from a cup that kept knocking against her teeth. She looked about fourteen, probably a runaway, with dirt embedded under her nails, and hair that hadn't been washed in a long time. Valentine introduced them, then left them alone together. Jude talked to her softly, mostly reassuring her. The girl hadn't seen anything. Hadn't heard anything. Just arrived at the house to find the carnage.

"Do you have anywhere to go?" Jude asked when she was convinced she'd get nothing else out of her.

She shook her head. "I want to go home."

"Where's home?"

"South Dakota."

"We'll help make that happen."

Jude found a female officer. "I think we have a runaway. Take her downtown, feed her, have a detective interview her in an interrogation room, then see if you can get a relative's phone number. Hopefully someone can come and pick her up, but let them know we'd like her kept in town a few days."

The officer nodded and Jude caught up with Uriah, who was preparing to leave. Outside, Jude checked her phone and was surprised to see three hours had passed. It was still dark, but birds were waking up and reporters continued to wait, dressed in winter jackets and knit caps. The previous day had been warm, but fall nights in the city could be frigid. A camera was shoved in Jude's and Uriah's faces, and questions were shouted.

"Press conference in the morning," Uriah said, his voice heavy with exhaustion.

"Here?" someone asked.

"We'll let you know."

Jude looked for her bike, then remembered she'd come with Uriah. On the way to the car, Uriah said, "I think I'm going to have to burn these clothes. This smell is never coming out."

She understood the scent of his clothing wasn't what he was really thinking about. "The trick is to not let it break you," she said once they were in the car and Uriah was easing the vehicle from the curb.

"Sorry I was abrupt earlier. Not making excuses, but what we saw back there will be with me for the rest of my life."

She'd told him everything would be okay, but she understood what he meant. It was impossible to look at the world in the same way once you'd witnessed such evil. Every crime and every crime scene imprinted your psyche with a new sort of blackness. "I'm not saying forget. I'm saying don't let the weight of it get you."

"Is that how you did it? How you do it? How you made it through?"

Past and present. It was the first time he'd asked such a direct question about her years of torture. "I don't forget. I don't try to forget, because when you forget, it comes back at inopportune times. When you're experiencing life. But if you never forget, it can't break you."

"You really never try to erase it from your mind? Pretend the bad things didn't happen?"

"Never."

He took a sharp turn. "Coffee." He pulled up to the drive-thru and placed an order for two. Jude paid, and they were back on the road in less than five minutes. She took a sip of hot liquid. "Drop me at my motorcycle," she said. "I'm going to go home to shower and change. I'll meet you at the office. I think we need to talk to the math professor again."

"Grab a couple of hours' sleep while you're there," he said. "You're going to need it."

Maybe Uriah had been right when he said she was just fooling herself, because later, while hot water ran over her, she began to shake violently. She locked her knees, forcing herself to remain upright. Finally, she shut off the shower, got dressed, strapped on her gun, and headed downstairs. Uriah had said to get some sleep, but she knew she wouldn't be able to do that here.

Pausing next to her motorcycle, wishing she'd paid more attention in math classes growing up, she pulled out her phone and did a Google search. The next number in the Fibonacci sequence was eight.

Elliot had heard Jude come home, followed by the sound of the shower and the knock of the water moving through the pipes. And then he heard the slam of her apartment door. He listened, expecting her footsteps to fade, indicating she'd gone up to the roof, where she sometimes slept. He'd seen her there more than once, but he'd kept his distance because he'd also seen the handgun beside her.

She didn't go to the roof. Instead, her steps moved past his door. She was heading to the parking garage.

Wide awake now, he threw on jeans and a flannel shirt and ran from his apartment, slipping into his car moments before she exited the garage on her motorcycle. He turned the key in the ignition, put his car in gear, and followed. He knew how to keep a good distance between them. He'd done this before.

CHAPTER 18

The world was asleep and the night was muffled, but her awareness of the key in the lock was familiar, and Jude felt a surge of anticipation—a response carried over from her imprisonment. She'd spent days and years imagining that faint sound, waiting for the shudder of her captor's footsteps overhead, waiting to hear his voice and feel his touch. Because whatever happened once her cell door opened was better than endless hours of darkness spent with nothing but her own thoughts.

But now she was the one doing the unlocking.

She closed the door behind her, pausing to rub her fingers across the metal of the key, warm from the pocket of her jeans. She hadn't gotten the locks changed yet, and she wondered if this had been *his* key. Finally she tucked it away and turned on her flashlight app, illuminating the basement stairs and blood spatter in front of her. With no hesitation this time, she moved down the steps, every footfall taking her closer to her goal, and every step bringing increasing reassurance.

Once she was inside the cell, the door open an infinitesimal crack, she turned off the light and sank to the cold concrete, resting her shoulder blades against the insulated wall, eyes closed, and let out a sigh. She'd told Uriah every crime had an impact on them. It was true. She would never be free of this one.

Her mind moved backward, to the days of her imprisonment and the self she'd discovered there. She might have dropped off to sleep, or she might have convinced herself that this was her life again. But at some point, she became aware of footsteps above her head. They confused her. Were they happening now? Or had her memories returned with such clarity that even her ears deceived her? Was it the squatters? Whatever the true source, she fell back into the old reaction of waiting for him the way she'd always waited for him, hoping he'd talk to her this time, hoping he'd stay awhile.

She heard someone moving down the stairs, coming closer. And she imagined *his* boots, and imagined *his* face. Some shred of self-preservation was tripped and she pulled her weapon, held her breath, and waited.

He was *right outside the cell door.*

As she listened, the footsteps moved away, back up the stairs, to fade completely. She opened the door in time to hear a car roaring down the street. *Was it him?* No, he was dead. She'd killed him. Like she'd killed her father and brother.

Her fingers went limp and the gun clattered to the floor. She pressed a hand to her mouth, stifling a sob. He'd been here, and now he was gone, leaving her alone in the dark again.

She knew she should go upstairs and lock the door. Instead, she curled up on her side and slept. Deeply, better than she'd slept in months. At some point, she awoke with a start and listened in the blackness. Nothing but the sound of her own breathing. Unsure of how much time had passed, she checked her phone. Morning. And not that early.

This was bad. Her compulsion and fascination with the house was sick. She knew it. She should tear it down, but how could she possibly do that when it was so much a part of her? When it might prove to be a source of strength?

She got to her feet, slipped her gun back into the holster, and stepped from the cell. The basement windows had been cemented over long ago, before she'd been taken prisoner. Upstairs, she was puzzled by how dark it was, then realized the windows had been boarded up. Surprisingly, Joe the Handyman had come.

She moved through the house, her boot heels echoing on the hardwood floor. She found herself thinking about what she might do to fix the place up. *Stop!* Paint the kitchen table and chairs, maybe a cream color. A fresh coat of paint on the walls, maybe something in a pale yellow. *Stop!* Wash the windows and hang some cheerful curtains. *Stop!*

This was so wrong. Before she lost her resolve, she looked up demolition companies and contacted one of them to tear down the house.

"It takes time to prepare all the paperwork," the woman who answered the phone told her. "Permits have to be issued, gas and electric lines have to be disconnected."

Knowing it would take time was a relief. "That's okay," Jude said. "Take as long as you like." Wondering if she'd back out.

In the bedroom, the mattress gave off the scent of body odor and cigarette smoke. It was a smell she remembered. There was a long, low dresser against the wall. The crime-scene team had combed the house, but she opened drawers anyway, pulling them out completely, looking under and behind, running her hand along crevices. She didn't know what, if anything, she was looking for. Just the detective in her, maybe.

With the last drawer, something snagged. When she tugged the drawer free, she heard a piece of paper drop to the floor. She set the drawer aside and pulled the dresser away from the wall. Trapped in the dust was a curved photo, facedown.

A Polaroid.

She'd forgotten about the photos. How had she forgotten about the photos? And if she'd forgotten about them, what else had she forgotten? What else had she bent and turned into something else?

She picked up the print, shook off the cobwebs and dust, turned it over—and sucked in a breath.

Hours ago, she'd told Uriah she hadn't deliberately tried to forget anything. Not completely true. She'd pushed the hard-core events

away, and with distance she'd come to almost romanticize her time
in the house. She could see that now. In this house she'd been more
spiritual, calmer, more accepting, in many ways a freer person. She'd
transcended the physical world, the world of cold and pain, and survived in the world of her mind. Maybe that was what she really missed.
Maybe she missed the deep connection to herself she'd found in the
house. The security of herself. The photo served as a shocking reminder
of the harsh reality of her existence here.

He'd taken many photos. More at first, and then fewer as she physically fell apart. In this one, like most of them, she was nude, arms tied
above her head, a gag in her mouth, eyes wide. He used to hang her
from the ceiling above a floor drain and hose her down with freezing
water. Later, he got lax, or maybe he knew she was broken, and he'd
have her stand with no restraint, just the warning of his Taser.

She stared at the photo. She didn't feel any embarrassment or
humiliation. It was like staring at someone else. A stranger. An abused
stranger. What she felt was compassion and outrage. Finally, she was
thankful she'd killed him.

Numbly, she cast her gaze around the room, noting the hundreds
of pinholes, spaced evenly. And she realized he'd tacked her photos to
the wall. He'd probably spent time in bed looking at the pictures while
masturbating.

Where were the rest of them? Had they been there when the crime-
scene team came? If so, why hadn't she been aware of them? Did Uriah
know? Maybe not. Maybe they'd been removed before that, either by
her captor or by someone else. By Grant Vang, who was now in prison
for setting her up? She hadn't looked at the evidence they'd collected—
she'd had no real reason to. But now . . . She tucked the photo inside
her jacket. Like the picture of the house, it seemed to have a pulse.

Outside, she breathed in cool morning air, trying to get her head
in the game, the game of multiple murders.

"I thought that motorcycle looked familiar." The words came from the homeless woman Jude had talked to before. Today she wore a snagged knit cap, torn tennis shoes, dirty jeans, baggy coat. Her shopping cart overflowed with treasures she'd scavenged. "You supposed to be in there?" She squinted at Jude.

"It's okay. I bought it."

"Oh." The woman was understandably surprised. "Why?"

"I'm not entirely sure."

"Well, better you than someone else. Still wish I could have helped you."

"Your name is Ruthie, right? Ruthie Logan? Maybe you can help in another way. You might have heard of the murders near Lake of the Isles." A lot of homeless people knew one another. But they'd also be reluctant to talk. "If you could keep your eyes open, let me know if you see or hear anything suspicious."

"I'm not sure." She was uneasy about the idea.

"We're talking murder. I just want you to stay alert. That's all." She zipped her jacket. "Do you still have my card?"

"Does it look like I ever get rid of anything?"

Jude smiled, then got serious again. "Don't put yourself in danger, but contact me if you see something that worries you."

The woman shuffled off, and Jude got on her bike. With both feet still on the ground, she dug out her phone and called Uriah to check on the day's agenda.

"I'm heading to the morgue before going downtown," he told her.

"I'll meet you there in an hour." She stuck the key in the ignition. "I've got something I need to do first."

Her personal story wasn't a priority, but she needed to see if someone had found the other photos of her when they'd processed the house. More than that, she needed to know if Uriah had kept them from her. If so, she might have to revise her current level of trust.

CHAPTER 19

The street directly in front of the police department swarmed with press. Jude avoided them by parking in the garage. She swiped her security card at a little-used door, then took the elevator to the basement and the evidence room, where an armed guard named Harold manned the counter.

He smiled when he saw her. They talked for a minute, then Jude got to the reason for her visit. "I need to see something from my own case. The Fontaine evidence."

"No problem." He clicked computer keys while staring at a screen she couldn't see from where she stood. If he was wondering why she'd want her old files, he didn't let on. Using a mouse, he scrolled, and squinted behind his glasses. "Got several entries here."

"It would have been submitted after my escape," Jude told him, "with the evidence gathered at the house where I was held captive. I'll need to look at anything that might contain smaller items. Paper, possibly photos."

"That narrows it down to two."

"Great."

He disappeared into the evidence stacks. She listened as he rummaged around. He finally returned with two cardboard boxes with cut-out handles that he slid across the counter, along with a pen.

"Had trouble finding one of these. It was filed incorrectly. That never happens."

The first box had been signed out by several people over the years, most of the signatures going back to her disappearance. The second one, the one that had required a search, had only one signature and was sealed up tight. That signature belonged to her partner, Uriah Ashby.

She signed the chain-of-evidence forms. Then, in a private room with tubes of blinding fluorescent lights overhead, she placed the containers on the lunchroom-style table. Without sitting down, she opened the box that had been signed out several times.

Nothing surprising. Small items, bagged and collected at the scene. The kinds of things found in a desk. She resealed the box, signed it, then broke the seal on the second container and lifted the lid. Photos. A hundred, maybe more, and they matched the one she'd tucked into her pocket at the house.

She dropped heavily into the nearest chair. Afraid of losing her nerve, she pulled the box closer. Without giving herself time to think, she sifted rapidly through the photos, grabbing several, shuffling through them, putting the viewed ones aside, grabbing another handful, distantly aware that her breath was coming short and fast, and that sweat had broken out on her body.

In every photo, she was nude. Filthy, hair matted, welts and cuts on her chest, legs, back, hips. The images weren't dated, but it was easy to track the passage of time by her physical decline and hair that had gone from brown to white. And not just the physical, because it wasn't her body that commanded most of her attention. Her face, the reflection of her essence, was the most shocking and disturbing thing of all. Over time, her expression had gone from angry and disgusted and resolute to blank, sometimes even submissive. She'd seen that look in the faces of girls who'd been kidnapped and tortured. The eventual emptiness in the eyes, the slackness of the jaw—indications of giving up and shutting down.

Some people had remarked on how she'd changed. Even if they didn't say it, she'd seen it in their unease. She'd clung to the idea that she was better now, stronger now, that the foolish person she'd been in those early photos was gone, replaced with someone better.

But seeing the blankness, she wasn't sure . . .

Not everybody wants to be an unemotional robot, Caroline McIntosh had said.

She went through the images again. It was like looking at someone else, someone who'd been victimized. Someone who needed help. But the person who'd done this was dead. And there was no one to save.

A rap on the door caused her to jump. Harold poked his head inside. "Everything okay in here?" He was too far away to be able to see the content of the photos.

She glanced at the clock on the wall and realized she'd been there almost an hour. "Fine. I'll be out in a minute."

He smiled and closed the door. She gathered up the Polaroids, dumped them back in the box. Sealed the container, signed and dated it, then returned everything to the front counter for restocking. "Thanks, Harold."

She left.

She didn't *care* that Uriah had seen the photos. They'd met right after her escape. The next day in the hospital she'd told him everything, so nothing should have shocked him. The idea of him seeing her so broken and humiliated wasn't what bothered her. Why had he kept the photos a secret? Who else had seen them? What else was he not telling her?

Her phone rang. She checked the screen, expecting to see Uriah's name since she was late to the morgue. *Unknown Number.*

In the hallway, as she waited for the elevator, she answered.

The voice at the other end belonged to a female. Young, hesitant. "Is this Detective Fontaine?"

"Yes."

"I called you the other night."

Jude struggled to pull her mind away from the photos. "The telethon? You gave me your number."

"Clementine."

As they talked, Jude straddled her bike and put the key in the ignition. "Do you need help?" She struggled for words that wouldn't come across as aggressive or threatening. "Are you in danger? From yourself? Others?" Too direct.

"Not right now."

"What can I do? I'd like to help you." Uriah was expecting her at the morgue. But those people were dead. This girl was alive. "I can meet you somewhere. Right now."

"I don't think that's a good idea." She sounded nervous, as if she regretted the call. Jude was trying to come up with another plan of action when Clementine hung up.

Jude hit "Return Call." She let it ring a long time and was about to give up when a distracted-sounding man answered.

"I'm trying to contact someone named Clementine," Jude said.

"I don't know anybody by that name. This is a pay phone. It wouldn't stop ringing, so I picked up."

Could be true, because Jude heard traffic. "Do you see a young girl nearby?"

"I just got off the bus. Some people got on, but I didn't pay any attention. I was looking at the damn phone."

"What's your location?"

"You sound a little too old for prank calls."

She didn't want to reveal her identity in case the man was Clementine's abuser. "Not a prank."

"I gotta go."

"Wait! Where's the phone located?"

"Can't talk anymore. Don't want to be a part of your game." He hung up.

There was nothing Jude could do except hope Clementine called back. She tucked her phone away, pulled on her helmet, and headed for the morgue and Uriah.

CHAPTER 20

U riah respected the past and the stories older buildings could tell. Because of that, he found the Hennepin County Morgue more fascinating than he probably should have. The squat concrete structure sat in the shadows of the downtown Minnesota Vikings' stadium. Almost everyone, from the mayor to morgue interns, agreed the facility had outgrown itself. Uriah was glad something was finally going to be done to remedy the situation, but he wasn't thrilled about the new site suggestions, all in third-ring suburbs. Yes, it would provide for future space to expand, but the drive, especially during rush hour, could be a severe time suck for busy detectives. And it would mean this building might be torn down. He didn't like that thought at all.

The backstory was that the current location was a repurposed food-storage facility. It had been a great idea years ago, due to a giant walk-in cooler that could store thirty-six bodies at once. Thirty-six! Alarmingly, that was no longer enough space. They were up to 1,400 autopsies a year, and it looked like they were on target to break that record.

The center had five postmortem stations. Most morgues in cities the size of Minneapolis had at least nine. "The overrun of bodies puts me in an odd position," Ingrid Stevenson had said to him not long ago. "I've been pushing for funding for a new facility, and the state keeps asking for proof of need. We certainly have it now."

Uriah turned off Chicago Avenue and pulled into the parking lot behind the morgue. Jude was there, standing next to her motorcycle, helmet tucked under her arm. She seemed even paler than usual, the circles under her eyes darker, her white hair in the kind of disarray people worked hard to achieve. He sometimes thought *heroin chic* when he saw her, then kicked himself for it. He was sure her look had nothing deliberate about it, and if she did any more than shower and brush her teeth, he'd be surprised. "Did you get any sleep?"

"A little."

Something was going on. She was putting off an unfamiliar vibe. He must have given her a once-over, because she glanced down and pulled a sticky cobweb from her jeans. It was the kind of cobweb a person picked up in a basement or an attic.

He couldn't give it the kind of consideration it deserved right now. Local media were on site. Not many. Most reporters were still at the crime scene, but a few had taken the opportunity to attempt to grab a sound bite at the morgue where the murder victims had been taken. Smart.

His phone rang. He glanced at the screen long enough to note that it was his father, and he remembered he'd never returned his call. He let it go to voicemail.

On the way from parking lot to morgue door, questions were directed at the two of them as they approached the building. Since the crowd was small, the queries weren't shouted and weren't even rude. "Minnesota nice" was a real thing, as passive-aggressive as it might come across sometimes.

"We're holding a press conference in a little over two hours," Uriah told them. "In front of the police station." Something they already knew, of course. They were all trying to beat the mob scene. "No exclusives. We won't be sharing anything until then."

That was followed by lowered mics and groans of disappointment.

Inside the building, he and Jude checked in at the front desk, then passed through Security into the relative quiet of the morgue.

"You know how I told you I bought the house?" Jude asked as they moved down the hall in the direction of the prep room.

Ah, that might explain the cobwebs. He hoped to hell she hadn't been hanging out there. Not healthy. "Let's talk about this later, okay?" He wanted to be able to give her and the topic his full attention. Inside the room, he opened a cupboard and pulled out a disposable yellow gown and handed it to her. "When we're done here." His back to her, he grabbed a gown for himself.

"I want to talk about it now," she said.

"The ME's waiting for us." She shouldn't have needed the reminder. He shook out his gown and slipped it over his arms, fastening it behind his neck, then reached around to grab the waist ties. If Jude were anybody else, he would have offered to tie her gown and asked for help himself.

"Now is better," she said.

Jude still struggled with social skills, and he doubted she'd ever get the hang of normal conversation again, or understand the difference between a good time to bring something up and a bad time. Normally that was okay. He was used to it, used to her saying things that were out of context or inappropriate for the situation. But sometimes, especially when he'd had very little sleep and was dealing with headaches that just wouldn't stop, her timing could be irritating. His voice, when he'd responded, had probably been sharper than he'd intended.

"What can you tell me about this photo?" she asked.

Distracted, he turned. She hadn't even started suiting up. Instead, she'd put the gown aside and was standing with her legs braced, helmet still tucked under one arm, an unreadable expression on her typically unreadable face. Between two fingers, she held a photo taken with an instant camera.

He might have flinched.

The photo was of Jude. Battered, bruised, eyes that were blank. Those eyes weren't blank now. "I want to talk about this," she said. "Now."

He took a step toward her, stopped. "Where did you get that?" Was someone stalking her? Was someone who'd been involved in her abduction still on the loose? Had Grant Vang sent it from prison somehow? His mind took another leap. "Did you receive that in the mail? Is someone threatening you?"

"I found it in the house."

The house. He let out his breath in relief. "Okay. I thought maybe . . ."

"You know why I couldn't meet you earlier? I had something to do. I had to check the evidence room for a box of similar photos. Come to find out, the only person to sign the chain of evidence was you. Ever."

He swallowed.

"You deliberately kept them from me," she stated.

True. He'd struggled with that decision, but in the end he'd figured they'd bring her nothing but pain. There was no sense in sharing them. And he'd deliberately misfiled the box so no one else stumbled across them, by intent or accident. But he'd discounted Harold's ability to find anything. "By the time we discovered them, they weren't necessary for the case," he said. "So I sealed them and that was that." What he'd done bordered on a lie of omission. He didn't add that if he'd been able to, if he hadn't been a detective who preserved evidence, he would have taken the next step and burned them. Every last one. But he prided himself on his integrity even when it hurt people he cared about. That very thing had gotten him into trouble with Jude in the past.

Their relationship was fragile, still in the building-trust stage ever since he'd surprised her with a seventy-two-hour mental-health hold after she'd lost it at the governor's mansion a few months back. He hadn't stuck up for her when she'd been kicked out of Homicide for her little stunt, either. He suspected Jude would never fully trust anybody again, but the last thing she needed was to pull away from him. He was likely the only person on earth who even kind of understood her.

"On top of everything, this"—she waved the photo—"wasn't found by the crime-scene team."

His fault too. Uriah was the one who'd discovered them. He'd been so dismayed by the brutality of the images that he'd been sloppy. He'd boxed them up and attached an evidence seal before dashing into the yard for air so he wouldn't pass out.

But Vang had been there and had seen them too. Jude might flip out if she knew about his involvement. Then again, Jude had never flipped out except that day in her father's house. Even now, her expression had shifted away from the liveliness of moments earlier. He suspected he'd witnessed a brief flare of the old Jude, but that person had vanished again, and right now she was looking at him with eyes that were almost as blank as the ones in the photo. As if the emotion of the conversation had been too much for her and she'd shut down again.

"It's okay." Her tone shifted to one of reassurance. That was odd, *her* reassuring *him*. "You did it to protect me," she said. "I understand." She tucked the photo inside her jacket, very near her heart. "Thank you."

He wondered what she planned to do with it. He had this notion of her putting it in some flowery frame and hanging it on her wall. Of course, she'd never really do that. Would she?

CHAPTER 21

Jude didn't like arguing, especially with her partner. She was relieved when their discussion was over, and almost regretted bringing it up in the first place. She was sorry she'd upset him.

In the prep room, she slipped into the paper gown and tucked her hair under a disposable elastic cap. Sometimes, with cases that were open and shut, they didn't wear the gowns, but in a situation like this, it was best to avoid anything with the potential to contaminate. A single hair from someone who wasn't on site when the crime took place could be detrimental to the investigation. So they were cautious. Gowns, shoe covers, caps, and even masks were in place before they stepped into the large room.

Jude had never been at the morgue when all five bays were in use. Right now, each bay contained one of the murder victims. Three females, two males. The males were waiting for autopsy; the females were in various stages of autopsy, with two gowned employees staffing each table—one doctor, plus one assistant or diener. Two other people in lab coats and name tags helped where needed. Jude knew Uriah would have preferred that Ingrid Stevenson, chief medical examiner, perform all five autopsies, but that was unrealistic. Instead, she was overseeing all five. Also in the room was Dominique Valentine.

"So far we've identified three of the victims," Valentine said. "We're still canvassing the neighborhood and hope to have all five names by the end of the day."

Uriah nodded, and Jude moved between the stainless-steel tables, familiarizing herself with the bodies that had been cleaned and sliced open. It was unnerving and distracting to be surrounded by so many murder victims. Ordinarily, an autopsy had a sacred, intimate feel. That was present in the room today, but it was overshadowed by the separate conversations and activity. As always, the victims seemed different here, away from the violence of the scene. "Two of them don't look over sixteen," she noted. "If they're runaways, it might be hard to ID them. Many runaways don't even use their own names." She thought of the girl called Clementine.

"We'll reach out to the public during the press conference," Uriah said, glancing up at the clock.

Hours ago, in the burned-out mansion, it had been hard to get a good look at the victims. Here, the lights were too bright, blinding. Uriah peered over his mask and asked, "Any sign of sexual assault? Before or after death?"

"One body had vaginal tearing."

"Postmortem?" Jude asked.

Ingrid shook her head. "I doubt we'll be able to determine that, but we've already taken vaginal and pubic-hair samples."

"Live semen!" Those excited words came from a young woman sitting in front of a microscope. She realized she'd shouted, and turned back around, shoulders hunched in shame.

Semen could remain alive in a corpse for up to thirty-six hours. "It might not belong to the killer," Jude said, moving to the body of the other young girl. This one had dark skin and dark hair.

"I'll put a rush on the most pressing DNA samples," Ingrid said.

Jude leaned closer to the body in front of her. "These don't look like stab wounds." Last night, or rather early that morning, the girl's nude body had been covered in blood, making it impossible to visually process. Today she was clean, her wounds exposed.

"I wanted you to see that." Ingrid stepped closer. "We still need to wash two of the victims, but so far three have similar wounds."

Jude, Uriah, and Valentine moved from table to table. "What makes that kind of wound?" Uriah asked. "I'm not seeing a typical bite pattern." He pointed to the stomach of one of the Jane Does.

"Looks like it *was* caused by teeth," Valentine said.

Jude glanced up. "They're biting out pieces of flesh."

"You're right." The words came from Ingrid, who appeared behind them.

Once they got past the shock of that realization, discussion moved to the murder weapon or weapons, and they all agreed that the neck wounds looked similar except for depth and length. They also noted that the lethal wounds had been created by more than one kind of blade this time, ranging from sharp to dull, serrated to smooth. No more trying to find sales of a specific type of knife.

One looked to have been created by a left-handed person.

"We're going to pay close attention to stomach contents," Ingrid told them. "We're hoping that might give up some clues. What they ate, when; were they together at the time."

Killers could cover up a lot of things, but most of them didn't think about food.

"Once we're done with all five autopsies," Ingrid said, "we'll bring in our forensic pathologist."

Valentine remained in the suite with Ingrid Stevenson while Jude and Uriah slipped into the prep room.

"Do you think it's the same person or persons?" Jude asked as she removed her mask and untied her gown.

"Yes, even though the MO isn't the same."

"The left-handed slice is telling."

"I agree. And the reason behind the ramped-up MO could be escalation and the fact that the perpetrators had the freedom to spend more time with the bodies inside a secluded and secret space."

"My thought too. Are the pieces of flesh trophies?" she asked. "Something they saved?"

He tossed his gown in the biohazard bin. "This is a sick-as-hell idea, but what if someone is actually eating them?" He seemed horrified by his suggestion.

She didn't pause as she removed her slippers from her boots. "Some killers see the murder of their victims as something spiritual, as the ultimate bonding of two people. It makes sense that they might want to partake of the victim's body."

"Let's say the killings are all related, going back to the first single body. Something triggered this," Uriah said. "Not just this killing, but all of them."

"Death of a family member?" Jude suggested. "It's usually a mother or mother figure, but that's not always the case."

"Then you have the numbers thing. College students are under a tremendous amount of stress. Not the ones attending college for the social life and parties, but the overachievers. The loners. I think there was some of that going on with my wife. I thought her return to school was something she was doing out of boredom. I didn't realize how much her less-than-perfect scores were having an impact on her. And being a nontraditional student, she didn't have friends at school. Or even here, since we'd recently moved to the Cities."

It was the most she'd ever heard him talk about his wife. "Many college students have mental breakdowns and don't become killers," Jude said. "Even professors."

"What's your profile?"

"I'll put one together tonight."

"I'd like to hear it right now. Your undiluted, instinctual thoughts. How do you see this person?"

"Okay . . ." She had no problem tossing out ideas. "I think our main killer is twenty-five to forty-five. White male. And he recently suffered a traumatic event and possible loss."

"Education?"

She crossed her arms and leaned against the wall. "I think he's educated. College, maybe a degree. Maybe self-taught. And, unlike most serial killers, I think he's social. He'd have to be, since we've pretty much established he's not working alone. And he must be charismatic. He has to be able to sway people to his way of thinking."

"Like a cult leader."

"I think he'd have to have that kind of power, anyway. Somebody who's possibly recruiting people for his benefit under the guise of something else."

"And if he's recruiting . . . Who are the most likely people to fall for something like that?"

"They come from all walks of life, so I'd hate to narrow our focus too much. They're black, white, rich, poor. Think Jim Jones. His followers were of every age and every background imaginable."

"But they didn't kill people. They were lost and searching for answers."

They left the prep room and headed down the hall.

"Okay. Then Manson," Jude said, pausing at the exit, unwilling to continue their conversation outside, in front of the waiting press. "I hate to bring him up, because he's too easy. What happened with him was unique, and it was very attached to the sixties underground culture. But yeah. Some similarities, for sure."

"He appealed to young, impressionable females."

"Right. Part of Manson's allure was that these young women— Susan Atkins, Linda Kasabian, Patricia Krenwinkel—found him attractive. They were in love with him, hard as that is to believe. I don't know about Tex Watson. Maybe he was attracted to Manson too. Or maybe it was just a case of one psychopath following another."

"We've been working on the assumption of a leader and a follower or followers, but we could also be dealing with a pair of equals," Uriah said. "In some crimes involving more than one perpetrator, it's been determined that the murders would likely never have happened if the killers hadn't had each other."

"Like the Railway Killers, John Duffy and David Mulcahy. Or David Alan Gore and Fred Waterfield." Not to mention her own family.

"The Killing Cousins." Uriah pushed the door open, paused when he saw that some die-hard media people were still there, then took a deep breath and plunged forward.

Questions about the bodies and autopsies were tossed at them. Jude recognized a guy who had a popular YouTube channel. Everybody wanted a sound bite. Normally friendly with the press, Uriah didn't slow his pace as he headed for his car. "Downtown," he shouted over his shoulder.

CHAPTER 22

The press conference took place in front of the Minneapolis Police Department. It was just past noon, and the weather was overcast and unusually humid. Jude and Uriah took their places behind an array of microphones. Nearby stood Chief Vivian Ortega, Detective Valentine, and Medical Examiner Ingrid Stevenson. Due to her aversion to being on camera, Jude hung back while Uriah, as head homicide detective, spoke for their department; Ingrid followed up with anything he'd left out.

The PD had a good relationship with the press, no hostility, based on mutual respect, which was fortunate, because they needed the media. They got the expected questions: *Who found the bodies? Was it drug related or an acquaintance murder?* Then the more disturbing ones: *Was this a spree killing? We're hearing the crime scene was reminiscent of the Sharon Tate murders of 1969. What are your thoughts on that? Who were the targets? What about the theater killings? Any connection?*

And one question directed at Jude.

"I've been told you recently purchased the house where you were held captive," a reporter said. "Is that true?"

The sound of the world dropped as Jude stared out at the expectation in front of her. In her mind, she stammered and searched for a reply. Beside her, she felt Uriah bristle and knew the newsperson was about to be chewed out. Jude stepped closer to the cluster of mics and said, "That has nothing to do with this case."

The reporter didn't give up. "Is it true?"

"Next." Jude pointed to a familiar face, someone who asked an on-point question. Jude replied. She was still rattled, though, and while her attention was focused on the reporter, someone outside her field of vision shouted.

"Murderer!"

A fraction of a second later, Jude felt something strike her neck. She staggered and caught herself as sticky red liquid bloomed on the front of her white T-shirt. People screamed. Jude and Uriah dropped to the sidewalk as Valentine pulled Ortega to safety.

Jude examined her bloody hand. The color didn't look right. Next to her on the concrete was a broken water balloon that had been filled with what Jude now realized was probably red dye and corn syrup.

Uriah seemed to grasp what had happened at the same time Jude did.

He sprang to his feet and dove headlong into the chaos of the screaming, dispersing crowd, running and weaving, his jacket flying behind him. Jude raced after him, the mass of humans parting in front of her, people with hands to their mouths as they watched the scene play out. Others held phones high to capture the moment.

As Jude cut through the throng, she caught a glimpse of Uriah several yards ahead. Like a boat moving through water, he left a wake of shifting people behind him. She increased her speed until she was close enough to see him tackle someone to the ground.

When she caught up, Uriah was lifting a skinny white guy to his feet by the back of his shirt. Young. Maybe seventeen or eighteen. Thin arms, sunken cheeks, dark circles under his eyes. Stringy yellow hair, about shoulder length.

"You're choking him," Jude said. "Let him go."

At first Uriah seemed unwilling to comply, but he finally gave the guy a shove and released him. The kid staggered, caught himself. "I didn't have anything to do with that." He pointed to Jude's neck and shirt.

Cops arrived. The suspect was handcuffed and led away. As Jude and Uriah walked back through the crowd, both breathing hard, a woman offered Jude a handful of tissues. "Here, honey." Jude accepted them and wiped at her face and neck.

They returned to the press conference area. Uriah, disheveled and still breathless, briefly explained that no one was in danger. "But just in case, let's call this a wrap and catch up later."

The reporters, the ones who'd stuck around, didn't argue. Microphones were dismantled and power cords were wound around elbows.

Inside Headquarters, Jude went straight to the restroom and tugged her white T-shirt over her head. Standing in a bra and jeans, she scrubbed and rinsed the fabric using liquid soap from the dispenser. The red wasn't giving up very easily. She placed the dripping shirt on the side of the sink, bent over, stuck her head under the faucet, soaped her hair, washed it, and was blindly reaching for paper towels when several were shoved into her hand. She rubbed them over her hair and straightened to see Vivian Ortega leaning against the wall, arms crossed.

"That was quite some drama out there." The chief pushed herself away from the wall with one shoulder, squeezed the excess water out of Jude's shirt, and stuck the fabric under the automatic dryer. "I like the pink hair. Not sure how that's going to go with our dress code, but considering the circumstances, I think we can look the other way."

Funny she would mention dress code. Or maybe she'd meant to be funny, since Ortega had to be aware of complaints about her own clothing.

The dryer was high powered, and within five minutes the shirt was damp but not soaking. Jude slipped her arms in the sleeves, then stuck her thumb in the collar and pulled the neck hole over her head.

Ortega was eyeing her closely, lips pressed together. The reporter's question was probably the first she'd heard about Jude's purchase of the house, and Jude braced herself for disapproval. But Ortega's words surprised her. "I haven't come right out and said this to anyone but my husband," she said. "I've hesitated for fear my words will just sound like someone else who wants reassurance from you, but I'm terribly sorry about your abduction. More than that, I'm sorry we didn't find you, and I'm sorry you had no one but yourself to depend on. I'm sorry you were so alone, and I'm sorry we let you down." Her eyes glistened, and Jude hoped she wasn't going to full-out cry. "I don't ever want you to feel that alone again," Ortega said. "We're family here. We're a team. We look out for one another."

Jude tried to remain unaffected by Ortega's words while giving her an honest response. "The truth is, we're all alone." She needed to escape this conversation and the open-wound rawness of it.

Ortega got a pained look on her face. "That's not true. I will always be here for my detectives. Always. Even when I'm at home."

Jude played that scene in her head. A call to Ortega's house would result in those sweet sounds of life. The kids. The dogs. Ortega's caring husband. How could that possibly make Jude feel better?

She busied herself by cleaning the paper towels off the sink and throwing them away. Her hands were shaking. Way too much brittle emotion in the air. She was rescued by a text from Uriah telling her she was needed downstairs.

Balloon boy is in an interrogation room.

Thank God. Jude told Ortega she had to go. Once out of the restroom, she wanted to run, leave the building, race down the street to anywhere that wasn't here. Instead, she caught up with Uriah.

"Name is Blaine Michaels," said the officer who'd booked him. "And he's got a record." She handed Jude a clipboard with the boy's details.

"Eighteen," Jude told Uriah as he opened the door to the interrogation room. She noted with relief that her hands were now steady even though her heart was still pounding.

Inside, Michaels was slumped in a chair in a pathetic attempt to look tough, eyes downcast, a glass of water in front of him. In the center of the windowless room was a rectangular table. Jude sat across from their new friend, and Uriah chose to create a more intimidating presence by standing at the end of the table, two feet from the young man.

Before they began their questioning, Michaels said again, "Wasn't me." He glanced up at Uriah, then back down, avoiding prolonged eye contact. He spent the next five minutes denying his involvement, but finally gave up when he saw they weren't going to back down.

"Somebody on the street said they'd pay me to throw the balloon at you," he finally admitted, staring at his hands. "That's what I meant when I said it wasn't me."

Struggling not to let the restroom meeting with Ortega distract her, Jude forced herself to focus. "By pay, you mean pay in drugs?" she asked.

"Does it matter?"

"Knowing the kind of payment gives us a better grasp of your motivation," she explained. "People do a lot of things for money. But drugs to a drug addict . . . Well . . . people will do almost anything for a fix."

He wiped the back of his hand against his nose. "Not an addict." His black T-shirt, with the name of a band Jude didn't recognize, was soaked with sweat. He was in need of a fix right now. Her next thought: *This is somebody's child.*

"Believe it or not, I'm more sympathetic to an addict than just an opportunistic criminal," Jude said.

"What are you addicted to?" Uriah asked.

Michaels chewed his lip and shook a leg up and down before finally muttering, "Heroin."

Jude pushed the glass closer to him, saying, "I'm sorry. That's a tough road." She leaned back in her chair. "What did you mean by the word you shouted? 'Murderer'? Was that directed at me? Or someone else?"

"I don't know what it means." Head tipped to the side like some bird trying to sleep, he shrugged. "I was just told to say it. Shout it, throw the balloon at you, then run to meet the guy who was going to pay me."

Uriah pulled out his phone and relayed instructions for officers to check out the area where Michaels had been brought down.

"He probably never planned to pay you," Jude said. "You know that, right?"

"Maybe. But maybe he would. And I thought it was harmless." He glanced at her hair and stained shirt, then away.

"We need a description."

He gave it to them while Uriah took notes.

"He was maybe twenty-eight? Thirty? Not sure."

"White?" Jude asked.

"Yeah. Mustache. Curly brown hair that I'm pretty sure was a wig." He pointed to Uriah. "Kinda like your hair, but longer. And a beard that mighta been fake. Looked real, but I think maybe it was a disguise. Like, I'm not even sure the mustache was real, so I don't know how much help a description'll be."

"Height?"

He frowned.

"Taller than me?" Uriah asked. "Shorter than me?" It was good to give them comparisons. "I'm five eleven."

"Maybe the same."

"Weight?" Jude asked.

"It was kinda hard to tell, because he was wearing a baggy coat. I'd say average."

"So maybe 160."

"Yeah."

"You mentioned a baggy coat," Uriah said. "Describe that."

"Like one of those canvas farm coats that are kinda yellow, kinda brown."

Uriah wrote it down.

"I can't stay here." He clenched his hands between his legs and rocked back and forth. "I can't stay in jail."

Yeah, he needed a fix. "We'll bring in an addiction specialist," Jude assured him. "She's good and will get you on medication that'll help."

He looked ready to cry. "I'm sorry."

"I know."

Outside in the hall, Uriah said, "What do you think? Is he telling the truth?"

"He doesn't have a hard-core record. A few minor drug busts, that's all. I'd say we let him go, but I'd also like to see him in a program."

"You're being too soft on him. He assaulted an officer of the law."

"And that's a serious offense. He did something stupid. I want to give him a break. He might not learn anything, he might not change, but he's so young, Uriah. And he should have more than an addiction specialist. If he's addicted to heroin, he's going to need to go through medical detox."

Hands on his waist, he gave it some thought before finally agreeing. "He could actually be in more danger if we release him."

"We don't know who was behind this. You're assuming it has something to do with the recent murders, when in fact it might have everything to do with my killing my father. Whoever hired him could be harmless. And that person is certainly a coward. And I don't think we want to waste much more time on this kid when we've got a serious case to solve."

"Let's see if there's an opening in a rehab center out of town," Uriah said. "I'll have someone look into getting him in a place where he can live for at least two weeks. Then we can reevaluate."

Jude returned to the kid and explained the plan.

"You're going to release me?"

"If you agree to go into a program."

"I don't have health insurance."

"We can get you set up with something state funded."

He began crying for real. She didn't know if it was out of relief from not having to go to jail, a reaction to her compassion, or desperation for a fix.

Outside the interrogation room, she and Uriah made plans to find Professor Masucci.

CHAPTER 23

Jude flashed her badge at the young man raking leaves in front of the two-up-two-down stucco apartment building. It was late afternoon, a few hours after she'd left Blaine Michaels in the hands of a social worker who planned to get him into detox. "We're looking for Professor Masucci." She and Uriah had gotten no response from the call box on the building. "Have you seen him today?"

The kid shifted nervously from foot to foot. He was shirtless even though the day wasn't warm enough. Had a bit of California surfer to him. Blond, blue eyes. Smelled of pot. Jude didn't care.

"Probably on campus. That's where he usually is."

"You a student?" Uriah asked.

"Yeah. Everybody knows Professor Masucci. Because he's weird. And some kids make fun of him and even tease him. Not me." He rushed to make that clear, which left Jude to question his denial. She guessed he was lying, guessed he was one of the people doing the teasing. "He walks around campus most of the day," the young man said. "I've heard he thinks he still works there."

"Wait. What?" Jude said. "He doesn't work there?"

"Nope."

So the article she'd read had been correct.

"He was tossed out of a lecture hall when he tried to take the podium." He stifled a laugh. "What is it about math that makes people lose it?" His eyes lit up and he pointed at the badge he could no longer see inside Jude's jacket. "Oh, hey! That's what this is about, isn't it? Those murders. Oh, man. I could see him going totally off the rails and doing something like that."

"Let me make this clear," Jude said. "The professor is in no way a suspect. We just need to talk to him."

"Oh, sure, sure. Okay. Sorry, man." He started raking again, faster now, head down.

Jude and Uriah looked at each other, eyebrows raised, and left, next stop the university located two miles away. Once there, they drove though the old part of campus, found a parking spot, and walked to the math department, located in a building made of red sandstone.

The massive structure had a clay-tile roof and copper eaves, along with the requisite ivy flanking a set of impressive steps leading to massive wooden doors fit for a castle. It was like a movie set. Students strolled leisurely to their next class, books tucked under an arm, and it almost made Jude want to go back to school. A glance at Uriah told her he wasn't having the same nostalgic thoughts. He was moving fast, as if eager to get the visit over with, perspiration glistening at his hairline. There were many colleges in the Twin Cities, but she wondered if this was where his wife had gone.

The head of the math department was in; they were escorted to her office, where they loosely explained the reason for their visit.

"Do you think he could be a danger to students?" The woman fiddled nervously with a necklace that looked like it was made of red pearls. She was tall, probably in her sixties, with dark-brown hair and a demeanor that came from years of living within the insular world of academia. "I don't know if you're aware of his history, but he lost his job here several years ago," she said from across an ornate desk that echoed the period of the building, with its marble floors, dark woodwork, and ceilings that went on forever. "He had a mental breakdown, and the university just allows him to wander around the campus. We thought he was harmless, and being here gives him a sense of purpose. He was a good professor. Most of the students like him. They talk to him, address him with respect, give him food. Sometimes he sits in on classes, and helps students in lab. If someone is having a problem understanding the curriculum, he's there for them." The worry lines between her eyes deepened. "Nobody ever thought he was dangerous. But I'll have to admit, there's been talk. You know. With all the bad things going on today, we don't want to scare off potential undergraduates." She lowered her voice. "We've considered banning him."

Uriah shifted uncomfortably in his leather chair, and Jude leaned forward, elbows to knees.

"He's not a suspect," Jude assured her. The last thing she wanted was to cause trouble for the professor. Not a good message to send to anyone trying to reach out to them. "We'd appreciate your not sharing this information," she said, "but we think he might be of help with a case."

"He had a life once, you know," the woman said. "A wife. Kids. One day he just snapped. He started throwing books and shouting at the students, telling them to run. And he never came back from that. As far as I know, he's on medication that keeps him level, but he's never been the same. It's a sad thing for students and colleagues to have witnessed."

She looked up at the industrial clock on the wall and told them where they might find him. They left their cards and went through their typical spiel. "Let us know if you think of anything or see anything unusual," Jude said. Then they were back outside and Uriah was heaving an obvious sigh of relief.

As they walked, he rolled his shoulders. "This weather."

"I know." She'd hardly even noticed, but now she saw it was another perfect fall day.

"I almost lost it here myself a few months back," Uriah confessed as they continued side by side.

Off in the distance, someone shouted to a friend and girls laughed. "My wife was going to school at the U when she committed suicide. Not long ago, I found out she was having an affair with her philosophy professor. So I came here one day." He looked surprised by his own words of admission. "I don't know what I had in mind."

They'd gone to another place that caused him pain. But there would always be reminders. There was no escaping them.

"I think at the very least, I'd planned to beat the shit out of him," Uriah said. "But when I was face to face with the bastard, I couldn't do it. I realized he wasn't the one who'd done wrong. It was me. I wasn't there for her."

"We're all responsible for ourselves," Jude pointed out.

"That's easy to say, but I might have been able to help if I'd known she was suffering. This job . . . It swallows you whole. It's not good for relationships."

"Do you think you'll ever be in another?" She couldn't imagine such a thing for herself, but Uriah . . . Yes.

"Right now, no. I can't. Not when I know I can't give a hundred percent. When I might not be there for her."

They found Professor Masucci sitting on a bench feeding pigeons in the grassy area across from Northrop Auditorium. From where they stood, Jude could see a silver section of the Weisman Art Museum, which overlooked the Mississippi.

He wore the same suit he'd been wearing the other day. Did he have something more for winter? And was she so very different from him? Sometimes Jude feared she was barely holding it together and it wouldn't take much for her to scream at people to run. After all, she'd purchased the house where she'd been tortured. And she'd even spent the night there.

"I thought I might be hearing from you." He threw a piece of white bread to the nearest bird, then handed a slice each to Jude and Uriah. "I saw the news last night."

"Your theory does seem to hold some weight," Jude told him. Now that they all had bread, more birds were descending.

Uriah broke off a piece, gave it a toss. "We're just checking in to see if you have anything else to add. You deal with math every day. You kind of have your finger on the pulse of the math world here on campus. Have you heard or seen anything suspicious?"

"That bird"—Professor Masucci pointed—"she's the dominant one of the bunch. Look how fat she is." He admired her for a few moments, then, keeping his eyes on the birds, he twisted the bread bag and tied it closed. Was he saving it for himself? "I wish I could help you," he said, putting the bag aside, his focus finally shifting from the birds to Jude. "You know it'll be eight people next time."

Her stomach dropped. She did know. And she hoped he was wrong, hoped they caught the killers before that happened. "Do you remember ever having a student who was fascinated with the Fibonacci sequence?" she asked. "Or someone you maybe just met at random?"

"That would be a lot of people." He tipped back his head and admired the orange leaves above his head. "I find it fascinating, don't you? And to bring death into the sequence . . . It's a lovely idea."

Jude and Uriah looked at each other in alarm. Could *he* be involved in some way? He was a frail man, but then, she herself had said that with enough adrenaline, a small person could have committed the crimes.

And there were documented cases of killers actually helping the police with an investigation.

"It takes the nature of the sequence to an entirely new level by adding a human component," the professor said.

"Doesn't that ruin it?" Jude asked, watching him closely. "It's no longer nature then."

"But isn't man always looking for ways to control nature?"

"Often to his detriment," she said.

"Exactly. The deaths are an art form."

Uriah jumped in at the mention of art. "Do you recall running into anybody who was an artist with a fascination for the Fibonacci sequence?"

Professor Masucci seemed to look inward. "I've known several over the years." His face clouded. He picked up the bread and put it down again, seeming agitated.

Uriah raised his eyebrows in silent question and Jude responded with a slight shake of her head. *Don't push him.*

"It was good seeing you." She gave her remaining bread back, and Uriah did the same. Then she pulled out her card and handed it to him. "I think you already have one of these, but just in case . . . If you want to talk to me, or if you ever have anything to tell me, just give me a call. It doesn't even have to be about the case."

"I hope you find it."

"It?"

"What you're looking for."

"We're looking for a person or persons."

"I mean you." He glanced at Uriah. "Both of you."

They nodded their good-bye and left him there, sitting in the late-September sun. Jude thought about what the kid in the yard had said about math and an unstable mind. And she wondered which came first.

CHAPTER 24

I t was late, six hours after their visit to the professor, and Jude was heading back to her apartment. She needed to feed Roof Cat. Take a shower. Try to catch a few hours of sleep. Her skin felt hot and tight, and her muscles ached. Any bed, any pillow, would be welcome right now.

After parking in the underground garage, she took the stairwell to her fourth-floor apartment and found a sticky note stuck to the door. Expecting it to be something about a failed delivery attempt or something from Elliot, she peeled off the note.

Your cat escaped when we came inside to fix your shower. The foyer door was propped open, and I think he got out of the building. Sorry. ☹

Sad face? Really?

She tried to reassure herself. Roof Cat had been feral, so if he'd managed to escape the building, maybe he'd be smart enough to avoid traffic. She hadn't had him long, and he'd never really acclimated to being an indoor cat. Part of her had wondered if he'd be better off back on the street, but in truth he hadn't been all that able to fend for himself. He'd been scrawny when she'd first spotted him on the roof, which had prompted her to feed him. Later, when he quit eating completely, Uriah had helped catch him. That had resulted in a trip to the vet, dental surgery, and recovery in her apartment, where she'd fed him warm milk while insisting she didn't want a cat. She'd tried to give him to Uriah, but he'd told her his building didn't allow cats. A lie, she guessed. Uriah had it in his head that she needed a friend, even if that friend was a feline. And so she'd become an accidental and reluctant pet owner. But with news of his absence, she had to admit she'd liked having him in her apartment when she came home. Now, when she stepped inside, she felt his absence acutely. He tended to hide under the bed, in the hole he'd made in the box spring, and didn't sit on her lap like cats were supposed to do, yet she always felt his presence. She'd liked that he was aloof and only slightly less suspicious of her than he was of anybody else.

Growing up, she hadn't had pets. Her mother was allergic and her father hadn't liked animals of any kind. Probably for the best, all things considered, since many killers began with animals. There was her old boyfriend's dog, but it had died while she was in captivity, so the idea of bonding with an animal was relatively new to her. And the sense of loss she was feeling was even newer.

She dropped her messenger bag on the couch next to another note, this one on a sheet of typing paper. It instructed her to not use the shower for twenty-four hours. She opened a window to air out the space and get rid of the scent of sealant. A cool night breeze rushed in, along with conversation from the street below.

She searched the building, from the basement to the roof, calling his temporary or nontemporary name even though she was pretty sure he didn't know it. Like Uriah had said, Roof Cat wasn't really a name, and she usually spoke it only to herself, in her mind.

The cat was gone.

Just a cat, she tried to tell herself. He'd be okay, she tried to tell herself.

Back in her apartment, she paced and wondered what to do. He wasn't a missing person. Calling the police didn't seem practical. From below her feet came the sound of faint music. Elliot. She left her apartment, ran down the worn marble stairs, and knocked.

"Have you seen my cat?" she asked before he'd finished opening the door.

His hair was messy and his face was the kind of puffy that hinted at sleep. He was wearing faded jeans and a faded T-shirt with another band name she didn't recognize.

He must have been one of those people who left music on all night. Then she had an awkward thought. Maybe he did it to cover the sound of her screams.

"No, sorry. Your cat's missing?" She saw *How in the hell does that happen in an apartment building* on his face.

She explained, and told him to let her know if he saw anything. He was already grabbing his coat, slipping it on. "I'll help you look."

"That's not necessary. I was just checking to see if you'd seen him."

"I want to help. Come in while I find a flashlight." He vanished and she stepped inside.

She could see nothing through the half-closed bedroom door, but in her mind she pictured a broom leaning against the wall for those times he pounded against the ceiling. He returned a moment later with a flashlight, and locked up after they stepped into the hall. "What's the cat's name?"

She thought about what Uriah had said about Roof Cat not being a real name. "He doesn't have one."

He frowned, puzzled again. "How long have you had him?"

"A couple months."

"That's weird," he said. "That he doesn't have a name yet."

"So I've been told." Then she confessed. "I call him Roof Cat. But I don't know if that's good enough. Maybe I need a version of it."

"I guess it would be tasteless to call him Roofie."

"Yeah."

They spent two hours searching outdoors, starting small, then expanding. A few people joined in, but by two o'clock Jude called it quits.

"Let's go back to the apartment and I'll make a PDF, take it to a twenty-four-hour copy shop, and get flyers made to put up," Elliot said. "I'll just need a photo of your cat, and your phone number for the flyer."

"I don't have a photo."

He gave her that look again. "You have a cat and you don't take photos of him? I've had a cat less than a week and I've already posted at least twenty photos on Instagram."

"I don't have Instagram."

"You should have Instagram."

"Why?"

"It's fun. And you can share things with other people."

"I don't need to do that."

Standing in the middle of the dark sidewalk, he pulled his phone from his pocket, moved closer so she could see, and began scrolling through photos. They were all of his new cat, a black long-hair. "His name is Blackie."

Not much better than Roof Cat. "I'd never do that," she said. "I'd never put myself out there like that."

"Because you're a detective? I think it would be good PR."

"I don't want to share myself like that. With strangers."

"Oh, right. Sorry." Contrite. Recalling her history and the reason she might have for not wanting anything to do with people in general. He put his phone away. "Not every stranger is an enemy, though."

They were walking again, getting very near their brick building. Streets were empty, and the city was relatively quiet. Her ears picked up a strange sound. It took her a moment to realize it was the occasional plop of rain against a fallen leaf. It sounded unusually loud in the semisilence.

"Let's go back to my apartment and do an online search," Elliot said. "We'll find a cat that looks like yours."

She surprised herself by agreeing.

Five minutes later, as they sat side by side on the couch, staring at Elliot's laptop screen, she decided on a yellow-and-orange tabby cat while Blackie watched them with suspicion. She wished it was this easy when dealing with sketch artists. "Good thing he's so generic looking," she said.

"Could call him Orangey once he's back home."

"You're very literal, aren't you? Orangey's not dignified enough. He has a lot of dignity."

"Sir Orangey."

She actually laughed, then got herself under control. The walk, the impromptu time spent with another human, followed by actual laughter, had pushed her close to overwhelming fatigue.

Elliot must have noticed. "I'll take care of this," he said. "Go upstairs. Go to bed. I'll design a flyer and have it ready in the morning. Stop by before you leave. Or you know what? I'll do it. You're dealing with those murder cases. I saw it on the news. Glad you weren't shot. I saw that too. But I actually kind of like the pink hair."

Normally she'd never accept a stranger's help, or anybody's help but Uriah's, but her brain was shutting down. Even her words, when she could figure them out, were getting thick. She gave him her number. "Do you need money now? For the copies?" She looked around, as if her bag with her billfold would magically appear.

"We'll figure it out later."

"Okay."

She went upstairs. She couldn't take a shower, but she probably wouldn't have attempted it anyway. Without removing her clothes or brushing her teeth or getting a drink, she dropped across the bed and fell asleep. When the dream came, she was too exhausted to scream.

CHAPTER 25

Wmenitle gotta get outta here."

Blaine Michaels stood hunched behind the homeless shelter, shifting from foot to foot. It was dark and the temperature was dropping, but he was more nervous than cold. The rehab center where Detective Fontaine had sent him hadn't been one of those places where they locked you up, so once everybody was asleep, he'd left and hitched a ride back to Minneapolis. Nobody was supposed to step outside the homeless shelter once the doors were locked for the night. He'd texted Clementine and she'd met him at the back door. It was against the rules to even open it, like she'd done.

When she didn't respond to his plea to leave, he spoke her real name out loud, something he'd been forbidden to do.

"Don't call me that."

"I'm done with this town," he said. It had been good at first, but lately . . . No. He wished he could turn back the clock. "You need to come with me."

"I can't."

He grabbed her arm and tried to pull her outside.

She jerked away. "Stop it!" She sounded scared. He was scared too.

"I've gotten myself in a mess. I have to get out of here. You need to come with me. I can't leave without you." To his humiliation, he started to cry the way he'd started to cry the other day when he was talking to the detective.

"Shhh."

"We've done bad things. I've done bad things." It was the drugs, he'd tried to tell himself. He never would have done anything like it if he hadn't been so high. Half the time when Blaine woke up covered in someone else's blood, he couldn't remember what had happened the night before.

"I know," she said.

He wiped at his nose with a shaking hand and tried to get himself under control.

He and Clementine had run away together, and he felt responsible for her. "We have to go," he said. "*Now.* We'll hop a train back to California. Come on."

She pulled in a shaky breath and said, as if coming to a big decision, "You're right about this place. And getting out. I'm afraid of what Leo might do when he finds out we've left, but I'm more afraid to stay." Before Blaine could express how happy she'd just made him, she added, "Wait out here while I get my things."

She closed the door behind her. Blaine exhaled in relief. Everything was going to be okay. They'd go back to California and forget about the bad things that had happened. They should never have left the West Coast. But some train hoppers had talked about Minneapolis like it was the best, and a buddy had said he'd show them the spots to dumpster dive. Where was that person now? Probably back in California. And the fucking winter. Holy shit. No way anybody back there would believe what winter was like here. He'd actually looked forward to snow. It was one of the reasons he'd come. And then he experienced it and he hoped he'd never see the shit again.

How long had Clementine been gone? Had she changed her mind?

He paced and smoked. Rain began to fall. The soft plop on the leaves made him feel safe. It must have been a sign, because he heard the click of the latch and there she was with her backpack.

"That all you have?" he asked. When they'd run away from California, they'd had sleeping bags.

"I didn't want anybody to notice," she whispered, letting the door lock quietly behind her. No going back. *Good.* She skipped lightly up to him, took his arm, smiled into his face. Her eyes were clear. Her long blond hair smooth and shiny and clean. This was how it should be. Just the two of them again.

She gave his arm a tug, urging him forward. He stumbled, caught himself, then fell into step beside her, their footfalls echoing on damp brick, sometimes muted by wet leaves. And he realized a heart could actually soar.

She was quiet, hardly responding when he said something to her. Normally chatty, she seemed focused on getting to the place where the track turned sharply and the train had to slow to cross the river. It was raining harder now. When they were near the spot, they climbed under an overpass where it was dry, sitting with feet to ass, knees to chest, and waited.

They'd given him naltrexone at the rehab center, but he was sweating and his stomach was making gurgling noises. The trip would be rough, but it didn't matter. They were going home.

He felt a rush of guilt. Detective Fontaine had believed in him and had given him a chance, even when her partner had been against it. Not many people had ever believed in him, and he was letting her down.

Clementine jumped to her feet. "It's coming."

The sound was buried by the pouring rain, but he could hear a low rumble that seemed to come from deep in the ground.

They grabbed their things. Bent at the waist, the two of them hurried toward the tracks and a giant concrete footing that supported the bridge. They'd hide behind the footing, watch the train cars, find the right one, then run like hell. They adjusted their backpacks. Just like the old days.

The rhythmic clacking of the train wheels grew louder, and suddenly cars were flying past. They were so close he could feel the heat, and the draft blew his hair back.

"Now!" he shouted.

As rain pelted down, they ran. Adrenaline raced through his veins, the train almost close enough to touch, their feet flying. He was panting, Clementine in front of him. Coming up beside them was a freight car with a sliding side door and metal steps with a handle to grab. It would be tricky in the rain.

"Careful!" His words were lost in the noise.

It was all about timing.

He shouted, "Now!"

She looked back at him. In the darkness, her face was a blur of white, and her hair blew to the side like a flag. She was beautiful, and his heart leapt again. And then she faltered. Instead of increasing her speed, she slowed too much and he almost crashed into her, both of them coming to a halt. One of her hands grabbed his arm and she spun around to face him.

Poor girl. She was scared. He understood. He was too. But their chance to get out of there was hurtling past. They could do it. He smiled at her with reassurance, hoping she'd see his face in the semidarkness. "Come on! Run!"

Then she did something really strange. She placed both of her hands on his chest.

And shoved.

His boots slipped in the loose gravel. His arms flailed. There were her hands again, only they weren't trying to help him. She was pushing him *toward the train*.

He grasped at the air, shouted her real name, his brain denying what was happening.

"I'm the bad thing you were talking about!" she screamed as he tumbled backward.

CHAPTER 26

Early the next morning, before leaving for Homicide, Jude knocked lightly on Elliot's door. He answered and handed her a stack of flyers. "Printed them up last night. Already hung a few. How do you think the imposter cat looks? Pretty good, right?" Elliot was wearing flannel pajama bottoms and a black T-shirt. Yet another band she'd never heard of.

"Perfect."

"You should probably hit the animal shelters," he said. "There's also a Facebook group for this neighborhood. I'll post there too."

She wanted to believe he was a good guy, but she still didn't trust him. Was it her overall distrust of everyone? She didn't think so. Despite his friendly attitude, or possibly because of it, he gave off a secretive vibe. "Why are you doing this? I haven't been that nice to you."

There had still been no mention of the screaming and the banging. From either of them. That was weird too, like the elephant in the room. Maybe he felt sorry for her. A lot of people did, and sympathy from anybody made her uncomfortable.

"I like to help people, that's all."

She juggled the stack of flyers, sliding them into her messenger bag. "Call or text me if you find him or get any leads."

He laughed softly. "Leads. Like I'm a detective too."

She didn't laugh.

"It's funny," he said, gesturing to aid his explanation, "because we're talking about a cat, not a person."

"I don't get it."

"Never mind." He closed the door and she hurried toward the parking garage, pausing in the stairwell when her phone rang. Uriah.

"I've got bad news," he said. "Blaine Michaels is dead."

She leaned against the wall, relieved that he wasn't calling to report the murder of eight people, but not relieved because *someone* was dead. "Suspicious circumstances?"

"He was running away. Tried to hop a train. It was raining and he must have slipped. The scene has been processed and the county coroner is on site and ready to bag the body. Neither of us needs to be there, but I knew you'd want to know about it."

"Call them. Tell them to leave Michaels where he is until I get there."

"I thought you'd say that. They aren't going to be happy, but I'll see what I can do. It's raining like hell out there," he warned her. "Not a good day for a motorcycle."

"I'll catch a cab."

CHAPTER 27

U riah was right. The day wasn't movie-set perfect, for a change. It had been raining several hours straight, the kind of cold rain that seeped into your bones and soaked through your clothes and shoes. From Jude's position at the foyer doors, she could hear the patter on the trees.

When the cab pulled up in front of her building, she ran across soggy grass and leaves. Sliding into the vehicle, she gave the driver the location and he entered it into his GPS. "Sure about that address?" he asked. "I don't think there's anything there."

"I'm sure."

He pulled from the curb and they headed for a place where the tracks turned onto a metal bridge that spanned the Mississippi. Long before the turn, train engines were forced to reduce speed, slowing enough for people to toss their backpacks into cars and jump inside. Train hopping used to be a culture reserved for the homeless and desperate, but more and more kids from all walks of life had at least tried it. Some loved it, some hated it. Some disappeared.

Twenty minutes later, the cab pulled to a stop. Beyond the rapidly moving wipers were a white coroner van and a few other official-looking vehicles.

"Don't you have an umbrella?" the driver asked.

"No."

He fumbled, then passed one over the seat. Black, a little wet. "Take it. I get them cheap."

She didn't have the best history when it came to cabdrivers. She took the umbrella. "Thank you." She paid and slipped from the car, open umbrella overhead, to navigate a muddy trail past a trestle covered in graffiti, toward a cluster of people in bright raincoats.

A few reporters were braving the weather. One young man spotted her and stepped forward. His suit was soaked and his hair was plastered to his forehead. He recognized her and asked, "Can you tell me anything about the body, Detective? Is this a suspected homicide?"

She held her umbrella higher—an invitation for him to step underneath, which he did. "I just arrived and probably know less than you," she told him.

He blinked water from his eyes and tried to hide his disappointment. Somebody young and new, hoping for a scoop. It wouldn't be coming from her. He thanked her and left the cover she'd provided.

At the drooping yellow tape, she flashed her badge. She didn't know why, since all the cops knew who she was. Maybe it was wishful thinking that one day someone wouldn't recognize her.

The death was being called an accident, but it would still be investigated. A glance around told her the scene had been processed in what was more a formality than anything else, quickly, with a small perimeter. Black umbrellas were everywhere. Leaving the scene were several men in suits, possibly from the National Transportation Safety Board. Whenever someone died from an encounter with a train, an investigation was required, no matter how obvious the cause.

The coroner spotted her. His expression didn't bode well for her presence on the scene. He wanted this to be fast, and he wanted to get out of the rain. She made an attempt to placate him, give him some assurance that she wouldn't waste his time. It did no good.

"We've been waiting to bag the body," he said. "Have a look so we can get the hell out of here." Rain beat against his yellow hood. Below that, his eyes were grim and his mouth was a straight line. It wasn't unusual to call a coroner if the death wasn't considered suspicious. He was old-school, which could be good—but in this case not so good, since he was known to prefer working with male detectives.

"The victim is someone I've dealt with," she told him, thinking that might make him a little less hostile.

He muttered something she didn't catch but figured was an insult. It was jarring to run into someone who seemed to think women shouldn't be cops. Thankfully those men were rare in their department, possibly because of the leadership of Chief Ortega, but they weren't as rare in other areas of the police force.

"It's pretty gruesome," he warned, his words a dare.

"I'll be fine." She had bigger concerns than this guy. If Michaels had gone to jail, he'd still be alive. This was her fault.

No one else was near the deceased. They either were finished or couldn't handle it any longer. A few stood in clusters, talking quietly while waiting to bag the body and leave the scene. Wordlessly, she moved past the hunched shoulders and black umbrellas. The scents of strong coffee and cigarettes wafted her way.

The ground slanted steeply where it had been terraced and graveled for the tracks. She focused on her footing while also remaining vigilant for anything that might have been missed in haste. She swung around and shouted to the coroner, asking how long the body had been there.

"Long enough to reach full rigor mortis."

"So eight to twelve hours?"

"I'm not a medical examiner, and the rain, plus low ambient temperature, would play a role." He shrugged. "I'd put it around there. We'll know more once the rigor mortis begins to reverse."

She approached the death site, careful where she stepped even though it hadn't been designated a crime scene.

It was bad. Really bad. The train wheels had severed the body in two. It might have been the worst thing she'd ever seen, even worse than the mansion slaughter.

She squared her shoulders, moved closer, and crouched down, sheltering Blaine Michaels's contorted face with her umbrella. Death had been quick, but not that quick. His heart would have continued to beat until he bled out. The knowledge that he'd probably lived a while was almost too much. She felt panic building and batted it away like the meditation balloons.

What a strange turn his life had taken over the past days. Someone had offered him drugs in return for tossing fake blood, and now here he was. Cut in two.

His hands were clenched into claws, held parallel to each other, as if he'd been reaching for something. Cadaveric spasm? It was rare, but it could occur in violent deaths that took place under extreme physical circumstances. She'd never seen it, but it would fit. And if it was cadaveric spasm, establishing time of death through rigor mortis wouldn't be possible, because it would never reverse.

Without touching anything, she shifted her feet to get a better view of his clenched hands. A single strand of long blond hair was trapped in his fingers.

She straightened and walked over to the lower half of the body. Disturbing, but not as disturbing as looking at Michaels's face. His jeans were still zipped and buttoned and he was still wearing a leather belt. Unlike victims of car accidents, who often lost their shoes, his boots were on his feet. Like the upper half of the body, this half was also contracted in extreme rigor.

She took her time and refused to allow the huffing and puffing and pacing man not far away to rush her. When she was done, she stood but didn't leave. Instead, she circled the area where the body had fallen. Interesting how little blood there was because the rain had swept it away. But a pair of deep gouges in the ground, about the width of the victim's boots, were still there. Signs of struggle? That, along with the hair in the hand, told a story. With her back to the crowd, she pulled out her phone and called Uriah. "You're going to want to see this," she said when he picked up. "It's not an accidental death."

He didn't question her. "Be there in fifteen minutes."

She tucked her phone in her pocket and turned around. This was a murder scene, and much of the evidence had already been lost, contaminated, or washed away. "Who found the body?" she asked a nearby officer.

"Some guy walking along the tracks."

"Is he still around?" She tipped her umbrella back over her shoulder and let the rain hit her face.

"I don't know."

"Find him." She tempered her command. "Please." Nobody was going to be happy about the next words she spoke, in a voice that carried. "The body isn't going anywhere. This is a homicide."

CHAPTER 28

"The cat's missing," Jude said.

Uriah glanced up from the severed body of Blaine Michaels. She'd had time to adjust, but he appeared understandably rattled. And queasy.

A tent had been erected over the scene. Trains had been rerouted, and the BCA was on site, taking photos and gathering evidence. More media were there too, along with vans equipped with satellite dishes that allowed for live, on-site broadcasting. And it was still raining.

"Roof Cat?" Uriah asked in surprise, appearing glad of the diversion. His dripping hair had soaked the collar of his jacket, and his black eyelashes were spiked. "How'd that happen?" Same expression she'd seen on Elliot's face.

She told him. "I was getting ready to put up flyers when I got your call."

"Well, shit." Hands at his waist, jacket open. She could see he was trying to gauge how to justify her leaving right now to go home and search for her cat. The fact that he was actually considering excusing her from the scene said a lot about him.

"It's okay," she said. "Somebody is helping me."

"I'm sorry." He seemed puzzled that she knew someone, anyone, well enough to help her find a cat.

"I don't think he liked being a house cat anyway," she said in an attempt to make them both feel better.

"He would have adapted."

"You keep saying that, but I don't know."

"Did you check the roof?"

"Yes, but I'll check again later. And I'll put food out for him."

"I've heard you should leave something of yours outside. Like a shirt."

"That could drive him away." She'd been his captor, not his friend.

They ducked from the tent. Standing under umbrellas, they interviewed the person who'd found the body. A man who claimed he just enjoyed walking along train tracks. Might or might not be true.

"We'd like for you to come downtown so we can take your official statement," Uriah said.

"Am I a suspect? 'Cause I was just letting you know about the body. I did a good thing, right? I mean, I could have just kept going and not reported it."

"We thank you for that," Jude told him. "This is routine, and the weather makes the present situation and location less than optimal."

He calmed down a little. "Okay."

"We'll have someone drive you," Uriah said.

As the partners left the scene, Uriah spoke on his phone, arranging for Detective McIntosh to interview the witness. As soon as he disconnected, he got a call about a lead on Michaels's whereabouts last night. "He slipped out of rehab and was spotted outside a homeless shelter called Light in the Darkness on South Washington Avenue," he said once his phone was back in his pocket.

Ruthie Logan had mentioned staying at a shelter on Washington Avenue. Was it the same place? Jude wondered.

They got in the car with their dripping, collapsed umbrellas, and latched the seat belts as Uriah made a three-point turn to head toward Washington Ave.

"What do you think?" He reached for his coffee mug.

"I don't believe the witness when he says he just liked to walk along the tracks. Who walks along tracks in the rain?"

"He could be a suspect."

"Why would he report it?"

"Stupid criminal? Because it looked like an accident?"

"Maybe." People didn't realize the majority of killers were easy to catch, mainly due to their stupidity. "I think he was a train hopper."

There were around twenty shelters of various kinds in the Twin Cities. Jude was familiar with most, but the one they were looking for had sprung up after the blackouts to address the increased homelessness and need for more beds.

"We can sleep twenty-four people," the director told them ten minutes later from her cramped, windowless office of concrete-block walls. Her desk and three bookcases were full of paperwork and bulging file folders.

Jude pulled out her phone and scrolled to a photo of Michaels taken the day of the dye incident. She turned her phone around so the director could see it.

"Blaine Michaels." The director was large, with dark skin and dreadlocks, kind eyes, kind face, probably about forty. "He's a regular. Visits us several nights a week. He and his girlfriend, although she's not here as much as he is."

"Girlfriend?" Jude asked. Could explain why he was in such a hurry to get back to Minneapolis.

The director pulled a ledger close and began riffling through the pages. "I don't have much information on her. We have a lot of underage kids come through here. I know you won't approve, being police and all, but our focus is to keep those children off the street and safe for the night. Feed 'em, give 'em a pillow, don't ask too many questions. I learned that fast. Too many questions and they don't come back. They go into prostitution or end up raped or dead."

"I understand," Jude said.

The woman found what she was looking for. "She was here last night." She glanced up. "We have everybody sign in, but we don't require ID, and many of our guests use aliases." She eyed the ledger again. "She checked in at six forty-five. That's odd, someone must have messed up—there's no checkout time written down for her. We lock the doors at eight p.m. and nobody leaves until we kick them out at six a.m." She turned the book around so Jude and Uriah could see.

"That's her." The director pointed to a single entry, written in big, round letters.

"Clementine?"

Uriah picked up on Jude's surprised reaction. "What does she look like?" he asked.

"Pretty. Long, straight blond hair."

Blond. "How tall?" Jude asked.

"Average."

"Age?"

The woman sighed. "She's one I thought might be a runaway. But she has an innocent face that could make her look younger than she really is. And she acts older. Wise and bossy. But if you just saw her, you'd probably think she was about sixteen."

They talked a little more, then Jude gave the woman her card. "We really need to speak to Clementine," she said. "If she comes back, don't tell her about us. Just call me."

"That goes against our policy."

Uriah wasn't as easy on her as Jude would have been. "Let me remind you, Clementine's boyfriend was killed less than twenty-four hours ago. Clementine might be the last person to see him alive. She's also the prime suspect right now. We need your help." He didn't add that if she didn't help, they had the power to shut down the shelter. It wasn't something they'd do, but the threat could serve as leverage.

"Okay." A nod. "I'll call if I see her."

"Thanks." The words were spoken in unison as Jude and Uriah got to their feet.

"Why did you react to the name Clementine?" Uriah asked once they were in the car.

"The girl who called and asked to talk to me the night of the telethon said her name was Clementine. I gave her my number, and she called me several days later."

"Unusual name." They were both thinking it was more than a coincidence. The light turned green and Uriah accelerated.

"She didn't tell me where she was or why she was calling."

"The dye-tossing incident is beginning to feel less and less like it was about your father," Uriah said, "and more and more like it was about the Fibonacci murders."

"That's what I'm thinking too. But I still don't get the connection. Or why the dye was thrown at me. It seems too risky for people who are ordinarily good at covering their tracks. It makes no sense."

The rest of the day was filled with briefings, another press conference, follow-ups, and poring over evidence results for various crime scenes.

"I'm going home," Jude finally told Uriah. It had only been dark two hours—a short day for her. "I need to put up flyers and leave a can of cat food on the roof." She stuck the stapler from her desk into her messenger bag, next to the flyers Elliot had made.

"Want me to help you look?"

"That's okay. You've had a longer day than I have, and I suspect you'll be here several more hours." She could also see pain lines in his face, an indication of another one of his headaches.

It was no longer raining, but she took a cab rather than a bus or the light rail. When they reached her neighborhood, she told the driver to stop at various corners so she could attach flyers to telephone poles.

At home, she was opening a can of cat food to take to the roof when a light knock sounded on her apartment door. It was Elliot.

"Is this Sir Orangey?" He held up a yellow cat. "I went up to the roof and he was just chillin' like he belonged there."

She slipped the cat from his arms.

"Guess it's him," Elliot said.

Jude nodded but didn't look up. She had her nose buried in the animal's fur. The door closed softly. That was followed by the sound of Elliot's footfalls on the stairs. Now that he was gone, Jude did something that took her by surprise. She started crying. The cat squirmed away, his feet hitting the floor with a heavy thud. He ran straight for the kitchen, jumped on the counter, and began eating the opened cat food. She didn't even tell him to get down.

CHAPTER 29

I ris's life was a cliché, but she was trying to do something about that. She wanted to be more than the daughter of a rich, business-suit-wearing, briefcase-clutching CEO who only cared about money. She wanted to be more than the brat raised by so many nannies she'd lost count.

But yeah. Cliché. Rich kid. Wealthy family. Despised the parents. Dropped out of college. Nineteen, old enough to be on her own, but she continued to kiss ass while resenting them.

Tonight was one of those kiss-ass nights.

Her mother had insisted Iris come home so she could attend a small dinner at her parents' multimillion-dollar house just off Lake Harriet in the upscale Lynnhurst neighborhood of Minneapolis. This was the price for letting them continue to support her. They paid for her apartment and had even bought her a new car. But none of it was *really* free. She had to attend their events, keep her spine straight and chin high, as she'd been taught. Smile, sound intelligent, be gracious, not get too drunk, engage guests in conversation.

She'd been doing it for years.

Her parents employed their own chef, yet this particular meal had been overseen by some fancy dude who'd waltzed in and out of their house, staying long enough to boss people around and berate their cook. Typical of her mother to bring in someone prestigious so she could attach his name to the meal. It was all about status. Get the best chef in town. Pay him a shit-ton of money. Invite the Minneapolis elite. This time it was a guy who owned the power company, along with his wife and son. The son was an obvious attempt at a set-up. Like that hadn't happened before. His name was Tristan Greer. She'd covered a laugh with her hand when she'd heard that. Pompous and lame.

"I'm glad you left your surly goth look at home," her mother told her.

They were standing in the kitchen and the guests would be there soon. They'd have drinks and talk boring talk before moving from the massive living area, with its expensive paintings, to the formal dining room.

Iris looked down at her black-and-white-print skirt. It was full, and it covered her well. No slutty stuff tonight. On her feet were black Mary Janes. Her top was red and sleeveless, with a neckline that allowed her to lean forward and flash some boob if she got the notion.

Lifting a cracker with caviar taken from some poor Russian fish, she paused with the black eggs on the way to her mouth, saying, "I gave up goth years ago." She smiled at the server as if they shared a joke between them. And they did. They both knew her mother was obnoxious, and the money she'd spent on tonight's dinner could probably put the guy's kids through college. It was shameful. The server looked nervous and didn't smile back.

Thirty minutes later, their guests arrived sans the potential mate, Tristan.

"He's coming later," Tristan's mother explained as she passed her coat to Iris's father. "Let's not wait for him."

Looked like Iris wasn't the only one dreading the evening. She wondered if Tristan would come at all.

They had drinks, they talked, Iris pretended to listen, her parents gave their guests a tour of the house, and finally it was time for the meal. The empty chair next to Iris's waited for the mysterious Tristan.

Next to it sat Iris's brother. She called him Damien, but his real name was Monroe.

She wouldn't be talking to him. She never talked to him.

Hardly anybody knew it, but the power-company guy had been behind the blackouts that had pretty much destroyed the city months ago. Iris had heard her parents whispering about a cover-up, how the man had taken bribes and swapped good equipment for cheaper stuff. The cheap equipment had weakened the whole system, and something had blown. Her dad said it was just a matter of time before they had another citywide outage, because the crook had only patched things instead of replacing them. "It would cost too much money."

Even her father had been horrified, and that said a lot about how bad it was. But there were also rumors of an activist group being behind the blackouts. She wanted the activist group to be the real story, because the country needed to jump to its feet and toss a table. Nothing had been exposed or proven, and now she had to talk to the liar. Another man just like her father.

They were halfway through the main course when she pulled her phone from her skirt pocket and checked the time.

"No cell phones," her mother said from the opposite end of the table. "You know that." She wiggled her fingers. "Give it here." Iris passed the phone to the power guy, and the device moved down the table until her mother set it beside her plate for safekeeping.

Five minutes later, Iris excused herself, ignoring her mother's look of displeasure. Instead of going upstairs to her old room, she leaned against the wall in the foyer and closed her eyes. As she rested and waited for time to pass, her ears picked up the distant sound of soft conversation. She marveled at how dull they all were and how excruciatingly boring the night was. Privilege and boredom seemed to go together. She'd rather be poor. She'd rather be homeless, living on the street. That kind of life was exciting and different every day. This . . . this wasn't living.

She heard a soft knock on the front door and opened her eyes. Her heart began to pound. She considered not answering, but what would be the fun in that? Crossing the room, she turned the deadbolt and opened the door.

Four people dressed in black, all wearing ski masks, stood on the dark step. Three men, one woman. Two of the men wore black sweatpants and long-sleeved T-shirts; one wore a tuxedo. Unlike the other three, who wore latex gloves, his were white cotton. One of the men in sweatpants held a can, cap off. Iris could smell spray paint.

She attempted to slam the door. Not fast enough. The one in the tux blocked her, then leapt silently over the threshold, pushing her to the side, a finger to the smiling lips framed by the mask. *Shhh.*

"No," she whispered. "Don't."

The smiling man grabbed her arm, squeezing hard.

From the dining room came the voice of Iris's mother. "Is someone here?"

As if of one mind, the four masked guests swiveled toward the voice.

CHAPTER 30

The door closed softly and one of the men locked it behind him. All four of the intruders peeled their ski masks to the tops of their heads, and faces were revealed. The leader in the tuxedo leaned close to Iris, smiled, and put a finger to his lips again. Behind him, one of the men clutched a handgun, his arm bent, the weapon pointing toward the ceiling. The girl's eyes were vacant and reflective, pupils large beneath her wispy blond hair.

Iris's breathing was coming in short little pants, her heart slamming, body covered in sweat. None of them had spoken any real words. All of them were staring at her.

She became aware of the sounds of normalcy coming from the dining room. That soft conversation and silverware striking china. She wished she were back in that room. She wished she hadn't opened the door.

The man in the tuxedo reached for her. She recoiled, then corrected so he wouldn't notice. He grabbed her and pulled her close, right hand to her spine. With his left, he threaded his gloved fingers through her bare ones. Almost silently, like the star of his own play, he began to waltz her around the room in what seemed like some crazy performance. But the threat was there. In the firm grip of his fingers. In the stiffness of his body. They were twirling so fast his shoulder-length dark hair flowed in a theatrical way. She closed her eyes a moment, almost tricking herself into thinking this was some prank, something one of her old school friends had devised.

"Honey, what's going on out there?" Iris's mother must have heard the shuffle of feet against the wooden floor.

The man stopped the mad dancing and kissed Iris on the lips, smiled, and whispered, "It's time." He held out a gloved hand and one of his team gave him a knife.

He brought the wide, shiny blade to Iris's face. Then he touched the cold steel to her throat, and chuckled at her reaction before flipping the weapon and pressing the blade handle into her palm. She curled her fingers around it.

The knife was heavy and warm, and seemed to have a life of its own. She wasn't a strong person, but adrenaline pumped through her veins. Maybe she could kill him. Take the knife and stick it in his jugular before anybody could stop her. He was the leader. Once he was dead, the rest would scatter.

She couldn't do it. She was too scared. Her brain seemed to shut down and the room faded. Even the man's tuxedo made everything feel like a dream. He pressed something else into her other palm. A pill, small and pink. Then he pulled her close and whispered in her ear, "This will make you feel better." He watched, waiting for her to take it. She obeyed and tossed the pill into her mouth. He smiled again and nodded, almost like he was proud of her. As if by some silent communication, because they'd done this kind of thing before and practiced this kind of thing before, the others moved in unison, two guns visible now. The leader turned Iris toward the dining room. With a hand to her back, he urged her forward.

Robotically, still gripping the knife, she began taking jerky steps toward her family.

Upon seeing the five of them enter the dining room, the people at the table froze in confusion. That confusion quickly melted, displaced by alarm. Iris's father got to his feet, braced to demand answers. But his status had no power over these people. Her mother asked Iris a question about the strange people in the black clothes. Iris might have replied. She wasn't sure.

One of the men with a gun, along with the blond girl, disappeared through a doorway that led to the kitchen. They were looking for others. Looking for staff. Her father, mother, brother, and the power guy and his wife were quickly and efficiently bound and gagged in the chairs where they sat.

It was interesting how none of them fought, not really. Her father and brother reached for their phones, but there was no struggle. They hoped their good behavior would lead to survival. *Be good, don't make noise. We'll rob you and be on our way.*

But this was no robbery. The intruders could be identified if anyone survived.

The two who'd gone to the kitchen returned. At first, it might have seemed they'd worn black to sneak inside without being seen. But now Iris noticed their faces were flecked in blood, their shirts soaked with it. Blood even dripped from their gloved fingertips to the floor, yet the red on their clothing wasn't obvious.

The next thirty minutes expanded to feel like a lifetime, like the night would never end. Seconds felt like days, and heavy movements were accompanied by sluggish vapor trails.

Her mother, behind her duct-taped mouth, was crying, tears running down her cheeks, body shaking. Iris's brother was crying too—the kid who tortured small animals was sobbing silently, his red eyes glassy with fear. The girl with the long blond hair stepped up to him. Like a baby offered candy, he stopped sniffling and his shoulders quit shaking. She wasn't much younger than him. Pretty, Iris supposed. Maybe he didn't notice how odd she was, how evil.

The blond girl bent down and looked into his eyes. Iris could feel Monroe's frozen anticipation. Maybe this girl would have mercy on him. Maybe this girl would even think he was cute. Because a lot of girls thought he was cute. A lot of girls had been destroyed by him.

The girl pulled off the duct tape in one quick jerk. Iris's brother gasped in pain, but continued to watch his tormentor, a hopeful expression on his face. The girl climbed on him, a leg on each side of the chair. She leaned forward and kissed him. Not a chaste kiss, but a sexy one, thrusting her tongue deep into his mouth.

Everybody in the room watched, transfixed, wondering what the hell was going on. Finally, the girl pulled back several inches. Monroe's mouth was red from the pressure of the girl's lips, and his eyes were confused.

As Iris stared at her brother's face, the red around his lips grew. A puzzled moment passed before Iris realized the blooming of red was blood. His eyes changed. Alarm replaced the question as a gurgling, sucking sound came from somewhere within him. And then Iris noticed the smile on his neck. A big gash that began to squirt blood.

He turned his head slightly, looking for her, his eyes making contact. What was he thinking? What did someone like him think about when he knew he was dying? Was he sorry for the things he'd done to her? Things her mother and father refused to believe? Was he sorry about that? No, he was probably just thinking of himself.

While this played out, sounds were emitted by the other captives. High keening noises, and chair legs banging against the wooden floor.

Monroe's eyes went flat and the blood stopped spurting. Iris felt a strange sense of relief, almost as if his death erased his misdeeds.

The girl with the yellow hair kissed him again, slipping her tongue inside his dead mouth. This time, when she pulled away and tipped back her head to laugh, her teeth were covered in his blood. Then the girl spun around, strode up to Iris, and kissed her on the lips. The taste was metallic and salty.

There was a roaring in Iris's head, a hundred times louder than the ocean. And yet, when the girl with the glassy, soulless eyes leaned back and spoke, Iris heard her. "That's how you do it."

If the scene had a soundtrack, it would be thundering dread. Or maybe something sad and soothing. Iris latched on to the idea of something sad and soothing.

She felt a hand at her back. The girl was pushing her forward, toward the dining table, where her parents still sat. Iris wondered if they'd have tried to run even if they hadn't been bound and gagged. The keening noises they'd been making had stopped, and their eyes held the deep shock and acceptance of the unthinkable.

Iris looked from one intruder to the next, pausing on the leader. His gloves were still white.

"Please," she whispered. The drug he'd given her had kicked in. The room shifted, and the walls moved. Colors changed, and the shivering cold in her veins began to warm. She turned back to her parents. They sat on opposite sides of the table, facing each other.

"Make a choice," the leader said.

He wanted her to kill one of them.

She began to hum a tune she'd forgotten until now, something one of the nannies had sung to her as a child. A song meant to calm hurts and fears.

The blond girl glided from Iris's father to the next person, her eyes on Iris. She dug her fingers into Iris's mother's hair and pulled back her head, exposing a long, bare throat that had seen a lot of special creams over the years.

"Now," the leader said, his voice a harsh command.

What if she disobeyed?

What if she obeyed?

"You never believed me," Iris said. She chose her mother because the woman should have protected her, supported her, defended her. "You never believed me when I told you what Monroe did to me. But

I think you *did* believe. I think you knew all along. I think you both knew and chose to ignore it. And you didn't want anybody to find out. So you called me a liar, a spoiled brat. But you knew it was true. Didn't you?"

Her mother squeezed her eyes shut and fresh tears ran down her cheeks. Iris stepped closer. With a burst of rage and a sweep of her arm, she cut long and deep. At first it seemed as if nothing had happened. But then a red line slowly appeared against her mother's white skin, and blood began to run.

At almost the same time, the other intruders ended her father's life, along with those of their two guests. Lucky Tristan.

The amount of blood was astounding, so much it seemed like a video game or TV show. Blood shot several feet into the air, hitting the walls. At one point, Iris slipped on it and crashed to the floor. She laughed and rolled and scooped blood up with her hands. The girl with the yellow hair joined her. She dipped her hands in the blood and crawled across the floor to write on the wall. When she was done, she rubbed blood on her face, laughing and talking to herself.

The room continued to swirl as the intruders went to work posing the people slumped at the table. Iris didn't participate in what they were doing. Instead, she looked away and began humming to herself once more.

Hours might have passed, or minutes. At some point, the leader pulled her to her feet and swept her into his arms as he began to dance with her again. She wanted to tell him to be careful, he'd get blood on him, but it was too late. When his hands touched hers, his gloves were finally soiled.

"There are only seven people."

The dance came to a halt and the leader looked at the boy-man who'd spoken. "Are you sure?"

"We've gone through the whole house twice."

"Seven." The man with the white gloves frowned. "With all our careful planning, how did this happen?"

"We don't know."

The leader slowly turned back to Iris.

It took several beats for her to understand his intent.

She ran.

Through the house, up the stairs, to her old room. She slammed the door, locked it, and dove under the bed.

They were right behind her. The door crashed open. The lock meant nothing to them. A hand grabbed her leg. Another grabbed her arm and dragged her out.

From a neighbor's house, a dog barked in alarm. Had she screamed? Yes. Maybe. Another dog took up the cry. One of the boy-men pushed the curtain aside with the barrel of his gun. "There's a car out there."

Tristan? Finally?

"We need to hurry," someone said.

The doorbell rang.

Iris was lying on her back as they loomed over her. "Don't. Please." From downstairs came the sound of a lame and happy cell-phone ringtone that went on and on and on.

She put up a hand and a knife slashed her arm. Another cut her throat. Looming above her, they were a jumbled snarling pack, and it was impossible to know which one of them had served up her death.

CHAPTER 31

Jude was lying on the couch, Roof Cat curled up on a pillow near her head, the sound of his purring hypnotic and soothing as she stared at the ornate light fixture on the ceiling. She should be sleeping, but this passive meditation was better, and certainly better than the nightmares sleep brought. She felt relaxed, and it was a state she hadn't experienced in a long time.

Her cell phone vibrated on the coffee table. Not taking her eyes from the ceiling, she reached blindly for the device, held it in front of her face, saw Uriah's name. Her body tensed, and relaxation vanished. Without answering, she continued to stare at the device. The tone stopped. Moments later, a voicemail banner scrolled across the screen.

After some hesitation, she listened to it.

"There's been another massacre."

Her reaction was to stroke the cat and aim her eyes back at the light fixture as Uriah's voice continued to fill her in. This one was different from the last two because it was in an occupied home in a wealthy area of town. He told her the names of the homeowners. She recognized them. Vincent and Meredith Roth. Vincent Roth was a real-estate investor her father had hung around with. That told her everything she needed to know about him.

"First responders are saying it's much worse than the last one. Not sure how that can be possible. And Jude? There are eight bodies."

She sat up. The cat slipped from the pillow and let out a small protest before jumping to the floor with a thud and sauntering to his food. Since his return, he'd been cocky and even friendly, enough for her to quit feeling sorry for keeping him captive.

Standing, Jude entered the address Uriah had given her into the map app on her phone. Her hands shook, but she ignored them as she memorized the location. Done, she tucked her phone away, pulled on her boots, laced them, strapped her gun belt around her waist, stuck her badge in the pocket of her black sweatshirt, and headed for the door.

And then she had a thought. What if she didn't go? Uriah had no way of knowing she'd listened to his voicemail. She could pretend it hadn't happened. Pretend she hadn't gotten it.

Music was coming from Elliot's place. She locked her door and went down the stairs, pausing at his apartment to listen. She pictured him in there, living his life, his simple life, which didn't involve murders.

With no conscious understanding of her motives, she knocked.

Moments later the door opened and the music grew louder. He looked surprised to see her. "Your cat isn't gone again, is he?"

"No. And thanks again for everything. The flyers. Finding him."

"I'm pretty sure you would have found him without my help, since he was on the roof." He smiled. "And when you consider his name . . ."

"Yeah, but still. You helped. You didn't have to."

"Glad to do it."

She was sorry she'd been mean to him. She hadn't been interested in whatever he wanted from her. Friendship, sex buddy, possible relationship. None of those things were her anymore.

He took a step back and she could see his black cat sitting on the couch, one leg pointed toward the ceiling as he groomed himself.

"You busy?" he asked. "Wanna come in?"

He was barefoot, wearing a torn pair of faded jeans and one of the flannel shirts he seemed to like, this one blue. He smelled like soap and shampoo, and his hair was damp. Behind him, the coffee table was strewn with schoolbooks tagged with yellow labels on the spines that said *Used*. Purchased at the campus store. Completing the student persona were an open laptop and a backpack. Next to the books was a Canon camera that looked fancy and expensive. But the strap looked less serious—it was black with white peace signs.

She remembered those days when all you had to think about was class. When you could fall into that insular world and stay there. Until this moment, she hadn't missed her old life and her old self with such deep longing, not really. But standing in Elliot's apartment, she felt a strong wave of loss and nostalgia for what had been taken from her. Not just a life, but *her*. The old Jude. The one who laughed and told jokes, and even sometimes had casual sex.

Instead of trying to ignore the person she used to be, instead of trying to forget she'd existed, maybe she should try to be her again. *Fake it till you make it.* If she tried hard enough to imitate her old self, maybe her old self would become her new self.

In her pocket, her phone vibrated. She ignored it, stepped inside Elliot's apartment, and closed the door behind her.

He turned down the music. "Want something to drink? Beer? Water? That's about all I have."

His apartment was the opposite of Uriah's. Her partner had created his own world with vintage furniture, antique rugs and light fixtures, floor-to-ceiling walls of collectable books inside a sterile apartment complex. This was sparse. Almost monastic. Or maybe more like Elliot hadn't committed to living in the space, knowing it was temporary. Which made perfect sense. He was a student.

Elliot's apartment was the same size as hers. Just a living area, kitchen, bathroom, bedroom, and only one window. At first, when she'd escaped her captivity, she couldn't stand to be inside and she'd slept on the roof, the roof being the reason she'd chosen this apartment complex, and it was how she'd met Roof Cat. But as time had passed, open spaces began to make her uneasy, and she found herself craving confinement.

"A beer would be nice." She pulled her phone from her pocket. Saw she had another message from Uriah. Put her phone away.

"I would have baked some Oreos if I'd known you were coming," he said, returning with a beer he handed to her.

She took a drink from the bottle, then looked at the label. A brand you could only get in Wisconsin. "I think there really are recipes for imitation Oreos."

"You might be thinking of whoopie pies."

"Maybe." Her phone vibrated again. She ignored it and took another drink. And another. It didn't take long for her to feel a little buzzed, because she rarely drank and she couldn't remember when she'd last eaten.

Elliot sat down on the couch. She could see her presence was puzzling him but he was being a good sport about it. Coming to an abrupt decision, she placed her bottle on the coffee table and said, "You know what?" She nodded, pleased with herself. "I'll have sex with you." A shrug let him know she didn't expect anything beyond the act. No cuddling. No pillow talk. No uncomfortable encounters in the hall later.

He laughed, then saw she was serious. "Hey, whoa." He put up his hands and leaned into the couch cushions as if to put more distance between them.

She felt the weight of her gun on her hip. "Don't worry about this. Here, I'll take it off." She reached for her belt buckle.

"It's not that. Well, yeah, I mean—" He jumped to his feet. "There's the gun, but—"

"I thought you—"

"No, no, no!" His denial was rapid-fire. No room for doubt there. Not even interest. Not even *Maybe someday*.

A flush rose in her face. "Well, this is embarrassing. And inexcusable. I'm so sorry."

"It's okay. Not a big deal." He smiled crookedly, trying to make light of an awkward situation. "It's flattering. Really."

"What do you want, then? I need to know. It would help me process this and any future possible sexual encounters." Like someone testing water, she stirred the air space between them.

"Not everybody wants something. I keep telling you that."

"I don't believe you."

"That's okay. You don't have to."

So much for her superpower. Just because she'd learned to read one man didn't mean she could read them all. And yet this guy . . . Something was off . . . "I have to go." Too mortified to look at him any longer, she left his apartment, ignoring his weak attempt to talk her into staying. In the hallway, she stopped to check the voicemails she hadn't yet listened to.

"I'm on my way to the scene. I've been told it's bad, but I know you can handle it. You handled the last one better than everybody else." The next message asked where she was. The third one began to sound alarmed. *"Call me when you get this."*

It was almost as if Uriah didn't want to go to the scene without her. Like he needed her there.

She stuck her phone back in her pocket and took the stairs to the parking garage, straddled her bike, started it, then hit the "Open" button on her key chain. The garage door groaned and inched its way upward. She shifted with her foot and let out the hand clutch. The bike leapt over the incline and into the street.

She didn't go to the crime scene. Instead, still in need of a reset or diversion, she took a route that would take her down a familiar street to a familiar house. Once there, she'd hopefully feel safe, at least for a while.

CHAPTER 32

If a person's footsteps could transmit dread, Uriah's were doing just that. He'd parked his car far from the lights that flashed silently against the city skyline. Hands deep in the pockets of his long coat, he walked with his face down, hoping the darkness would keep him hidden from the media. At one point, he paused under the deeper shadows of a tree, pulled out his phone, and tried Jude one more time.

She didn't answer.

His inability to contact her was alarming, because she had no home life, and if she didn't pick up, she always called him back within minutes. Under any other circumstances he'd drive straight to her apartment to check on her, but he was needed at the crime scene. He left another message while trying to ignore the throbbing in his head.

The responders around him seemed to be moving in slow motion, some coming, some going, all silent and quiet, their thoughts internal as they tried to cope with what they'd seen or been told about. The nearer he got to the house, the more surreal the setting felt as cops wordlessly strung yellow crime-scene tape and news teams set up in prime locations, not proud of their accomplishment for once and maybe even regretting their haste to arrive.

A few reporters recognized him, but none tried to approach. And it came to him that this felt like a funeral. Everything was hushed. Even the footfalls were muted by the leaves that covered the sidewalks.

Uriah wasn't an angry detective. He sometimes worried that his lack of anger was a weakness. Sometimes getting mad, getting really pissed, was a form of protection. Anger gave your thoughts a solid focus, a diversion from things that were too hard to look at with unfiltered eyes.

The sidewalk to the front door was wide, the steps flanked by concrete urns containing some kind of purple plants that looked like cabbage, along with the mums people liked to plant in the fall. He thought about how they didn't smell like flowers, but more like earth and the moss that grew in the forests along Lake Superior. His mother said mums were a waste of flower space since they didn't bloom until late fall. He just remembered that. A conversation that had taken place when he was a kid. He supposed that memory would now be replaced with a new one, of this night and the horrors he hadn't yet seen but knew were coming.

He was met near the door by a first responder. "Officers are having a hard time here." She was pale, her voice shook, and she was shivering. From where he stood, he could see two officers doubled over, throwing up into unused evidence bags they clutched in both hands.

"Any sign of forced entry?" Uriah asked.

She tried to say something, then just shook her head.

Which might or might not indicate that the occupants knew their assailants. "Take a breath," he said softly.

She did. After a pause, she was able to speak. "We have people canvassing nearby houses and taking statements. The neighborhood is in lockdown. Residents have been alerted and told to stay inside."

"Who reported it?"

"A guy named Tristan Greer." The relaying of straightforward information seemed to calm her a little more. She knew how to do this part.

"Greer?" He recognized the name.

"Son of the couple inside, Declan and Blythe Greer. Says he was invited to dinner, was running late, and when he got out of his car, he heard someone scream. Tried to call both of his parents, who were inside. No answer from either of them even though their car was parked in front of the house. He called 911."

"Security system?" Uriah asked. A house like this would likely have a good one.

"Got people looking into that right now." She pulled in another deep breath, and her next words were free of trembling. "There are cameras at the front and back doors, but they were blacked out with paint. We're hoping one of them picked up something beforehand."

"Good work." Uriah gave her a nod and made his way inside.

The interior of the building was a hive of controlled chaos. Eight bodies to process required a lot of manpower. A coroner was on site, along with an ME, two night-shift detectives, the BCA, and Homicide's own crime-scene specialists.

"In there." An officer jerked his head, indicating that Uriah should step out of the foyer and into a dining room.

Uriah entered the space and people moved back. He didn't look at anybody, but he felt their eyes on him and sensed their expectation of his reaction. He was only slightly aware of the stillness of his stance as he took everything in.

The place was brightly lit—blinding, really. He fought the urge to slap a wall switch and turn off at least some of the lights. This was not the kind of thing you wanted brutally exposed.

He wished he had anger in him. He could use that anger now.

What he had, what was washing over him, drowning him, was a grief so deep and so painful he didn't know what to do with it other than lay it aside. Just find a chair that wasn't soaked in blood and put his grief down there.

He remembered this feeling. From when his wife died.

He'd felt responsible. He should have been able to stop it. Should have seen it coming. In this case, he should have figured out who was doing this and stopped them by now, locked them up, done whatever had to be done before they struck again.

His fault.

"It doesn't look real, does it?" someone said.

Uriah agreed. "Just what I was thinking."

The dining-room scene was like something out of a B movie, the images so horrific that the mind rejected them while trying to explain them away as something fake.

Where was Jude? Not that she could make it any less unspeakable, but she'd bring a practicality he needed right now. With a sense of panic, he looked around, not at the bodies, but at the room, searching for exits, searching for a place to run and maybe hide. He, a grown man. Not only a grown man, but the head of Homicide.

He didn't run.

They were all going to need some serious therapy after this. All of them. Every person who'd stepped into this room. And with that realization, he found himself thinking that maybe it was a good thing he hadn't been able to reach Jude. Maybe she shouldn't see this.

"We don't even know where to start."

It took him a moment to realize someone was standing a few feet away. One of the crime-scene team members, waiting for instructions, his eyes large, that familiar telltale sheen of perspiration on his face.

Uriah wiped at his own upper lip with the back of a hand. Someone gave him a pair of latex gloves. He took them and watched himself snap them on. He was going to have to make eye contact at some point. Then, oddly, he felt a hand on his arm. "Eight bodies?" a familiar voice asked.

Jude. Solid and dependable Jude. And she was actually touching him. He wasn't sure if she'd ever touched him other than by accident or task—like the time she'd helped him home when he was too drunk to get there under his own power. When he finally looked up, he saw the compassion in her face and it almost undid him. He swallowed, and they both nodded in silent communication. "Five here, two in the kitchen, one upstairs." They could get through this. They *would* get through it. Her hand was still on his arm as she said, "I'm here now." So level. So together.

CHAPTER 33

An average human body contained approximately one and a half gallons of blood. Five bodies in the dining room. At least five gallons of blood on the floor. And the table. And walls. A slaughter, deliberately meant to horrify, Jude decided. On the wall was the affirmation:

All I seek is already within me.

And as far as she knew, that message, seen at the last homicide, had never been leaked to the press.

She hadn't gone inside her house after all. Maybe the last message from Uriah had done it. She'd heard the tightness in his voice. She hadn't even shut off the bike. Instead, she'd headed for the crime scene with a heart full of dread. But when she saw Uriah standing there, his body language, even from behind, radiating something close to panic, she was glad she hadn't given in to her selfish desire to hide.

Jude had never seen such an elaborately staged scene. She'd heard of them, read about them, but they were rare and almost a thing of fiction. "Have you ever seen a staged murder?" she asked.

"Nothing like this."

All five bodies had not only been stripped of clothing; they'd been posed in various positions.

"An inside job?" she asked. "It would explain no forced entry."

"Possibly. We need to talk to every person who works here and who's been in this house in the past few weeks. Everybody. Deliveries, anything."

"Here's the lineup of all of the victims." An officer handed Uriah a sheet of paper. Uriah read off the names.

Jude not only recognized the homeowners; she actually knew the two guests. The life she'd lived long before she'd become a detective and long before she'd been kidnapped had involved upscale private dinners. At a few of those she'd met the couple here tonight. They'd been considered Minneapolis elite, people her father had courted and fed and probably involved in some of his shady dealings. She couldn't recall any details about them, so she pulled out her phone and searched Google. "Declan Greer was the chairman, president, and chief executive officer of the biggest power company in the three-state area." His death was going to cause ripples. "I met them years ago. All four of them were associates of my father's." She lowered her voice. "I'm not certain, but I think both men were corrupt."

Uriah frowned in thought. "Could this possibly have anything to do with your father?"

"That's a stretch. And what about the other people from other crime scenes? As far as I know, none of them knew my family."

"Maybe the intention shifted. Maybe the person behind this is feeling guilty but he can't stop, so he's looking for justification. He could consider himself a hero."

"All killers are the heroes of their own story."

An officer came up behind them. "Were they having an orgy when they were killed?"

Jude shook her head. "It's meant to humiliate."

Blood was spattered across the table, mixed with food and splintered wine glasses. They'd been taken by surprise while eating. "They were killed, stripped, and arranged this way."

"This had to take more than one person," Uriah said. "And probably more than two. Who could hate someone this much?"

"I don't know." She meant she couldn't understand it. To hate with that kind of fire. She didn't ever think she could feel that way. When it came to the bad people in her life, she'd simply wanted to stop them, not kill them. And after . . . The regret was almost too big sometimes. This kind of hatred . . . No.

They'd been arranged in sexual positions. The youngest person, a male who might have been in his late teens or early twenties, was being abused by the adults.

Jude wanted to cover them up, but as the killers had known, that wasn't possible. They would stay the way they were until all the evidence had been collected and all the photos had been taken. Those photos would document this event, and they would be used in court once the killers were apprehended. Later, the disturbing images would be filed and stored in the evidence room. Hopefully none of the officers on site had taken any pictures, but it was much more common for digital photos to get leaked to the press today. And disturbing photos of prominent citizens? Those images could be sold for a large amount of money. Everybody knew it was wrong, but cops didn't make much money, and Jude understood the temptation. *Opportunity knocks.*

"This is forever," Uriah said.

She wasn't sure if he meant it would stick in his mind forever, or this was how these people would now be remembered. This sick and cruel tableau.

Both. Because this kind of visual never left you. Never. Thirty years from now, anybody and everybody who was here today would recall it. At fancy dinners with tapered candles. Whenever someone poured a glass of red wine. All of them would be imprinted with the horror of this scene.

"We need to figure out who hated these people," she said.

"Everybody is hated by someone." It was almost the opposite of what Elliot had recently told her.

"This kind of hatred wouldn't have gone unnoticed."

Arteries had been cut and the victims had bled out. Then the killers had dipped their hands in the blood and smeared it on walls that were the color of gray sky.

"I'd have to say Tristan Greer is our prime suspect," Uriah said in a low voice intended for her alone.

Seeing her doubt, he said, "If he'd been here, it would have meant nine bodies. That's highly suspicious if we're thinking this is the Fibonacci killer."

"Where is he? Tristan Greer."

"Downtown for questioning. I think Dominique is interviewing him. And hopefully we can hold him."

They went to the kitchen. No poses here, and no nudity. Just sliced throats. More like most of the earlier crime scenes. Cool, calculated.

The room was getting crowded. They excused themselves and headed upstairs.

"This place is so damn big," Uriah said. "Why does anybody need a house this big?" The space had to be over four thousand square feet.

"If my father were still alive, he might be able to tell you," Jude said.

People came and went in the hallway, some silent, some speaking in whispers. Faces were downcast in an attempt to hide the shame of deep emotions. They were professionals. Professionals who were supposed to be able to handle murder and death.

But should they be? Really?

Maybe every one of them needed a crying room.

Without thought, reacting purely from a need to comfort, Jude found herself silently reaching out to touch some of the people moving slowly and awkwardly past. She gently squeezed an arm or patted a shoulder. She nodded in shared sympathy. If eye contact was made, she held it a moment. Even with officers who'd looked askance at her when Chief Ortega had allowed her to come back to work. And the officers who'd put together a petition to remove her from the force, claiming she was unstable, spooky. Those people responded to her presence with a softening of eyes and a slight relaxing of shoulders.

The victim, the eighth victim, turned out to be the homeowner's daughter, Iris Roth. Nineteen or twenty, from the looks of her. She was lying on the floor in a bedroom that appeared to be more suited to a high-school girl. Bathed in blood, her face smeared with it by some sick person's hand. A crime-scene officer took a few photos with a flash, then moved aside and out of the room, leaving the detectives alone with the body.

Unlike the other family members, the young woman was dressed, lying on the floor next to her bed, where she'd probably run to feel safe. She'd almost made it. To the pile of stuffed animals and the blankets she could have curled up in, feet off the floor and away from the monster in the closet or the monster under the bed or the monster on the stairs. But the monster had caught her before she'd reached safety. Silly thoughts for Jude to have, but she wished the girl had made it to the bed, even though the outcome would have been the same.

Iris had not been posed. Maybe there hadn't been time. Dogs were barking, according to neighbors. Someone was knocking on the front door. Tristan, if his story held up.

The girl was lying on her back, arms wide, hands like claws. Even from yards away, Jude could see flesh under her nails. Somewhere, someone was running around with deep gouges on his body, hopefully on his face. This was information they could release to the press, and something that could lead to an arrest. One clue could break a case.

But the girl . . . Back to the girl. Her hair was straight and dark and long, fanning out on the floor in a way that looked deliberate. Like the others, her throat had been cut. In addition, she had a defensive knife wound on her arm.

Jude knelt beside her. "Left-handed cut," she noted, presuming, from the position of the body and the pattern of blood spatter, that Iris had been slashed from the front. A wave of sweet sadness washed over her. She'd thought it many times before, and now she was struck by the thought again. Death was beautiful. Even this kind of violent death. She would not say these things aloud. She'd learned her lesson about that.

While she observed the victim in silence, Uriah moved around the room, looking at photos on the walls, pulling open drawers. If this was the girl's room, it hadn't been redecorated since she'd graduated. Maybe she still lived here. Maybe she'd moved out and was just visiting.

"Nineteen."

Jude looked up to see Uriah holding an expired driver's license.

"Her childhood room," Jude said. "It makes sense that she'd run here."

It might have been the shadow of Uriah moving between her and the ceiling fixture, but a shift in light made Jude lean closer. "Is a window open?" she asked, not taking her eyes off the girl.

"No, why?"

Had she imagined it? Or had she detected a slight flutter of the single strand of hair lying across the victim's face?

Focusing on the girl, Jude said, "Iris?"

"Oh, for God's sake." Uriah's voice was a loud and immediate whisper of annoyance. "Don't do that. We've talked about this before. Don't hold hands with the dead. And don't *talk* to them. I mean it, Jude. If you're going to do that, then get the hell out of here."

Yes. Faint eye movement beneath the lid. Could be a postmortem spasm. It happened. But then one of the girl's fingers twitched. In a slow, almost drugged movement, the young woman reached for Jude, eyes struggling and failing to open.

She was alive.

How long had she been lying there as officers moved through the house? An hour? Two?

Jude took her hand. Through the latex glove, the girl's skin felt like ice. Jude wrapped both hands around her fingers, trying to warm them. "Get me a blanket."

She sensed Uriah behind her, heard his sound of irritation, followed by a gasp and a shocked curse under his breath. Then he was shouting for paramedics and an ambulance.

A quilt appeared. "Here," Uriah said. Then, "How in the hell did this happen? How did somebody miss this?"

The quilt was pretty. Pink and purple and white. Innocent. Jude released the hand long enough to spread the blanket over the young woman, tucking her cold arm below the fabric.

The girl's mouth opened and closed, the action conveying urgency and the need to tell Jude something. That slight movement sent blood spurting from her neck. A major artery had most likely been cut, but not severed. It had somehow clotted enough for the bleeding to stop. Until she'd tried to move. "Don't talk." Jude pressed her hand against the wound.

From behind came sounds of scrambling feet.

A folded stretcher was placed beside the girl. "I can't get a vein," a nervous EMT said. "She's lost too much blood."

"We're wasting time. Let's go," another replied. Three people lifted in unison and placed her on the stretcher. With another synchronized movement, she was raised.

"You can move away now," someone said.

Through it all, Jude had kept her hand on the girl's throat. She removed it. A thick white cloth replaced her bloody hand.

"Soft pressure," Jude said.

"We know."

"What hospital?" Uriah asked.

"Hennepin County Medical Center."

They walked down the hall, then the stairs. Outside, ambulance doors were wide, and the stretcher was slid inside.

Without hesitation, Jude pulled herself through the door. She wasn't going to leave the girl alone with strangers.

"Call me when you know something," Uriah said from the street. She nodded.

The door was closed firmly. Within a minute, an IV was going. A different tech, a young woman with short dark hair, managed to find a vein as the vehicle careened around corners. A heart monitor beeped, the sensor attached to Iris's finger, as worried looks were passed around the interior of the brightly lit vehicle.

Ten minutes later, they roared up to the hospital. The emergency room had been notified of their imminent arrival. Doors were pushed wide and two nurses and a doctor burst out. The stretcher was unloaded. Jude jumped to the ground and the group ran for the building.

"Surgery's ready," a guy in green scrubs said as they busted through the doors.

The medic who'd found Iris's vein rattled off details and vitals.

"We need a blood type *stat*," the doctor said. She was ready for surgery, with scrubs and a bright cap. "Make sure the hospital blood bank is well stocked. She might need more than we've got. Call around for a backup supply."

One of the nurses nodded. Grasping her stethoscope, she hurried away to relay the orders.

"Relative?" the doctor asked Jude.

"Homicide."

The doctor's face changed upon recognition. "What about the victim's family?"

Jude glanced at the young woman on the stretcher. Her eyes were open a crack. "Not now."

Iris surprised Jude by reaching for her hand. Still ice cold, she felt like a corpse. Did she know her parents were dead? And her brother?

Jude leaned over the stretcher. "I'll see you in a little bit."

The girl blinked as they wheeled her away.

Jude left her phone number with someone at the ER desk. "Call me when she's out of surgery." She wanted to stay, but she was needed back at the crime scene. She caught a cab, and on the way she contacted Molly, their information specialist at the police department, and asked her to find everything she could on Iris Roth and her family.

CHAPTER 34

Three hours later Iris Roth was out of recovery and in a private room, and Jude was back at the hospital, this time with Uriah. She felt bad about questioning the girl right now, but they didn't have the luxury of time. On the drive there, they'd decided Jude would go in by herself.

"She's obviously responded to you," Uriah had said.

"The cut was clean, and the repair went well," the surgeon told them as they stood in the hospital corridor a few doors from Iris's room. "She's breathing through a tracheostomy tube right now. That'll come out in a few days, but I'm guessing you want to question her right away." She didn't look happy about it, but she also understood the urgency of the situation.

"I'll try not to tire her too much," Jude said.

"She doesn't know about her family. I thought it would be better for you to handle that. She asked, though. We're trying to track down an aunt and uncle, but we haven't been able to reach them. We'll keep trying."

"Is she out of danger?" Jude asked. "From the injury," she added. The girl's life might remain in danger as long as the killers were still out there.

"She's stable. Lost a lot of blood. I've never worked on someone who was that close to dying from blood loss. But we have a good blood bank here, and it's remarkable how quickly a person responds to trans-fusions, especially someone so young." She checked her pager. "I have to go." She gave them a curt nod and left.

"Maybe I should question her," Uriah said, backpedaling on their earlier decision. The parallels in their traumatic stories weren't lost on either of them: Iris hadn't been held captive for years, but she'd been severely traumatized.

"It's okay," Jude said. "I'll do it. I think she'll be more comfortable with me." The girl's reaction to Jude, a female, could have been the result of male intruders.

Molly had dug up what she could in the short time she'd had. Iris had recently been a student at MCAD, Minneapolis College of Art and Design. A legitimate school, but probably not the first choice of a wealthy family that could afford any school in the country or beyond. And art focused, not business. Maybe her high-school grades hadn't been good enough to get her into one of the more elite colleges, or maybe she was rebellious. Detective McIntosh was interviewing Iris's friends. Right now they still didn't have a solid picture of who she was.

Uriah leaned against the wall, hands in pockets, and looked down at his feet. He was trying to hide another of his headaches, but Jude could read the pain in his face. "This is maybe the toughest part of our job," he said.

Sharing news of the death of a loved one. It wasn't easy, but it was best to leave yourself and your own emotions out of the equation. Concentrate on the victim. All victims experienced guilt. All victims blamed themselves. It was how the brain worked. *Something I did led to this. Or something I didn't do.* Iris would walk that road too.

Jude was still learning to tamp down her guilt about the random choices she'd made the day of her capture. If she hadn't gone jogging that morning on that particular trail, with easy access from a street and the van she'd been stuffed into. If she hadn't been wearing earbuds, if she'd been more aware of her surroundings.

Uriah waited outside.

The room was bright, and Iris was awake. She had a white bandage on her throat, and her long, smooth hair had been brushed, waiting for visitors who'd never come.

On the tray in front of her were a can of soda and a plastic cup of ice. It seemed like a bad idea to drink anything carbonated, but comfort was comfort. Jude introduced herself even though the girl probably knew who she was by now. "Would you like me to open that?"

Unable to speak, Iris nodded. Jude popped the top on the can, lifted and tipped the cup, and poured a few inches, setting both containers on the tray.

The girl picked up a tablet and pen, wrote something down, turned the tablet around. The letters were large and round, almost happy.

You were at the house.

"Yes."

She wrote something else and turned the tablet again so Jude could see it.

Mom and Dad? Where are they?

She wrote more.

Are they OK?

Jude had hoped to ease into this. Talk a little, get some details if possible, before addressing the death of Iris's family. That wasn't going to happen. She couldn't evade a direct question.

"I have some bad news."

The girl's expression changed quickly, going from expectation of a welcome reply to dread.

"Have you pressed your button in a while?" Jude asked, indicating the morphine drip Iris could administer in regulated doses.

The girl shook her head, seemed unwilling to dose herself, changed her mind, then pressed her thumb against the button. Jude waited until she saw that Iris was relaxed, a slight smile on her lips and a question in her eyes.

"Your parents are gone. Your brother is gone too." Because people rarely understood the word *gone* in this situation, she was forced to elaborate with words she didn't like to speak. They seemed so cruel. "I'm sorry. All three of them are dead."

The soda sizzled and snapped, and the clock above the bed came into play, the sound of the second hand something Jude hadn't noticed before. The girl's eyes flooded with tears and her face contorted in grief. Her hand lashed out, dramatically sweeping the cup away so hard it hit the wall, the contents exploding. And then she opened her mouth in what looked like a scream. No sound came out. Blood bloomed on the white bandage on her neck.

The door burst open and Uriah appeared. The noise of the plastic cup hitting the wall had alerted him. His eyes went from Jude to the silently wailing girl. Immediately reading the seriousness of the situation, he vanished, shouting for assistance.

Jude had been prepared for overwhelming grief, but she hadn't been prepared for the violence of Iris's reaction.

Nurses appeared.

The room was chaos. Someone got permission to sedate the young woman, and a needle materialized and was inserted into her IV. The silent screaming finally stopped. Her doctor joined the chaos, unwrapped the bandage to check the wound. "A suture has ripped. Bring in a kit and I'll take care of this here." She turned accusatory eyes to Jude and Uriah. "I'm guessing you gave her the news and didn't do a very good job of it. My God, you detectives can be heartless. Get out."

The girl pounded the bed with her fist, demanding attention.

"You can talk to them later," the doctor told her. "Right now we have to get this bleeding under control."

"I'm sticking around," Jude said in the corridor when Uriah gave her a look that said *Let's go.*

He glanced at the clock on the wall. "We need to prep for the press conference. We need to brief the task force."

"I'll wait. She's going to want more information."

"Somebody can call us."

"And *I* need information. I want to talk to her before anybody else, before her statement gets muddied."

Uriah was her superior, but he hardly ever pulled rank. Except now . . . "An hour. If she hasn't talked to you in an hour, I want you in the office. You can swing back here later. In the meantime I'm putting a couple of officers at her door. Once the news is out that there was a survivor, she could be in danger."

It was too bad they couldn't have kept news of a survivor from the press. The media didn't know the details yet, but it was hard to keep a mass murder a secret for very long. And the fact that an ambulance had roared away from the home, full sirens and lights, left people to conclude the obvious. Someone wasn't dead.

"An hour," he repeated.

She nodded and he left.

Thirty minutes later, a nurse found Jude in the waiting area, sipping coffee. "She's asking about you," the nurse said. "Her surgeon has reluctantly okayed your visit, but please keep it short, and try not to upset her again."

Jude set the cup aside and hurried down the corridor.

Inside the room, Iris was propped up in bed. Her bloody sheets had been changed, and her throat had a new white bandage. Someone had replaced her tablet with another, but the pen was the same.

"Would you like me to wash that off?" Jude asked, indicting the blood on it.

Iris shrugged and shook her head.

Aware of the time and her need to be back at the MPD soon, she said, "I have to ask you some tough questions. Are you up for it?"

Iris blinked in the affirmative.

She told Jude there were four intruders, all wearing ski masks.

"How did they get inside?" Jude asked.

They knocked and I let them in!

Iris started crying with odd abruptness, continuing to write as Jude watched over her shoulder.

They started hurting people and I ran and hid. I don't think they knew I was gone for a long time. I should have tried to call the police, but I didn't have my phone.

"You did the right thing," Jude said. "Did anybody talk? Did anybody's voice stand out?"

Iris shook her head. She was getting tired.

"Were they all men?" Jude asked.

Not sure.

"Can you describe any of them?"

She shook her head.

They were wearing black ski masks.

That information matched the poor-quality video footage supplied by a house on the block.

Iris couldn't ID them, but the intruders might not be sure of that. And more, they might still want their number eight.

"That's enough for now," Jude told her. It was late. Almost midnight. "I'll be back in the morning to check on you," she said. "If you think of anything else, write it down and have a nurse give it to one of the officers who'll be standing guard at your door." She was leaving when Iris tapped the tablet, then held it up for Jude to see.

Catch the people who killed my parents and brother.

The eyes looking at Jude were flat. It wasn't unusual to see such lack of emotion in a victim, but Iris had been crying just minutes earlier.

There was no denying the girl had been through the unthinkable. She'd almost died, but something was off. It was too early for Jude to mention her vague and unformed suspicion, if you could even call it that, to Uriah. Instead, she planned to take a mental step back, watch, and wait. But she couldn't shake the feeling that the last ten minutes had been a performance put on for her benefit.

CHAPTER 35

U riah walked through the skyway.

The art-deco Emerson Tower had once been the tallest and most impressive building in downtown Minneapolis. More recently it had been converted from a hotel to apartments as part of the mayor's "Stay in the City" campaign, but half the building was still empty. It was close to one a.m. and the lobby, with its Italian marble floor, was deserted.

He stepped into the elevator and punched the button. The door closed. As the car ascended to the seventeenth floor, he leaned against the wall of African mahogany and closed his eyes.

He wasn't sure when he'd last been to his apartment. Seemed like twenty-four hours, but maybe it was longer. Maybe it had been two days. Back at the police department, Jude had seen he was fighting another migraine.

"Go home," she'd told him. "Even if it's just for a couple of hours. Take a shower. Rest. I'm going to run home too. Feed the cat, catch some sleep."

He didn't argue. He needed sleep. In a bed, not just five minutes grabbed here and there, waking up hunched over his desk, drool on his face. Real sleep, plus the right meds, might reverse the headache. From experience, he knew if he caught it early enough, he could sometimes halt the progression.

The elevator lurched to a stop. He stayed where he was, too tired to move. With a jerk of awareness, he finally stumbled into the hallway. As he approached his door, his tired brain registered something odd. A person. On the floor. Male, dressed in jeans, chambray shirt, salt-and-pepper hair. The man was curled on his side, his back to Uriah, head on a canvas bag he was using for a pillow. Homeless? Maybe slipped into the building by following a resident through the main door. Pretty much anybody could get into a secure building that way. Everybody wanted to be helpful.

Uriah's brain was so far gone he couldn't prioritize what to do next. Let him sleep, or check to see if he was all right. Checking on him seemed like the best choice.

He shook the guy's arm. "Hey, buddy. Wake up. You okay?"

The man groaned, then rolled onto his back.

Staring up at Uriah was a familiar face.

"What the hell are you doing here?" Not the best greeting, Uriah realized.

His father, Richard Ashby, pushed himself to a sitting position and scooted his back to the wall. "I came to see my son. You have a problem with that?"

Uriah extended his hand and his dad grabbed it. "No, but I have a problem with my sixty-year-old father sleeping on the floor." He pulled him to his feet.

"Sixty is the new fifty."

Uriah's head was throbbing harder now, and odors had intensified, always a bad sign. He could smell the leather of his father's regulation shoes, and the deodorant he'd used since Uriah had been a kid. Old Spice. People said Uriah looked more like his mother than his father. It was true, but he had his dad's curly hair.

"You don't look so hot," his father said.

"I feel like shit."

"I've been watching the news about the murders. You never called me back, so I decided to drive up."

His dad was recently retired from the police force, and it wasn't going well at home. "He doesn't know what to do with himself," Uriah's mother had told him. She still worked full time, and Uriah imagined his father sitting alone in their two-story house, waiting for his mother to return. It was a sad situation, the loss of identity and the feeling of no longer being useful. Suggestions of things that might occupy his time were met with scowls. He was not someone who'd be happy with a hobby.

"I'm sorry," Uriah said. "I meant to call back, but you know how time gets away when you're deep in a case."

Even though his father had worked in a small town his entire career, he was no stranger to evil and horrific crimes. He'd spent three years on something called the Skunk River case. A family murdered while they slept, the location—a sleepy rural community—along with the motive of robbery, reminiscent of *In Cold Blood*, the case documented so well by Truman Capote. Uriah had an original copy of the book.

His father had eventually solved the murders, but his absence during that period, even when he was physically present, had been a pervasive part of Uriah's childhood. Once the case was closed, once it was found to have been perpetrated by two men who were just looking for money to buy meth, the resolution had been unsatisfactory, and Uriah's father had gone into a deep depression. Uriah and his brother quickly learned to slink around the house, learned not to converse with him, spoke in low tones, kept the TV turned down, went to bed when they were supposed to, tried not to fight, because any of those things could set him off.

"I'll fix you something to eat," his father said once they were inside the apartment.

Uriah's migraine was too far gone for food. The thought of eating made him feel nauseated. Amplified odors wafted to him from the antique books lining the wall shelves. He could even smell the molded plastic of the television and the lingering aroma of the coffee he'd brewed last time he'd been home. "Maybe later. I need to crash."

"Another headache? You're getting those more lately, aren't you?"

"Yeah."

"Stress?"

"Could be." He had to stop talking. "You can use my room. I'll take the couch."

"Absolutely not. You need sleep more than I do."

Uriah didn't argue. He managed to find a blanket and pillow for his father, down some pain medication, and fall into bed, an arm across his eyes.

Sleeping never came easy with skull-splitting migraines, but for Uriah it was a deep escape once it did arrive.

He woke up three hours later, the haze of the drug still in him, but at least the blinding pain was gone. He'd walk through the next twenty-four hours in the lethargic second phase of the attack, something called postdrome. It wasn't the drugs that caused the lethargy. His world always became cloudy and buffered afterward, no matter what. Lewis Carroll had suffered from migraines, and it was suspected he'd written both *Alice in Wonderland* and *Through the Looking-Glass* during the postdrome stage. Descriptions of postdrome varied, but Uriah likened it to moving through air that had turned liquid.

Time was five a.m. Pigeons were cooing somewhere, and early-morning sunlight managed to cut through a crack in the black bedroom curtains. He showered. When he stepped out, he caught a whiff of freshly brewed coffee.

The apartment was a small one-bedroom with a kitchen off the living room. Shortly after Uriah's wife had died, he'd sold their house and moved here, even though apartment living had never been on his radar. He'd deliberately wanted to distance himself from reminders of the traditional life they'd shared, so he'd chosen something out of character, and here he was. It suited his new lifestyle of all work and no play, but he'd been unable to part with some of his belongings, especially his book collection.

"How many eggs?" came a shout from the kitchen.

Uriah pictured a serving of slimy grease and his stomach lurched. "Just coffee."

He dressed and joined his father in the kitchen.

"You need to stay nourished." His father stood in front of the stove, towel over one shoulder. "It's especially important when you're working long hours like you are now." He poured a cup of coffee, then put the carafe back on the hot plate.

"I'll survive." Uriah sat down at the small table.

His dad slid eggs onto a plate and parked himself across from his son. "Will it bother you if I eat?"

"No." It would. "I thought you were supposed to quit eating eggs."

"I don't eat them that much."

Uriah was sure he'd heard something from his mother about a strict diet of oatmeal and fruit for breakfast.

"Mom sent you to check on me, didn't she?"

His dad let out a snort. "We were both worried, but she made the suggestion. Can't get anything past you." His father put one slice of dry toast on the table in front of Uriah. "These homicides, the unreturned calls. We were worried."

Uriah picked up the toast, eyeballed it, munched a corner, but mainly sipped coffee while giving his father a rundown on the murders—"For your ears only"—starting at the beginning. "We have reason to believe it's about numbers," he said. "Have you heard of the Fibonacci sequence?"

"The patterns of nature?"

"Yeah. The murders, if we include killings in a nearby Wisconsin town, all follow the sequence. Seven deaths in the latest massacre. Should have been eight, but one person lived."

"What's the next number?"

"Thirteen."

His father got a *holy shit* expression on his face.

Uriah looked at the clock on the wall. "I've gotta go." He rummaged through a kitchen drawer, found a spare apartment key, and put it on the table in front of his dad. "I don't want to find you sleeping on the floor again."

He finished getting dressed, slipping his badge into the inside pocket of his jacket and belting his gun around his waist as he returned to the living room.

"I'm coming with you," his father announced. When Uriah hesitated, he added, "A ride-along. You do those, don't you?"

"Not in the middle of a big investigation."

"I'd like to meet your partner."

Uriah imagined the encounter. Encounter? Yes, it would be an encounter. She'd be polite and distant, the way she was with everybody. And there was also the element of family and fatherhood that might be awkward.

"Partners are important. A good partner looks out for you."

"She does. Okay, come on."

Just after six a.m., Uriah and his father passed through the double glass doors into Homicide. The place was already buzzing, officers moving quickly, coffee in hand, some on phones, some looking at desk monitors as unforgiving sunlight poured in the floor-to-ceiling windows. Even Detective McIntosh, who typically slid in at seven, was at her desk. Someone shoved a stack of papers into his hand. "Tip-line calls from last night," the officer said.

He thanked her, rallied everyone nearby, and dove into instructions for the day, allocating tasks. "One thing we need to focus on is Tristan

Greer. Why was he late for the dinner? If he'd been there and been killed, that would have made nine people. How did the killers know the number attending? Was it random? Luck? I think somebody in that house knew the killers. Right now Greer is a prime suspect."

Jude swiveled her monitor so he could see the screen. She'd been watching interview footage of just the person he was talking about.

Even though there'd been a lot of press about Jude, Uriah's father did a poor job of hiding his double take. Uriah tended to forget the way her quiet presence filled a room. He introduced them, and Jude stood and put out her hand.

She was still too thin, and that thinness made her look even taller. Her dad, not a tall man, had to look up. She surprised Uriah by smiling warmly and greeting his father with something close to affection, her voice gentle and smooth. Uriah could see his dad's shoulders relax, and saw a return smile that was usually reserved for friends and family.

The squad dispersed, and his father wandered off while Uriah sat down to go over the paperwork he'd been handed. Minutes later, he looked up to see his father talking to Chief Ortega in her office. Richard Ashby sure knew how to work a room.

"You're not completely over the migraine," Jude said from a few feet away. Her direct and penetrating investigation of his face would never stop making him squirm.

"How'd you know?"

"Your eyes."

"Bloodshot?" He scooped up a pair of sunglasses from his desk.

"A little vague."

He put on the glasses. "Only you'd come up with that description." He could see she was worried about him and he appreciated that. "I've had these headaches since I was a kid."

"You're getting them a lot more frequently now." Not the first time she'd pointed that out.

"We're under a lot more stress lately." And yet she never varied, no matter what they were dealing with. Unruffled, calm, her presence bringing a soothing quality to even the most horrendous murder scene.

"You should see a doctor," she said.

"When things slow down."

"I'm going to remind you."

"Do that."

"You won't go."

He redirected the conversation. "Any more news about Iris Roth?"

"No. I'm heading over there soon. And about Tristan Greer—I don't think he had anything to do with this, unless he's an incredible actor. His parents wanted him to meet Iris, two rich kids forced together, and he deliberately didn't go. His mother sent him a few texts, and he decided to finally make an appearance."

He trusted her assessment, but it meant their only lead was no lead. "He's worth keeping an eye on."

"I agree."

His dad emerged from Ortega's office.

"Let me borrow your car," he told Uriah.

"Seen enough here?" Uriah handed him his set of keys. "Why don't you do the tourist thing today? You could go to the Mall of America, or one of the museums. Maybe walk around a lake. There's a new Springsteen exhibit at the Weisman that's supposed to be pretty good."

"Let's all do that together some other time." His father said. "How about when your mother and I drive up in a few days for the Crisis Center gala? You should come too," he told Jude.

Uriah took note of the confusion on her face. Had she thought about music since her escape? He knew she'd been listening to an iPod when she was attacked and kidnapped. "That's a good idea," Uriah said, eyebrows raised in question, nonverbally asking Jude if she was game.

"Maybe," she said.

"What's the address of the last crime scene?" his dad asked. "I'm thinking about doing some investigating of my own. That'd be a better use of my time and brain."

It wasn't such a far-fetched idea. His father was no longer a cop, so he could downplay any involvement in the investigation. Just a guy, curious like anybody else.

"There's a café near the crime site called the Grind," Uriah said. "Maybe you could hang out there, have a cup of coffee, listen in." He and Jude could do the same, but even in plainclothes they gave off an air of authority, and people recognized them from the news, especially Jude.

"Good idea," his father said.

All three took the elevator, with Uriah's father getting off on the second level and Jude and Uriah continuing to the basement.

"*Is* that a good idea?" Jude asked once they were alone. "Sending your father out like that?"

The elevator doors opened to the dark concrete underground and the echoes of cars they couldn't see. "He'll be fine," Uriah said. "He's been feeling lost since retirement. This will give him a sense of purpose, at least for a while. And he might just pick up some information."

They got in an unmarked car and headed for the hospital for another interview with Iris Roth.

CHAPTER 36

Richard Ashby found the house easily by using the GPS app on his phone. Funny how he'd hated the thing at first, but more and more he found himself relying on it.

The house was a mansion, at least by his standards. He knew nothing about architecture, but the building was made of large gray stones, with a roof of slate and flashing of copper that was now a fine shade of green. The lawn—yes, it was a lawn, not a yard—was manicured and had probably been designed by some fancy guy in a building downtown. The house Uriah and his brother grew up in was a two-story white stucco in a neighborhood so dead Uriah and his friends had played street hockey in front of the house on their Rollerblades. Not all that long ago, but a different time. Citizen awareness of child abduction had been fairly new then. Richard had lectured his kids and others in the neighborhood, but they'd still played unattended and unwatched for hours. Not sure he'd let that happen today even in a small town. One of the state's most tragic abduction cases had taken place in a rural community.

The house where the seven murders had occurred was an active crime scene. Tape had been strung everywhere, and news crews were using the structure as a backdrop for the latest update. There were maybe thirty people from the media on the sidewalk and in the street, and probably more to come since the national outlets would be hungry for the story. The rest of the crowd was made up of gawkers. Neighbors. Not-neighbors. Friends. Enemies. The curious. The morbidly curious. And maybe the killer.

Stacks of flowers were already in place, many resting along the curb, as near to the house as they could get without crossing the yellow tape. Along with the flowers were the requisite candles and photos. Richard noticed there were even photos of the girl who was still alive. And it dawned on him that no information had been released to the public yet. He himself had heard hints of a high body count, but he'd been unaware of details until talking to Uriah.

Nobody noticed him. Even back when he was a cop and out of uniform, he'd been good at blending. Now that he was older and no longer what his wife still called quietly handsome, he could really go unnoticed. A sixty-year-old guy who was losing his hair and not losing enough weight, moving through the crowd . . . Invisible. It normally bugged him—the invisibility of no badge and getting older. Not today. Today being invisible was a good thing.

He watched the people leaving flowers and candles. Many were young. One girl with long blond hair caught his eye. Something about the vacancy of her blue eyes, and the paleness of her skin. She looked like a doll.

She left flowers. Like many there, she stood for a time, staring at the house. He pulled out his phone and tried to grab a discreet image, but she turned and vanished into the crowd.

He moved slowly through the mob, taking photos, pausing now and then when he caught a drift of conversation that sounded interesting. Occasionally he even broke into that conversation.

"Did you know the people who lived there?" he asked a woman with a brightly colored scarf wrapped around her head.

"I used to work for them. Cleaning."

"Oh, I'm sorry."

She didn't look sad.

"They weren't the best people to work for. They fired me. And their daughter?" She shook her head. "She was a mess."

"How so?"

"Mean. Out of control. I was only there a few months, and she went through two nannies."

"Ah, it was a long time ago. I think I heard she was an adult."

"If you could call it that. Spoiled brat is what I'd say." She caught herself. That's how it was with him. People tended to talk as if he were insignificant, or as if he were a friend. Combine that with the fact that people loved to gossip and loved to connect themselves to the drama, even in a peripheral way, and it was easy to get information without even trying.

"I'm not glad about what happened," she said.

"Of course not. Nobody is."

"But that family . . . That girl . . ."

He moved on.

He talked to a young man with red eyes. "Are you okay?" he asked in a grandfatherly way.

The young man sniffled and wiped a hand against his nose. Hard, like he wanted to break it. "I went to school with Monroe Roth."

"That's gotta be a shock."

"No shit."

"Did you hang out with them lately?"

"No, I'm in college and I only saw them from a distance the past couple of years. I'm just home for a few days."

"I'm sorry."

Richard was walking back to Uriah's car when he noticed a man with a large camera and a telephoto lens, snapping photos. No visible press ID, and casually dressed in jeans and a flannel shirt. He watched him a little while, then headed to the coffee shop Uriah had told him about.

Inside, everybody was talking about the murders. It turned out Iris Roth had worked there for a short time, and people were whispering about her. As he sipped his coffee, he heard more discussion about how difficult she was.

"She was fired," a guy said. "And Josh doesn't fire anybody. So you know it had to be bad. I think her parents wanted her to have a job even though she didn't need the money. She resented that."

Richard got a text from Uriah letting him know a press conference was going to take place at the Roths' in under an hour.

He drank his coffee, bought some carryout, and returned to the house. The guy with the telephoto lens was still there, and now he was taking photos of Uriah and Jude. Probably a freelancer who'd sell the pictures to news outlets. Not unusual. Richard pulled out his cell phone, opened the camera app, and snapped a photo of the guy.

The press conference got under way. Everybody wanted to know about the survivors.

"Who was in the ambulance?"

Uriah shared that information. And he went on to discuss their theory of it being about the Fibonacci sequence.

In a case like this, the sharing of information had to be weighed. There were negatives to such transparency, because the killer now knew what they knew. But Richard thought Uriah had made the right call. Rumors would have gotten out, and they might not have been factual.

Press conference over, Richard caught up with Uriah and Jude and convinced them to do something they wouldn't want to do.

CHAPTER 37

Isn't fall the best season in Minnesota?" Richard asked.

Jude agreed, but it seemed wrong to be enjoying the beauty of the day. Not only enjoying the smell of leaves, the deep and dark shadows, and sun falling warm on her face, but enjoying it in a park. A damn park. At a picnic table. Kids were playing in the distance, their laughter carrying across the grass. But, as Richard Ashby had pointed out when pressuring them to stop and eat, they needed fuel. And he'd been generous enough to bring them sandwiches. Right now, he was unloading items from a bag.

"Vegetarian," he pointed out. "Didn't know if you ate meat."

Jude picked one up and unwrapped the white paper. "Thank you." She wasn't sure when she'd last really thought about food, but as soon as she took a bite she realized she was starving. The sandwich was an odd combination of hummus, avocado, and orange marmalade, of all things.

They'd made it through the press conference and managed to slip away from a few straggling questions. Once it was over, they'd driven to a nearby rose garden and park, Richard behind the wheel of Uriah's car. It was a serene place. The scent of so many roses, white sails on the lake, people on bicycles and Rollerblades, stacks of canoes, and the skyline of Minneapolis in the distance, jets crisscrossing in the blue sky above.

Closer to earth, dragonflies soaring. It was a lovely respite, physically and emotionally.

Uriah must have been having much the same thoughts. "Thanks for the lunch," he said. "This was something I needed. Not just the food." He waved one hand to encompass the peace of their surroundings.

"How's the migraine hangover?" Jude asked.

"Almost gone."

Holding his half-eaten sandwich in both hands, elbows on the table, Richard said, "You know, the girl wasn't very well liked."

"Iris?" Uriah asked, coffee in his hand, sunglasses shoved back, hair sticking up over them.

"It's kinda strange," Richard said. "In my experience, everybody likes a victim, even if that victim was a bitch."

"They don't want to talk poorly of the dead," Jude said.

"That's it." He took a drink from his bottled water. "Well, anyway, people didn't like her. People she worked with, neighbors."

"What does that have to do with anything?" Uriah asked. "Not-so-nice people can be victims, and they deserve justice."

"Not saying they don't."

"Your father's right," Jude said. "There's something wrong."

Uriah gave her a sharp look.

"I don't know what it is, but something's off. And she's holding back. That was pretty easy to see when we talked to her this morning."

They hadn't gotten any new information. Mostly recapped conversation, with Jude watching more closely the second time, still feeling there was a lot of acting going on.

"I didn't pick up on anything like that," Uriah said. "She seemed confused to me. And out of her mind with grief. Are you sure you aren't projecting?"

She'd had the same thought. "I don't know." She squeezed her sandwich wrapper into a tight ball, surprised she'd eaten so quickly. "Maybe. Hopefully the next interview will give me more to go on."

Uriah looked around. "This was one of Ellen's favorite places."

"Oh, kid," Richard said. "I'm sorry."

"It's okay. First time I've been here since she died. It feels kind of good, actually."

His dad was quiet a moment. "I keep telling your mom we should all buy an island somewhere and get rid of our phones and internet and TV. Just swim and catch fish and wash our clothes on rocks every day."

"We should do that anyway," Uriah said. "Not buy an island, but take a trip." He glanced at Jude. "You could come too."

"Somebody's got to stay home and work."

"Maybe just grab a few days. Once this is over."

"Come down to our place," Richard said. "You can fish there."

Jude was surprised to find herself warming to the idea. To the visit, anyway, not the fishing. She didn't think she'd like to fish anymore. "Maybe I will."

"He doesn't even have to come." He nodded toward his son. "If you have a day off, just drive down."

She laughed. Uriah didn't seem insulted by the idea of being left out. They dropped into a conversation about what kind of island they'd buy. Tropical. Or something where it was always green and foggy and a little cold but never snowed.

Finally, Uriah lowered his glasses over his eyes, gathered up trash, put it in a paper bag, and asked his father, "Did you see anybody who looked suspicious?"

"The usual crowd of people. Gawkers, press. Took a few photos." He pulled out his phone and scrolled through images. "You never know when you'll see someone again." With each photo, he turned the phone so Jude and Uriah could see. A woman with a bright scarf, a skinny young man.

"Old classmate, back home from college for a few days," Richard said. "Could be a source of info. Could be more than that."

With the last image, Jude leaned closer, squinting, then said in surprise, "I think that's my neighbor." Shoulder-length dark hair. Army-green backpack.

Richard looked at the photo. "Oh yeah. That guy. He looked like press, but I didn't see an ID. He had a fancy camera with a telephoto lens."

"He's a student at the U," Jude said. "Photography major."

Richard closed his photo app and put his phone away. "That's a fancy camera for a student."

"Not for someone serious about photography," Uriah said. "And this is the biggest story in town right now."

Jude extricated herself from the picnic table, but didn't mention her early suspicion of Elliot. She didn't want to distract Uriah from the case, and especially didn't want to point a finger at someone who had just as much right to be there as anybody.

"We're going to go through the house one final time," Uriah said. They needed to get back to the real world. The dark world. "Sorry, but you can't come inside, Dad."

"That's okay. Chief Ortega offered to give me a tour of the jail," he said. "I'm especially interested in the booking area. After that, I'm going to Skype with your mother. She'll want to hear about my day and how you're doing."

Their trip to the park had felt like truancy, but when Jude checked the clock on her phone, it told her they'd only been gone forty minutes. The dead could wait for the living to eat.

"Your father's nice," she said once Richard had dropped them back at the crime scene and she and Uriah were sidestepping through the growing mob of onlookers and press. For such a large number of people, the crowd was surprisingly subdued—a change from the more raucous crime scenes of a couple of months ago. Horrific murders were taking place, but some people were becoming more civil. Jude didn't know what that said about their city.

"He took a shine to you. You'd like my mother too. I think I've told you I had a fairly normal childhood, all things considered."

"Is that a bad thing?"

"No, but I used to feel guilty about it. Until all of that normal bit me in the ass."

She made a sympathetic face.

Reporters shot questions at them. Photos were taken. Microphones shoved in their faces. The intrusion didn't stop until they ducked under the yellow tape.

CHAPTER 38

U riah paused just inside the dining room and Jude noted his pallor. The bodies were gone, but it still wasn't an easy place to be. The only sounds were a ticking clock, the low hum of a refrigerator coming from the kitchen, and the buzz of flies. Flies always found their way in.

"Are you okay?" Jude asked.

Uriah gave himself a small shake. "Fine."

The chaos was over, but it was still a crime scene. Plastic evidence cards were everywhere. "I've never seen such high numbers," she said.

"I didn't even know they went so high."

"They don't." She pointed. Some of the cards had been hand numbered.

Uriah rolled his shoulders like someone getting ready to dive into a pool.

The house smelled of death. It was mostly the blood, warming in the heat of a fall day, but it was also other bodily fluids and excrement.

Later, once the building was no longer a crime scene, a company would come and erase all signs of the murders. They'd roll up carpet and deep clean the floors to remove bloodstains. They'd wash the walls and ceilings. Any contaminated furniture would be wrapped and hauled away.

Odd to think the house might belong to Iris now. It gave Jude a better understanding of the way people had reacted to her father's and brother's deaths, knowing she was the beneficiary even if she refused everything and anything.

They heard footsteps. A young guy with a BCA logo on his blue polo shirt appeared. "We're almost done," he said. "I think the house will be released soon."

"How soon?" She didn't like hearing they were going to lift the crime-scene status, especially considering the scope of the murders. But she wasn't surprised. She'd gotten the memo about their plan to be more efficient due to budget cuts. Get in, document the scene and collect evidence, and get out.

"I don't know, but I'd advise you to do what you need to do," he told them. "Go through it again. You can have it all to yourselves."

He left the building.

Sometimes that helped. To be alone at the scene without the mental and physical clutter of others. In her mind, she went over the events of the previous night. The killers had come in the front door. That had been established. From there, they'd moved to the dining room and kitchen. They'd probably broken up so the murders in the two locations could take place simultaneously. It had to have been fast, with no time for the kitchen staff to signal for help.

Cameras on the target house had been blocked, but security footage supplied from other homes had revealed the four people dressed in black moving up the street at around seven thirty. No vehicle, and so far no cameras had provided the starting point for their approach. From the coroner's approximate time of deaths, the murders had taken place soon after.

"At some point, Iris ran upstairs and hid," Jude said, trying to work out the timeline. "Possibly while her family was being killed."

Uriah held a pad of paper. He'd already drawn the layout of the rooms, but he was adding notes to the bottom of the page as he examined the bloody affirmation on the wall.

All I seek is already within me.

"She screamed," Jude said, "and dogs barked, alerting neighbors. Tristan Greer arrived and called 911. The killers ran, and her life was saved."

"They wouldn't have gone back downstairs to pose the bodies," Uriah said. "That must have been done when she was hiding."

"Or she witnessed it."

"Entirely possible," Uriah said. "The 911 call was logged at 9:02 p.m. That's an hour and a half to account for. Why didn't she call for help?"

"She said her mother took her phone away during dinner. It was found downstairs." They'd discovered nothing on it that seemed suspicious, but her contacts were being checked out and flagged for interviews.

Done with the dining room, they turned to head to the kitchen.

"Are you sure you're okay?" He didn't look okay.

"Fine."

No sooner was the word out of his mouth than he swayed, stumbled, and dropped like a stone. Jude tried to catch him, but fainters were fast. She managed to slow his descent enough to keep his head from hitting the floor with full force as she fell to her knees beside him. He was breathing, and his pulse was faint and fast. She loosened his tie and unbuttoned the top two buttons of his shirt. He would not want her to call 911. She pulled out her phone anyway, and in less than three minutes, she heard sirens.

Uriah roused, gradually becoming aware of his surroundings. He let out a groan of embarrassment and insisted upon sitting up. Tried, let his head fall back to the floor. All the while she held a hand to his chest, trying to keep him down.

"I'm okay," he whispered weakly, eyes closed.

"That's what you said seconds before you hit the floor." Was it the migraines? Something else?

"I don't need an ambulance."

The EMTs looked confused when they stepped inside. The blood. The flies. A man on the floor. They were expecting a gunshot victim. Jude explained the circumstances and who they were, although they probably already knew.

Uriah's vitals were checked. He had a weak, rapid pulse. His blood pressure was low. The EMTs started a fluid IV.

"I can walk," Uriah said when the stretcher appeared.

"You might as well get the full treatment," a tech told him. "We're here anyway."

After another struggle to sit up, he quit arguing. He was helped to the stretcher, his pad of paper placed on his stomach, and wheeled out of the house.

For the second time in less than twenty-four hours, Jude climbed into the back of an ambulance and took a seat on a side bench as doors slammed and the vehicle roared off toward the hospital, siren blaring and lights flashing.

In the hospital emergency room, Jude borrowed Uriah's phone to call his dad.

"They want to run a few tests," she told Richard.

"I knew something was wrong."

"It could be nothing."

He was there in thirty minutes. "I called your mother," he told Uriah. "She's renting a car and will be here tonight."

"That's not necessary. Where's my phone?"

Jude handed it to him. He poked at the screen, then put the device to his ear. "Mom, I'm fine. No, I'm okay. I shouldn't even be in the hospital. You don't need to come. Really." He disconnected and looked from Jude to his father. "She's coming," he said with irritation.

A doctor appeared and did a quick basic exam, pinching Uriah's skin, looking at his mouth and eyes, listening to his heart, and perusing his vital readings. "I suspect you're suffering from dehydration and exhaustion."

"So basically, I just fainted." To his father, Uriah said, "Call Mom again. Tell her not to come. I don't want her driving all the way here by herself when she's worried and distracted."

Richard pulled out his phone and attempted to dissuade his wife. "Wait until morning," he said. "I'll call you and let you know how he is." He hung up. "She wouldn't listen. She's going to come, regardless, but I think she's less worried, anyway."

"Dehydration can be serious," the doctor said. "And then there are those headaches. We'd like to keep you overnight for observation. Run some tests. An MRI, for one thing."

"I can't stay here. I've got too much to do."

"Exactly why you *should* stay," Jude said. "I'll return to the crime scene and go over everything. When I'm done, I'll text you. If anything new comes up, I'll call." Then she appealed to his logical side. "You aren't going to be of much use if you don't take care of yourself. It's just overnight."

He finally gave up and instructed her to go back to Headquarters, fill everyone in, follow up on anything urgent even if it didn't relate to the latest murders, then get back to the scene of the crime. Outside the room, the doctor spoke to Jude in a low voice. "He might be here longer than overnight, but I'll deal with his reaction to that when the time comes."

Her heart pounded. "Do you think it's something serious?"

"The headaches concern me, and I just want to make sure we don't miss anything." He paused.

"Is there something you aren't telling me?"

"It's not for me to discuss with someone who isn't a family member." He excused himself, and Jude went to find that family member.

With her direct question about Uriah's overall health, Richard pulled her aside. Most people knew not to touch her, but one of his hands gripped her arm as he urged her to a less busy area of the hallway.

He seemed to be struggling with information he didn't feel comfortable sharing. Finally he said, "He's supposed to have checkups every three years, but as far as I know, he hasn't had any since he was a teenager."

"Checkups?" She frowned. "A lot of people get headaches. Why does he need checkups?"

"Nobody's supposed to talk about it," he said, then seemed to come to a decision. "Uriah says it's history, but I'm going to tell you because you're his partner and I think you should know. He had leukemia when he was a kid. And when he started getting these headaches so frequently, his mother and I couldn't help but worry. I came up to check on him."

Her knees went weak and she felt faint herself. "Does Chief Ortega know?"

"I don't think anybody in the department knows. When he was cured, he closed that chapter of his life."

"Thanks for telling me, Mr. Ashby."

"He's not going to be happy about you knowing," he said. "Whatever you do, don't make a big deal out of it. He'll hate that."

"I won't."

Before returning to Homicide, she checked on Iris. The girl looked happy to see her, and told her the trach tube was coming out early—tomorrow, in fact—but it was no surprise that she had no new or helpful information. And everything, even the Fibonacci murders, seemed unimportant now in light of what Jude had just found out about Uriah.

Her strong reaction to his health scare left her with an unsettling self-awareness. As soon as something was dead, tenderness and mercy bloomed in her. She could easily love the dead, even a dead plant, even a cat who'd gone missing and might not return. But after all she'd been through, she was terrified to care about a living, breathing person.

CHAPTER 39

Six hours later, after filling in for Uriah at the police department, Jude took a cab back to the crime scene. In the hours since Uriah had passed out, the status had been lifted and After the Fact cleanup-crew vans were parked in the driveway. Inside, removal was under way. Three men were on site, all wearing white biohazard suits that looked like something appropriate for a moonwalk. Large, heavy-grade plastic bags were everywhere, tagged with hazardous-waste stickers.

She flashed her badge. "Who released this scene?"

She got a name and made a call to someone new in the BCA. She chewed him out, didn't get anywhere. Not wanting to bother Uriah, she called Chief Ortega to see if she could put a halt to the cleanup.

"Once the crime-scene status has been lifted, it's lifted," Ortega said. "The scene is contaminated now and no evidence can be collected from this point on. I'm sure the BCA wouldn't have lifted it if they didn't think they'd been thorough."

"It's premature." Frustrated, Jude ended the call. "Who's in charge here?"

A man dressed head to toe in protective gear crossed the room and pulled his breathing apparatus to the top of his covered head. She didn't know his name, but she was pretty sure she'd seen him somewhere else, probably at other crime scenes. It was hard to get a solid take on someone dressed in a moon suit and snug white hood. Funny how clothes and hair were such important factors in identifying a person.

"I'm in charge," he said. "And I'm not crazy about you walking around with no gear." He wasn't angry, just matter-of-fact. "I can get you suited up."

"That's okay." Wearing the suit seemed like overdoing it, since people had been walking about hours earlier without protection. But gear was standard protocol for cleanup companies.

The guy grabbed something from a box. "Here. At least put on a mask." It was one of the higher-grade white ones with a carbon filter. It would help with odor and bacteria.

She accepted the mask. Walking away, she had a thought, paused, and turned back. "You were at one of the Crisis Center telethons, weren't you?"

"Yep. I missed the last one, but I was there for the first and I plan to be there for the last, unless I'm working."

"It's a worthy cause," she said, surprised at her small talk.

"One more thing." He handed her a pair of shoe covers. "Go ahead and look around, but please don't touch anything. We're all about containment; we don't want anything tracked outside, and we don't want anybody picking up anything harmful."

"No problem."

She slipped the thin blue covers over her boots. He went back to what he was doing and she cupped the mask in her hand, placed it against her face, and brought the two elastic bands, one at a time, behind her head.

Like always, whenever she walked through a place where horrific things had happened, she felt a sense of peace that was almost spiritual. Maybe it was self-preservation, something her mind did to calm itself so she could sweep the sense of horror aside and take in the necessary.

They'd gotten a surprising amount done in a short time. Area rugs had been rolled up, bagged, and tagged for disposal. Most of the blood was gone, but the affirmation quote was still there. Even through the charcoal filters of her mask, she could smell bleach and cleaning products.

The crew hadn't moved upstairs yet, and the carpet leading to the second floor was still stained with footprints. She pulled out her phone and took pictures. Some of the prints were large and some were small enough to belong to a woman. Maybe Iris. Maybe some would match the prints from the theater.

Upstairs, in Iris's bedroom, Jude opened the closet and turned on the light. It was tidy and appeared undisturbed. After a moment, she shut off the light and closed the door.

Everything personal—like diaries, laptop, phone—had been logged into evidence and was gone, but Jude went through drawers again anyway, removing them, checking behind and under. Remembering the photo she'd found in her house, she pulled the dresser from the wall. Nothing. Not even any dust. Iris said she'd been hiding under the bed and they'd dragged her out. Sheets and blankets and mattress pad had been bagged as evidence and removed.

Jude sat down on the floor next to the bloodstained carpet, her back against the bed, legs straight, ankles crossed. She pulled off the mask and closed her eyes.

Ever since Richard Ashby had told her about Uriah, she'd been walking around with the sensation of something stuck in her throat, and a nagging feeling she couldn't identify. Now she recognized it as a profound and insidious fear. There was no reason to be afraid, she told herself. He would be fine. He *was* fine. Just exhaustion and dehydration.

A clock was ticking somewhere nearby. Muffled voices carried from downstairs. Soft conversation, doors opening and closing. That was broken by the sudden and intrusive roar of a vacuum.

She slid down until she was flat on the floor, so she could put herself in the same physical space as the victim. Eyes open, she looked up. The white ceiling above her head was spattered with blood. It was amazing how far blood could travel. And it was amazing that Iris had survived. Or maybe it wasn't. *What are you covering up, Iris?* Was she protecting someone? Had she known one of the killers? If at least part of her story was true, she was the one who'd let them in to begin with.

Oh hell. There were stars on the ceiling. Yellow plastic, the kind that glowed in the dark. They'd been arranged in constellations. Jude recognized the Big Dipper.

When things were good, Iris might have looked up at the stars just like this. And she'd looked up at them last night, while her blood soaked the carpet and her life faded away. Navigating the world was hard for any young woman, but you never expected the uncertainties to come from the evil of others. That wasn't in a young girl's dreams.

Jude made a pass through the rest of the upstairs. Three bedrooms and two bathrooms. Toilets had been dismantled, the pipes searched, because criminals often tried to flush evidence. But it seemed it had all ended in Iris's room.

She went back downstairs, returned the mask and shoe covers to the person in charge. He told her thanks, tossed them in a box with a hazard label, and walked away, back to the dining room and the affirmation he was removing. She watched him a moment, then left the building. Outside, she called Uriah to see how he was. It had been a struggle to keep from calling him every hour. And it was a struggle to keep her voice normal as she attempted to calm her pounding heart.

"Heading to Radiology for the MRI," he said. "My mother is here, and my brother is thinking about flying in." She heard the irritation in his voice, and that made her feel a little better even though a large part of that irritation was probably due to her calling 911 in the first place.

"They care about you," she said, fresh fear of the MRI results rising in her. She pictured the safety and security of her basement cell. "We all do."

Getting an MRI was a little like flying. Both required the relinquishing of control. No phones to answer. No crime scenes to attend to. No press conferences. No witnesses to interview. Uriah figured his embracing of the tube and the noise and the disembodied voice in his ear was confirmation of just how much he needed a change in something, probably attitude. In what other life would an MRI be considered a vacation?

The roar of the machine faded and the voice of the man behind the glass told him he was done. With a jerk, he was out of the cylinder and staring up at the ceiling. Earplugs removed, bare feet to the floor. The IV was slipped from the back of his hand. Someone grabbed his arm, asked if he was okay. Another someone told him a radiologist would be reading the scan soon.

The other weird thing? He wasn't worried. He'd seen the concern on his father's and mother's faces, and had reassured them everything would be fine. And it probably would be fine. But if it wasn't . . . He'd deal with it. If he got bad news, he didn't want anybody treating him differently, and he wouldn't want anyone at work to know. He'd do what he could for as long as he could, and when he couldn't do it any longer, someone else would take his place.

But when he was back in his room, drinking soda, eating food brought to him on a tray, and watching TV, his mother and father watching with him, he thought about what Jude had said earlier, about caring about him. Sure, she'd wrapped it up to include his parents, but she'd said it, and she never said anything lightly.

And it occurred to him that he was the one person who might be indispensable to her. She might actually need him.

CHAPTER 40

It was late when Jude emerged from her house. *The* house. Two hours ago, she'd sworn she'd only stop for ten minutes. But she was like an addict who couldn't stay away, who kept telling herself "once more" and "just a little longer." She didn't have time for this, so she'd tricked herself, saying the house was on the way to her apartment and she'd drive past, make sure nothing suspicious was going on. But she'd stopped, shut off her bike, gone inside. Into the cell, closed the door. Shut out the world and embraced the person she'd been when she was there. No yesterday or tomorrow. No murders.

No dying Uriah.

Now she straddled her bike and called him.

"Any news?" Would he even let her know if that news was bad?

"Nothing. Hopefully they'll tell me everything is fine in the morning and release me." They talked about the day, then he asked her where she was.

"Home." Not really a lie, but he would think she meant her apartment.

"Good. Get some sleep."

He disconnected and she sucked in a shaky breath, put on her helmet, and rode back to Powderhorn, the sky dark above her, lights from cafés and shops giving the streets a magical promise that would be gone once the harsh sunlight returned. At home, she entered her apartment building, helmet tucked under her arm. She checked her mailbox, then paused in front of Elliot's door.

Outwardly, she'd downplayed his appearance at the crime scene when she'd seen the photo of him. But there was a reason she'd been wary of him to begin with; only the disappearance of her cat had prompted her to lower her guard. Now she felt the need to find out if he was who he said he was.

She listened at his door, then knocked lightly. There was no answer, no music playing. She considered talking the caretaker into letting her in, but that would require time, and questions she didn't want to answer. The locks on the doors were old enough that a credit card might work. She pulled one from her billfold and slid it between the door and frame, angling the card down. Slowly but firmly, she pulled it toward her while turning the handle. The plastic slid between the mechanism and the frame. With the card holding the retracted bolt in place, she pushed the door open and whispered Elliot's name.

No one answered, and she closed the door behind her and turned on the overhead light. Books. Dirty plate on the coffee table. Cat hitting the floor to come rub against her leg. She petted him, then stepped deeper into the apartment.

This time she was better able to examine the books on the table. Psychology. Sociology. A couple of photography books. And math.

She'd never been past the living room. She put her helmet on the couch and strode into the bedroom. Unmade full-size bed shoved in one corner. Beside it was a broom. *The* broom, used to wake her up. Some cheap plastic thing. Funny, she'd always pictured it as an old-school straw one with a wooden handle. She imagined swapping it out for one of better quality—either her brain's attempt at something humorous, or proof of her questionable mental state.

The rest of the space had been designed as a work area, and the windowless walls were covered in photos. At least a hundred, maybe more. Most of them were three-by-five images, but some were as large as five by seven. The real deal, printed on photo paper. Anybody else would have let out a gasp, but she felt no surprise, only disappointment, to find that a man was once again taking photos of her and tacking them to the wall of his bedroom.

She heard a key in the lock, followed by footsteps. The cat meowed and Elliot replied. Jude stayed where she was, arms crossed, legs wide, staring at the images of herself. Even though she couldn't see him, she knew Elliot was right behind her in the bedroom doorway. He always smelled like soap he probably bought at the organic shop down the street.

"It's not what you think," he said.

"You don't know what I think."

"I can guess."

"Try."

"You think I'm a stalker. A creeper."

"Continue."

"You think I moved here to follow you."

"I'm a hundred percent sure you moved here to follow me." She probably shouldn't have been standing with her back to him, but a feeling of defeat had immobilized her. She finally forced herself to turn around.

That made him more nervous. "Well, yeah." He stammered, nodded. "Yeah, but . . . yeah." He struggled to explain something he wasn't going to be able to explain. "But it's the *why* of it. I don't have some crazy obsession with you."

"I've heard that before. It didn't end well for the other person. In fact, I killed him."

He swallowed. His nervousness was telling. He was no pro, and unless he was a helluva good actor, he probably wasn't an immediate threat. But that didn't stop her from reaching for her belt and the snap on her holster. He saw the movement and began talking fast.

"I'm a freelancer." He held up his hands, palms out. "I'm just doing a job."

"So you're saying somebody hired you to spy on me?"

"Well . . ." He was trying to formulate a lie or half truth. So transparent.

"All that cat stuff," she said. "Feeble."

"I wanted a cat. And it seemed like a good way to open up a conversation with you."

She laughed. Not a real laugh, but a sarcastic one. "That went well too."

"I'm an investigative journalist."

Her first suspicion had been right. She'd allowed herself to be charmed by him. Shameful. "Not a student."

"That was my cover."

"I knew you were lying about something."

"I'm writing a book."

"About me."

"Kind of. Yes. You've turned down requests for biographies, so I pitched an idea to a publishing house. *The Detective in the Apartment Upstairs.* Told from my point of view. No need for an interview. They liked it, so here I am."

"An unauthorized biography."

"Yeah."

"That's pathetic."

"People want to know about you. You're a part of our culture."

"Nobody owns me and I don't owe anybody anything." She let her leather jacket fall closed, and turned her back to him again while keeping her ears tuned for any sudden movement. "I've been interviewed."

"Nothing in depth. I suspect the short interviews I read were meant to satisfy people and keep the press away. Instead, they just made people more curious." She heard him shift, imagined uneasy foot movement.

"I like to write with photos, because they help me visualize my story while keeping accurate track of events," he said.

It was true. Everything on the wall was dated and followed a progressive timeline. Many were exteriors of crime scenes. There were several photos of her house, including ones taken the day of the auction. So he'd been there. Interesting.

"I'm going to have it torn down," she said, not knowing if she could really go through with it. "The house. I'm just not sure when."

"See, I could document that too."

She moved to stare at more photos of her. Some looked as if they'd been taken with a telephoto lens from the roof of their building. In one, she was walking down the sidewalk. Another, on her motorcycle. Her initial sense of defeat had been replaced by anger. Now she was so mad she shook inside while remaining cool on the outside. "You're never going to get your deposit back," she told him, her voice aloof.

"I've heard you can put toothpaste in the holes left by the tacks and nails."

"They make something called spackling."

"Here's what I'm thinking." He took a step closer, then stopped when she turned to give him a hard look. He'd dropped his hands. "I can help you."

"Really." The word was loaded with disdain.

"Yeah, yeah, yeah. I've been to every crime scene. And as you can see, I've taken a ton of photos. I didn't get as many of you as I would have liked, because you're so vigilant and aware of your surroundings."

"I think you have plenty of me."

"Can I come closer? You aren't going to shoot me, are you?"

He didn't seem like a physical threat. Just an idiot. She jerked her head, letting him know he could step all the way into the room.

"I want to show you something. And you probably aren't going to believe this, but I was going to come clean to you. I really was."

Maybe. Maybe not. It didn't really matter at this point. He'd lied to her. That was what mattered.

"I think I have something that might be of help in your investigation. Look at this image." He pointed. "See anything strange about it?"

The photo, about a foot above her head, was an external shot of the burned-out house at Lake of the Isles where the five people had been killed. He tended to take a lot of crowd photos, and this was no exception. Maybe twenty people, all staring at the house cordoned off with yellow crime-scene tape.

"Onlookers. Gawkers," she said. "They always come out for these things."

"Do any of them look familiar?"

"Too far away."

He seemed disappointed. "Okay." He ducked out, then returned with his laptop. He clicked some keys and scrolled through digital photos, finally stopping on the one he was looking for. A few more key clicks and the image was enlarged. Cradling the laptop in one arm, he pointed to a female on the screen. "It's her, right? The girl who survived the massacre yesterday."

Jude looked closer, then grabbed him by the arm and pushed him into the living room, where she felt less threatened. "It does look like her."

"I think it is. I'm pretty sure it is."

He pulled up shots of Iris Roth he'd apparently screen-grabbed from the internet. Pointed back and forth. "It's her."

"I'm not a hundred percent convinced," Jude said. But she was ninety-five. And if it was Iris Roth, what was the significance? "It might not mean anything. Just a weird coincidence. The whole city is following this case."

"I was thinking you could ask her. See what she says. See if she lies, or if she acts funny. I mean, you can kind of read people, right? I've heard that about you."

She didn't tell him Iris was already acting funny. Not his business. "That's an exaggeration. I'm no better than any good detective. I can tell you came from an outdoor café. Probably had a cup of coffee there. You sat under a tree. The only nearby coffee shop with trees along the sidewalk is Common Ground."

He was watching her like a kid who'd just been handed a quarter pulled from his ear. "How'd you do that?"

"Your breath smells like coffee, your shirt smells like fresh air and secondhand smoke, and you have a small leaf in your hair. It's not that hard."

"But you knew something was going on with me. From the first day we ran into each other at the mailboxes."

"What's your full name, real name?"

"Elliot Kaplan. I swear."

She snatched his laptop from his hands, Googled him. Several images verified his claim. He had a few journalistic credits, a couple for big magazines. She returned the laptop.

"So, are we going to work together?"

Back in the bedroom, she began pulling photos from the wall, ripping holes in the tops where the tacks were.

"Hey, hey!"

"We're not working together, and I'm confiscating these photos as possible evidence."

"You can't do that. You need a warrant."

"So what?"

"I can help you. I can blend."

"I'm not really crazy about the idea of working with someone who's writing an unauthorized biography on me."

"Understandable." He nodded. "Completely understandable. Forget about that. Let's shift gears. I could see this turning into an *In Cold Blood* thing. The Fibonacci killings are a big story, and I've been here from the start."

"I doubt I'll be able to forget that you deliberately moved to Minneapolis to stalk me."

"It's not stalking. I'm not stalking you."

He didn't deny the move. She looked at the photo of the girl again. "I call it stalking." It did look like Iris. But more interesting? She was standing next to a girl with long blond hair and a partially obscured face. And she hated to say it, but his idea of asking Iris if she'd been there might be a good approach.

"Are we okay?" he asked. "I can be beneficial."

"Like a beneficial parasite?"

He ignored that comment. The bite and humor and speed of her response held an echo of her old self that she kind of liked. It was exactly something she would have said years ago. And people would have laughed.

"If you don't want me helping with the case, I can feed your cat. And I swear I won't write about the other night when you tried to have sex with me."

"Is this blackmail now?"

"No!"

"You really need to stop talking. You just keep digging yourself in deeper."

"Okay."

"I want all these photos. Every one of them."

"I don't have to give them to you."

She stared at him.

"But I will," he said quickly. "Just because I'm a good guy and I want to help." He started pulling out tacks, tossing them on the floor, grabbing photos.

It took five minutes. When he was done, he stuffed the pile into Jude's hands. "I still have the digital files, you know. And I'm not going to delete them. And don't get the idea to take my laptop, because I use cloud storage."

Clutching the stack of photos, she scooped up her helmet from the couch and walked out. Upstairs in her apartment, she fed the cat, gave him fresh water, opened the freezer, and stuck a frozen dinner in the microwave. While it cooked, she sat down on the couch with Elliot's photos in front of her and sifted through them.

Roof Cat jumped on her lap. He'd parked himself next to her head a couple of times, but he'd never attempted to sit on her. She leaned back, both hands braced on the couch as he walked back and forth on her legs, purring faintly. She slowly brought one hand up and let him sniff it. Then she touched him on the head, a light stroke. When that didn't spook him, she gave him a few short, harder strokes. "Maybe we might actually become friends," she whispered.

The microwave dinged. The cat jumped, hissed, attacked her hand, all in a fraction of a second, then skidded around the corner to vanish into the bedroom, probably to hide in the burrow hole he'd created in the box spring. In the adjoining kitchen, she grabbed a paper towel and dabbed at the blood on her hand, then used a hot pad to pull the nasty-looking dinner from the microwave. Seeing the congealed mess, she hoped the stomachache it gave her would be over by tomorrow morning when she confronted Iris and checked in on Uriah.

CHAPTER 41

Early the next morning, Jude went directly to the hospital to confront Iris. "Is this you?" she asked, holding up the photo she'd taken from Elliot's wall.

Iris leaned close, so close her face was hidden by long sheets of dark brown hair. When she finally looked up, her eyes were blank. Her breathing tube was gone, but she wasn't supposed to speak. She shook her head.

"You sure?"

Iris grabbed a tablet and wrote angrily,

Not Me! I Wasn't There!

She was such a terrible actor. "What about this person?" Jude pointed. "The girl with blond hair. She's been spotted at two of the crime scenes. Does she look at all familiar?"

This time Iris didn't even glance at the photo. She just shook her head vigorously. A tell.

Jude tucked the photo away. She'd been told Iris could be released as early as tomorrow.

"Where are you going to stay?" Jude asked. "We want to make sure you're safe once you're out of the hospital."

With my aunt. She'll be here soon.

"Where does she live?" For the sake of the investigation, Jude hoped Iris stayed in town, but care would have to be taken. And they couldn't force her to remain nearby.

Saint Paul.

As if she'd been waiting in the wings, someone rapped on the door and a woman with a dark shoulder-length bob and red glasses stepped into the room. Crisp jeans, pale-blue T-shirt, and white sneakers. She introduced herself as Iris's aunt. "I just wanted to bring some clothes and a phone."

After getting the woman's address and both of their numbers, Jude told Iris she'd check in with her later, then headed down the corridor. Moments later, she heard hurried footsteps behind her. "Detective Fontaine. Can I speak with you?" The aunt glanced over her shoulder, toward Iris's room. "There's a little alcove down the hall where we can talk."

Once they were in the private area, she pressed her hands together in a nervous gesture. "Iris is not coming home with us. She thinks she is, but she can't stay in my house. I have children, and their safety is more important to me than making sure Iris has a place to stay."

"I understand." Jude *did* understand. She might make the same choice under similar circumstances. And the truth was, Iris herself might be a danger.

"It's not like we were ever close," the woman said. "In fact, my kids are scared of her. She teases them." She leaned closer. "Iris is not a nice person. She accused her own brother of molesting her. And he was the sweetest kid." Her eyes teared up. "She caused so much trouble for that family, and now this . . ."

There it was. The explanation of the empathy Jude felt for Iris even though the girl was lying. She believed her about the molestation. If she'd been standing there, Jude would have told her so. Was this another piece of the puzzle? Tamping down her flare of unexpected emotion, Jude asked evenly, "Are you saying she had something to do with it?"

"I'm just saying trouble follows her like a dark cloud of her own making. My brother would have paid for her to go to college anywhere, but she stayed in town. That's fine, but her grades were terrible and she dropped out after a year. She uses people and she's a negative, mean person."

"Teenagers aren't the easiest to deal with."

"She's not coming home with me. If I cared about her, it might be different. We'd figure something out. Right now, I'm here for my brother. That's it. And I'll help from a distance. But she can't be in my house. I think a nurse got the wrong idea and said something to her. I'm sorry."

"Does she have any other relatives she could stay with?"

"No." She relaxed a little now that her feelings were out. "Could you tell her? In a nice way?"

It was the last thing Jude wanted to deal with, but it sounded like she'd do a better job of breaking the news. In the meantime, it also sounded like she'd have to figure out what they were going to do with Iris.

Minutes later she told the young woman that she wouldn't be going to her aunt's house. Iris took it well, but a place to stay probably wasn't her biggest concern after losing her family.

Upstairs, Jude found Uriah's bed empty and made. She felt a moment of panic until he appeared from behind a door, dressed, a bag of belongings in his hand. "The MRI was fine and I've been released," he announced.

A wave of relief rolled over her, and yet she couldn't shut off the worry that immediately followed. What if he wasn't telling the truth about being okay? What if it was serious and he didn't want anybody to know?

"It was the migraines," he said. "Because of them, I wasn't drinking enough fluid. Along with that, I wasn't getting much sleep."

"Where are your father and mother?"

"Headed home. My mom had to work. I'm sorry you didn't get a chance to meet her, but they'll both be back for the gala in a couple of days."

His parents leaving lent validity to the positive news he'd just related. They wouldn't have gone if his test results had been bad. She wanted to bring up the cancer, but she also wanted to respect his desire to leave it in the past.

"Roof Cat?" he asked, nodding at her scratched hand.

"Yeah." She told him about the photo of Iris standing next to the blond girl at one of the crime scenes, but avoided going into the stalker aspect of Elliot's behavior. And she didn't tell him about her neighbor's photo wall. If Uriah knew, he'd probably head straight to Elliot's apartment to confront him, then faint. But she did share the news about Iris not having a place to go. "I showed the picture to her and she denied being there. I'm pretty sure she's lying."

"If it *is* her, if she knows the people who killed her family, why would she lie?"

"Because she's involved somehow and she's scared. Also, you probably won't like this idea, but I think I'll offer to let her stay with me."

He looked skeptical.

It *was* unusual. A detective taking in a victim. "I can keep her safe that way. Not only keep her safe, but maybe gain her trust and find out what she's hiding."

A nurse appeared with a clipboard and passed it to Uriah for his release signature.

"Do you need a ride?" Jude asked. She was on her motorcycle, but they could call a cab.

"My dad left my car in the ramp."

"Should you be driving?" He gave her a pained look, and she didn't push it. "I'll talk to you later," she told him.

Uriah was deep in discussion with the nurse and Jude wasn't sure he heard her say good-bye. She left and dashed down the hall, spotting the red *Exit* sign. She crashed through the door. In a fresh rush of overwhelming relief over Uriah's good news, she sat down heavily on a step, elbows to knees, and buried her face in her shaking hands.

CHAPTER 42

Uriah surprised everybody by showing up for work a few hours later. He roamed the office and sat at his desk, getting *welcome backs* and updates from the team. Someone had tied a helium balloon to his landline phone. Also in celebration of his return was a bouquet of flowers, along with a box of candy. The gifts were things Jude would have done prekidnapping, but today's Jude hadn't even thought about it. That bothered her. But then, she hadn't expected to see him back on the job hours after being released from the hospital.

He opened the box of chocolates and offered her one.

She took a piece, for no real reason other than the distraction and surprise of his presence. "What are you doing here?"

"I'm not sick, and I'm not dying. I'll take it easy. I'll make sure to drink plenty of fluid and sleep at least a few hours a night."

"Five hours. At least five hours."

Caroline McIntosh interrupted their conversation to hand Uriah a sheet of paper with a list of names and addresses. Were the flowers from her? There was a card in the vase, attached to a tiny plastic fork, but Jude couldn't read the writing from where she stood. She bit into the chocolate. Beige interior and an unpleasant flavor. Faux coffee? Caramel? Neither seemed right.

"I've been researching local residents with strong math ties," Caroline said. "I found a few with records. Nothing serious, but a couple of odd public disruptions that ended in arrests. One guy attacked a woman on a bus for wearing numbers on her shirt. I also pulled a couple of people who wrote articles on number sequencing in nature."

Looking up from the list, Uriah said, "Good work." Caroline blushed.

Chief Ortega emerged from her office to give them the now-familiar talk about not enough manpower. The Fibonacci murders, as they were now officially calling them, weren't their only case. "We can't allow ourselves to become so focused on these killings that we forget we have others to investigate."

Everyone murmured in agreement.

Uriah offered Ortega candy. She dug a chocolate from the box, then gave Uriah a hard look. "That said, I don't want anybody making foolish decisions because of lack of sleep. Take care of yourselves first. Eat decently, drink plenty of water, sleep. Every night. I do not want to lose any of you. Not because I don't want to be down more detectives. I don't want to *lose you*. Either by your reaching a breaking point, or by getting yourself killed. Lack of sleep and lack of proper nutrition lead to mistakes in the field." She bit into the candy and seemed pleased with the surprise she found inside.

"Do we still have to do yoga meditation?" Caroline asked. "Is that a requirement?"

The chief chewed, then talked around the candy in her mouth. "I plan to have the yoga instructor here once a week, but until the Fibonacci murders are solved, it won't be a requirement. But it's my opinion the people working the case are the very ones who need it right now."

"I'll try to participate," Uriah said. Probably not a good endorsement that the person who'd enjoyed the yoga meditation the most had ended up in the hospital.

Ortega returned to her office, and McIntosh returned to her desk while Jude and Uriah looked over the list of names she'd given him.

Their friend the math professor was on it. Jude checked the clock. "I say we try to catch him at home. Maybe we'll get lucky this time."

Uriah was already reaching for his coffee. "And McIntosh and Valentine can hit the other names on the list."

She drove while Uriah sat in the passenger seat. He'd brought the box of candy along, and he offered it to her again. She shook her head and said, "The unknown is too risky."

"There's an easy way around that." He squished a few of them to see what was inside before choosing one.

She stopped at a red light. "That's not the healthy diet Ortega was talking about."

"At least it's not hard liquor."

"You know those things usually come with a cheat sheet underneath so there are no nasty surprises."

"What's the fun in that?"

He did seem to be feeling better. His color was good; the circles under his eyes were gone. He looked relaxed as he leaned back in his seat. Maybe rest and hydration had been all he needed. She'd just have to watch him more closely.

"I know my dad invited you down to his place, but do you even like to fish?" he asked.

She made a right turn at a red light. "I used to. I don't think I'd like it anymore."

"Kinda wondered about that. Bad memories?"

"Not because I used to do it with my family, if that's what you're thinking. I did, but I just never thought about the fish before. Or the worm. I'd think about both of them now."

"Even the worm?"

"Yeah."

"Okay, well, when this is over, let's go canoeing down the Saint Croix. It'll be a great time to go, with the leaves turning."

"Is this something the doctor suggested?"

"Yeah, more recreation, but that's not a bad thing. He suggested I actually put relaxation and recreation on my calendar, no matter what we're dealing with."

"I'd like to do that. The river." It was a nice thought in a dark time. Something to look forward to. And it put a wishful deadline on the case. Fall would be over soon, and there would be no canoeing once winter hit.

At Professor Masucci's apartment building, Uriah pressed the number on the box next to the entry door. Under the awning were stacks of thick, weather-curled phone books and moldy newspapers in yellow plastic bags. There was no intercom response, but unlike on the previous visit, the door buzzed and unlocked.

The interior smelled of a combination of curry and cigarette smoke, along with the more unpleasant scent of disinfectant. From behind a wooden door came a deep and phlegmy cough, the kind of cough that was a permanent part of life until there was no life left.

Up one flight of stairs, Jude knocked on the door and spoke through it, hoping the professor was nearby. "Professor Masucci? It's Detectives Fontaine and Ashby. We're wondering if we could talk with you."

After a moment, the door opened.

He was dressed for the day in the suit and burgundy tie he'd been wearing the last two times they'd seen him. "I was just leaving for work."

The odor here was coffee and toast, not unpleasant, but it mingled with the others in the building, rendering them all slightly disagreeable.

"Just ten minutes of your time," Uriah said.

He stepped back and they stepped in.

Not a surprise to see they were in the presence of a hoarder. Not one of those people featured on TV or in the news. There was no garbage to climb over. Here, things were neatly arranged in piles of mostly newspapers and books, four feet tall, with a narrow path of bare floor that wound through the stacks. A single chair in the corner was dwarfed, a side table and lamp next to it, the table also loaded down with reading material.

"I'm a book collector," Uriah said, not seeming the least taken aback by the professor's living situation. Jude decided this was exactly the kind of thing she could imagine happening to Uriah over time. When she was last in his apartment, everything had been neat and on shelves, but he was running out of room.

The setting probably felt familiar to him. Surrounded by old books and papers that smelled of mildew and age. It probably brought both men comfort. She'd have to make sure Uriah didn't end up like this.

"There's a little more room in the kitchen," the professor said.

They followed him through the stacks. He'd been right about the kitchen when he'd said "a *little* more room." Three chairs and a small table were squeezed against one wall. He rearranged some piles. "Have a seat."

Jude and Uriah each took a chair. The professor sat down. "You're here about the most recent murders."

Uriah pushed at a small Jenga-like tower of books, trying to clear a spot for his elbows on the surface of the table. It seemed impossible, but the kitchen was even more packed than the rest of the apartment. Jude could hardly move her arms. "Have you thought any more about students you've known who might have had a special interest in the Fibonacci sequence?" she asked.

"You're talking about a lot of people." He seemed a little more lucid today, not distracted by pigeons. "Many of my past students were fascinated by it. Who wouldn't be?"

"Any people more fascinated than others?" Uriah asked.

"We'll understand if it takes you a little time," Jude added. "You've had so many students."

"And still do."

She played along, the way everybody played along. "Yes."

The space was so cramped it was a struggle to open her messenger bag and pull out some of the images she'd gotten from Elliot. Back at her apartment, she'd sorted through them, choosing various ones to present—the equivalent of a photo lineup—to see if he'd pick the shot Elliot had fixated on.

The professor looked over the images, lifting one at a time, giving each careful consideration. When he'd gone through them twice, he placed one down on the table and tapped it. "This girl looks familiar." It was the blond standing next to the girl who might or might not have been Iris.

"What about the girl next to her? The one with brown hair," Jude asked.

He bent forward, shook his head, and checked his watch. "I have to get to work. I have to go."

Jude wasn't sure if his sudden burst of anxiety was caused by a memory he didn't like, or frustration over not being able to remember. "Look at her again, please." She slid the image closer. "Where do you think you've seen the blond girl?"

"Was it recent?" Uriah asked. "Or years ago?"

"I don't know." He shifted, and a book crashed to the floor. Jude picked it up and placed it beside him. "I have to go," he repeated.

"The photo." Jude's voice was soft but insistent. "This is important," she reminded him.

"Numbers are exact," he told them. "That's why I like them. There are no gray areas. No confusion. They are what they are. I don't like to be wrong. I don't like to guess."

"A guess could help us," Jude said.

He looked at the photo again. "She might be a friend of an old student. Maybe I saw her with him."

"What student?" Uriah asked. Jude could see he was struggling to keep his voice casual so his question wouldn't be the end to the conversation.

"I can't remember." He sounded vague, and he seemed to float off, then come back. Nodding, he said, "He wrote an essay on the Fibonacci sequence and its close relationship to art."

"His name?" Uriah prodded.

He shook his head. "I don't remember."

"What did he look like?" Jude asked.

"Dark hair. Average build."

"Ethnicity?"

"White, I believe. The girl might have been his girlfriend."

"Would you have that paper here?" Uriah asked.

"The students get them back." He eyed Uriah with suspicion. "That would be unethical. In fact, this whole conversation is unethical. Students have rights. And you'd need a search warrant to see such a paper. I'm done talking about this." He struggled to extricate himself from the confines of the table. Standing, he said, "I can't discuss any of my students with you. You both need to leave right now."

Jude tucked the photos into her bag and got to her feet. "Thanks for your time." She'd given him her business card twice before, but in case he'd lost them or thrown them away, she gave him another. "If you think of anything we should know, please call."

In the car, Uriah said, "I'll have the photos of the girls cleaned up. We'll run them through facial-recognition software and see if we get any hits. I'm also going to put out a person-of-interest alert on the blond girl."

"Who gave you the flowers?" Jude asked as she turned onto University Avenue.

"Flowers?"

"The flowers on your desk."

"Oh. Chief Ortega."

"That was nice of her. I'm guessing the balloons and the chocolate were from her too."

"Caroline McIntosh." His phone rang. He answered. When he hung up, he said, "Iris Roth is being released today and Detective Valentine wonders what he should do about her."

"I'll drop you off downtown and head to the hospital to pick her up."

"You sure about this?"

Having a victim stay with a detective might have been unusual, but it would address a few issues. Jude could be the one protecting her so fewer cops would have to be pulled from their current beats, and when Jude wasn't home, her fourth-floor apartment would be safer than most places. "I want to keep a close eye on her." For various reasons. And she wouldn't let her guard down or trust her for a second. No keeping anything personal in the apartment, especially case files.

"Do tuxedo shops deliver?" Uriah asked.

"I'm pretty sure anything can be delivered today." With all that was going on, she'd forgotten about the upcoming gala and his live interview. "You have a good excuse to not go and avoid the stress."

"I've worried about it for too long to back out now. And I hope you'll come, houseguest or not."

"I'm not sure." She'd bought a dress, but she didn't know about leaving Iris alone. Or maybe that was her own excuse.

"There'll be dancing."

He said it like that was a plus. "Nope. Not me."

"If my dad's there, you'd better come prepared to dance. He taught me to waltz when I was seven."

"Are you trying to talk me *out* of going?" Dancing . . . Touching someone, standing so close. It terrified and intrigued her.

"Do you know how to waltz?" Uriah asked.

"Yes." Her dad had taught her too.

CHAPTER 43

Peeking from behind a massive tree, Elliot spoke softly into his handheld recorder. "Fall in the Twin Cities is beautiful," he whispered. "The sun is warm on my back, and every slight breeze dislodges red and orange leaves, adding to the colorful carpet at my feet. And the smell. I've never smelled anything like this. Fall in Texas will make me long for Minnesota once I'm back home."

Movement in the distance had him tucking the recorder into the pocket of his hoodie and lifting the camera around his neck. The sound of car doors echoed across the hush of the cemetery. He spotted Uriah Ashby. Beside him was Jude, her hard-to-hide white hair partially covered with a black cap. Next to her was the girl with long brown hair, Iris Roth. She was staying with Jude and had arrived yesterday. Handy for him.

He adjusted his telephoto lens, set the camera for "Burst," and pressed the shutter release, knocking out a series of shots.

Now that Jude knew the student angle was a cover, he was working diligently to document everything he could, wrapping up his spec job in what he hoped would result in some serious cash. He was broke. He'd even gone to a free pantry for cat food. Getting a cat had been a dumb idea, considering his financial situation, but he'd really wanted one. It hadn't just been a ploy to engage Jude in conversation.

Jude had suffered a lot. He knew that, but suffering could sometimes blind people to the pain others were experiencing. Like him, for instance. He'd recently lost a father. Friends tried to cheer him up by telling him he was lucky to have barely known the guy. Nobody to really miss. They didn't understand that the loss he felt was for the relationship that might have eventually been. That hope was gone. And his father hadn't completely abandoned him. He wasn't a deadbeat. He'd sent money over the years, and he'd paid for Elliot's college education.

Elliot wished he could get closer to the crowd. Did he dare? If Jude spotted him, what would she do? Probably nothing, at least until later. Then she'd storm into his apartment and demand the image files.

It was a sad situation, to be the only one left after the murder of a family. As someone who'd grown up with a single mom, he might not completely understand how it would feel, but he'd experienced enough loss to at least empathize. That didn't stop him from taking more photos.

The day was bright. Too bright for black clothes and deep sorrow. Oh, that was good. Juggling his equipment, he pulled out his recorder and mumbled the words into the mic.

He wasn't the only lurker. The burial had drawn a ton of media. Attendees were scattered around, positioned at various vantage points, clicking away. Too much competition here, but photos would round out his story, even though the funeral would be old news by the time his project went to press or book or whatever.

He spotted a girl with long blond hair, lifted his camera again, adjusted the aperture to bring her into sharp focus. She looked like the person in the photo he'd pointed out to Jude. "Turn around," he whispered.

She didn't. Instead, she vanished into the crowd.

He moved the lens to Iris Roth. Snapped a few images. He was surprised to note that even in grief, she managed to maintain that kind of spoiled look you couldn't quite source or get a lock on. It wasn't her hair or her clothes, and he didn't even think it was her expression. It was just there. He clicked away, then moved to Jude's face.

Jude.

She was interesting and intimidating. If she told him to lie down on the ground and do fifty push-ups, he wouldn't even ask why. He'd just drop and do it. *Yes, ma'am.* His heart began to pound as he thought about finding her in his apartment. He'd been scared shitless even though she'd been the one violating his space.

Right now, her face was blank. She did that well. The blank thing. Being a journalist, he'd learned to read people over the years. Jude Fontaine was impossible to read. Did she even have any emotions? He wasn't sure.

At least not when she was awake.

And then there was her partner, Ashby. Nice-looking guy, and another puzzle. Wasn't your typical cop. There was something too soft about him, too beta male for his line of work, but maybe he was the best kind of partner for Jude.

Elliot fumbled and whispered that into his mic. Ashby turned, and it almost seemed as if he was looking at him. But no, he was checking the crowd for possible suspects. He bent his head and whispered something to Jude. She scanned the crowd too. Elliot moved his camera, searching for the blond girl, and spotted her walking quickly away from the burial site, heading his direction. And now he could see her face. It *was* the girl in the photo. He was pretty sure of it. And shit. She was heading straight for him. Too late to try to hide.

He fired off a couple of quick shots, then lowered the camera and pretended to fiddle with the settings. She walked right past him, so close that her arm almost brushed his. Close enough for him to catch a whiff of her hair. It smelled like cookies.

He waited until she had a good head start, then he followed. Five minutes in, he lost her. He took the likeliest path, which led out through the cemetery gates to on-street parking, but after searching for another ten minutes, he gave up. He'd gotten enough shots. Instead of returning to the funeral, he sprinted for his car and headed to a place nearby, a place where he'd taken photos Jude hadn't seen. Of her entering and leaving the house where she'd been held captive. Later, he'd review the photos of the blond girl and send JPEGs to Jude, but now, while she was occupied with Iris Roth and the funeral, he took the opportunity to expand his journalistic investigation.

Rather than parking in the driveway or the street in front of the house, where his car would be seen, he pulled into the alley, edging his vehicle off the blacktop, tall weeds and shrubs scraping the panels. The car wouldn't be hidden, but there were no houses on the opposite side of the lane. Just a couple of abandoned buildings that might have been storage facilities, or maybe even small factories at one time. A high fence, broken windows, and a lot of graffiti advertised them as vacant.

Out of the car, camera around his neck, he popped the trunk and grabbed a crowbar. This time he planned to get inside the house. He thought of it as a place of history that needed to be documented for the world. One day Jude might thank him for it.

He climbed the chain-link fence, clutching his camera to his chest, and dropped to the ground on the other side. A glance around, and then, head down, bent at the waist, he moved quickly across the backyard, slipping into an alcove where a set of crumbling stairs met the back of the building. The house had been boarded up, and even though there were still signs of a traditional basement having existed in a previous life, at some point the windows had been removed and filled with cement. That kind of a basement treatment was suspicious and often typical of meth labs, but he had to wonder if the windows had been filled in with Jude's capture in mind.

Using the crowbar, he pried at a piece of plywood. The squeaking nails were bent in more than one spot, a sign the board had been removed and replaced at least a couple of times. It was harder than it looked to free, because the window was high. The last nail finally came loose, and he tossed the board aside. Most of the glass was gone, but not all of it. He took off his sweatshirt and draped it over the sill, covering any possible remaining sharp pieces. He wasn't the most athletic person in the world, but once he lowered his camera inside and let go of the strap, he was a hundred percent committed. It took a couple of failed running jumps before his belly was balanced on the sill. He wiggled and inched his way in, careful not to fall on his camera when he dropped to the other side.

Because of the plywood over the rest of the windows, the interior was murky. Sitting on the floor, he pulled out his cell phone and opened the flashlight app, letting out a sound of irritation at the appearance of the red battery icon. Not a huge issue. With the flash on his camera, he didn't really need the phone.

He'd landed in a bedroom with a bed and dresser and desk. Out of breath, he pushed himself to his feet, shook the glass from his sweatshirt, put it on, and reslung his camera.

He photographed everything he felt needed documenting. The stains on the mattress, the opened dresser drawers. A flyer for pizza someone had dropped. In the kitchen, the sink was overflowing with so many dishes it looked like a cartoon. Those dishes were covered in dust. He took flash photos of them.

He'd been in the house once before, when he'd followed Jude inside before freaking out and running off, but it was still strange to think of her imprisoned here, and even stranger to think she might have eaten off the chipped plates in the sink. Behind him, the kitchen table was littered with more-recent items. Empty food wrappers, plastic soda bottles, a lighter, and cigarette butts put out right on the table.

The odor in the house was oppressive. There was the stuffy house stench. Along with that were the odors of old cigarettes and beer, combined with a lingering scent of food that had gone bad long ago. He had another thought. The man who'd died here had rotted before his body was found. Yeah, that was what it was. The odor was embedded in the walls.

He'd saved the best or worst for last, depending on one's perspective. The best for him, worst for Jude. The basement.

He took several photos of what he guessed were bloodstains on the walls. This was where she'd shot her captor. She'd found his gun in the kitchen. It had been darker than this, pitch black, he'd read. She'd aimed at the sound of movement, pulling the trigger in total darkness.

"He tumbled down the stairs," she'd said in one account.

Hence the blood.

His heart was pounding and he tried to tell himself it wasn't in excitement, because this was the scene of some horrific events, but he was standing in the center of history and in the center of a place where a person's life had changed forever, and another had died.

He moved down the steps. To his left was a green garden hose.

"He used to hose me down with cold water."

And there it was. The cell.

"I screamed for days, but it was so well insulated no one heard me. I was only screaming to myself."

He took several photos of the hose and floor drain.

He had trouble with the cell door and ended up hanging his camera on a nail so he could grab the door handle with both hands. It was a tight fit, and it dragged and shuddered against the framework.

The cell was even smaller than he'd imagined. Too small to lie down in unless a person curled up. She'd said that in the interview, but he'd always figured it was an exaggeration. Jude was tall, probably five foot eight or nine. Elliot was five ten. By looking at the doorjamb, he confirmed that the walls were almost ten inches thick and layered with soundproofing material. There were three external deadbolts.

His heart pounding, he stepped inside, and with shoulders hunched he passed the light over the walls. Someone, Jude most likely, had scratched words everywhere. Every inch of space was covered, much unreadable because she'd been writing in the dark, and most or all of it had been written over many times.

He sank to his knees and curled into a ball on the cold concrete floor, trying to imagine what it had been like for her.

In here for years. *Years.*

He got brave and pulled the door shut, but not all the way. He wasn't *that* brave. He left it cracked an inch. His phone went dead then, plunging the room into darkness.

This is what it was like.

The silence. Total darkness.

He became aware of the sound of the house, like it was a living and breathing thing. Had that brought Jude comfort? The sound of the house?

A pop now and then of wood expanding or contracting, of something settling. From somewhere came a faint scurrying, maybe of a mouse or even a rat. Yes, because he heard movement in the walls. Digging, something falling.

Okay. Enough.

He was unfolding himself from the cramped position when his ears picked up a new noise. A shuffling, like something sliding against wood. Then, through the slightly ajar door, he heard footsteps. Real, human footsteps.

Jude?

The footfall changed in tempo. Jude, it must have been Jude, running now, down the steps. She hurled herself at the cell door and it closed completely.

The room went soundless.

He pushed back against the door. Not that hard at first, but then he threw his shoulder into it. Inside, there was no handle. "Hey!" he shouted, even though he knew she couldn't hear him. "Let me out!"

He tried to turn his phone back on, but it was dead. He reached for his camera, but remembered he'd hung it outside the cell.

Locked in, Elliot continued to shout and bang.

CHAPTER 44

Several hours after the Roth funeral, Jude stepped from her bedroom, wearing a long strapless black gown. She'd even put on a little mascara and red lipstick. Iris seemed to be coping okay, mostly lying on the couch, playing video games on her phone, so Jude had decided to attend the Crisis Center fund-raiser and gala. She was more concerned with keeping an eye on Uriah than on Iris. And as long as the young woman didn't do anything stupid, she'd be fine by herself in Jude's apartment.

Iris glanced up. "Nice," she whispered, admiring Jude's outfit. That single word was a broken croak. The doctor had said her vocal cords had been damaged but they'd heal. She wasn't supposed to speak, but it was reassuring to know she could. She could call 911, and she could probably even scream if she had to.

"Are you sure you don't want to come?"

Iris shook her head. Understandable.

Jude didn't trust her. Not for a second. Was she capable of murder? That was the question. Was her life in danger? Maybe. The building was secure, and the door to Jude's apartment was solid wood, with three locks. The windows looked down four stories to the ground. It would be almost impossible for anybody to get inside. If Iris kept her head, she'd be fine.

Iris wasn't a child and shouldn't need to hear the obvious. Jude laid it out anyway. "Don't leave the apartment. Lock the door once I'm gone. There's ice cream and Popsicles in the freezer. Juice and Jell-O in the refrigerator, soup in the cupboard." All liquid-diet items Jude had grabbed yesterday before picking Iris up from the hospital. "Sorry I don't have a television. Call or text if you need me."

Iris nodded, then scribbled on the tablet she'd used at the hospital.

Thank you.

It was strange to have someone staying in the apartment with her. One night so far, with Iris sleeping on the couch. Jude valued her privacy, and it had been hard to keep from going to the roof. Instead, she'd forced herself to stay in her bedroom, staring into the dark, listening to Roof Cat purring inside the box spring. One night. How many to go?

Her phone rang. She checked the screen, surprised to see Professor Masucci's name.

"I have something important to show you," he said when she answered. "Please come by my apartment immediately."

If it had been anybody else, she would have asked what he was calling about. With the professor, every question risked redirecting his thoughts or shutting him down completely. "I'll be right there." She hung up and got in touch with Uriah to tell him she'd be late, hoping the professor didn't forget why he'd called by the time she arrived at his place. Then she grabbed her messenger bag and leather jacket, told Iris good-bye, and hurried out the door. But no matter how little time had passed between the professor's phone call and Jude's arrival at his door, he still acted surprised to see her. And he liked her dress.

As she followed him through the maze of his apartment, she told him about the Crisis Center fund-raiser and gala. In the kitchen, he suggested she sit down. Since she didn't want to do anything that might cause him to withdraw, she sat. "You had something you wanted to show me?"

"Would you like a cup of tea?" He opened a cupboard and caught a landslide of papers and pill containers, shoved them back, and found what he was looking for. "It was a gift." He opened a box that contained a variety of tea and placed it on the table, then turned on the burner below a red kettle. This was not going to be the quick stop she'd hoped for. And her bigger worry—was this just a ploy for company?

She chose something called Spiced Ginger Plum. The tea came in little cloth bags. "It's shaped like a pyramid," she noted, holding one up.

He seemed delighted by that. Probably a math thing.

It seemed like forever before the kettle began to whistle. He preferred his tea with milk. Jude decided adding cold liquid to hot might speed things along. She poured a large amount of milk from the plastic jug. "Why did you call me, Professor Masucci?"

He fumbled in his pocket and pulled out a small piece of paper ripped from a notebook. "Sometimes answers come to me in dreams, especially things I can't remember when I'm awake." He pushed the paper at her.

Fibonacci = death.

Under that was a name.

Leo Pisa.

"I don't understand."

"I used to have a student who was obsessed with the Fibonacci sequence. One day he seemed to have an epiphany and started writing what he thought was an equation, filling the chalkboard in the front of the room. Nobody understood, not even me. But the gist was that Fibonacci equals death."

"And this Pisa person was that student?" She tapped the paper.

"Yes. I suspect he had his name legally changed."

He'd mentioned a dream. It was possible none of what the professor said had occurred in real life. She took a sip of tea, wondering how many sips it would take before she could politely slip away. The tea wasn't bad. She might start using milk herself. "Pisa," she said. "Like the Leaning Tower of Pisa?"

"Yes."

"Oh." Another drink. A glance at the clock. If she hurried, she could get to the TV studio before the telethon began.

"Pisa, Italy, is where the great mathematician Fibonacci was born."

Poor man. He was looking for vague connections where there were none. If Uriah had been there, they'd have been out the door by now.

"You don't know anything about Fibonacci, do you?" the professor asked when his information failed to impress her.

"No."

"Fibonacci's real name was Leonardo Pisano."

She might have let out a small gasp, giving him the reaction he'd been hoping for. Leonardo Pisano. She pulled out her phone and Googled the name Leo Pisa. Several articles popped up. It seemed Pisa was famous in underground circles for orchestrating elaborate performance art, some of which had to do with numbers. One of the articles had a photo attached. It was a face she recognized.

"I have to go." Jude scrambled to her feet.

"Was that helpful?"

"Yes. Very." She was sharply focused now. "I'll be in touch."

"One more thing. Leo is the person I was trying to remember when you were here before. I saw him at Dark Soul not too long ago. He stopped at my table and talked to me. I think he was with the blond girl in the photo."

Dark Soul. That sounded familiar, and then she remembered stopping in front of the coffee shop when she and Uriah were interviewing people after the theater murder. Killers were known to return to the scene of the crime. And they might even stop for coffee.

Had the professor just solved the case? If so, she'd bring him a giant box of tea bags shaped like pyramids.

"Thank you."

Outside the professor's apartment building, Jude called Uriah to tell him about Leo Pisa. No answer. He'd probably set his phone on "Do Not Disturb" for his Crisis Center interview.

After leaving an urgent voicemail, she straddled her bike, tucked in the hem of her dress, and tugged on her helmet. Easing her bike around, she squeezed the clutch, shifted into first gear with her foot, and roared down the street.

CHAPTER 45

The cat sat in the middle of the floor, watching her. What was it with him and all that staring? Iris didn't think he even liked people. He and his owner were just too weird.

"Are you hungry?" she whispered hoarsely.

The cat didn't blink. It was bizarre the way the cat and Jude were so silent. Iris had caught the detective staring at her a few times, and it had made her scalp tingle. She suspected something. Iris was sure of it. That was probably why she'd invited Iris to stay at her place. So she could keep an eye on her and maybe crack her. Neither of them were idiots. Iris should have refused, but she was scared. And Jude made her feel safe.

Iris picked up her phone. She was never supposed to call Leo with her personal phone. He'd gotten disposable burners for that, and she'd been warned about leaving any kind of clue or trail. "Never use your phone," he'd said. "That's how people get caught." But she knew his main number. And it was so tempting . . .

She'd done it for him, for his approval. Hoping he would finally like her more than he liked Clementine. It had been fun at first, the game, the performances. The idea of revenge had been particularly appealing, because she hated her parents for not believing her and for calling her a liar. And she loathed her brother for molesting her. And yet the night of the murders she'd changed her mind—but it had been too late. She'd already unlocked the front door and let them inside. And now that her family was dead, she missed her mother and father. But not her brother. No way would she ever miss him. Still, it had stopped feeling like a game the night they died. The night she almost died with them. They'd tried to kill her! Her tribe, her friends. So why was she thinking of calling Leo?

She touched the bandage on her throat. She'd always have a scar, and her voice would probably never sound the same, but she hadn't betrayed him. She hadn't betrayed any of them.

She didn't call. Instead, she began playing a game on her phone. A few minutes later, she heard a light tap at the door and froze. The knock sounded again. This time it was followed by a whisper. "It's me. Let me in."

Iris's heart pounded. She glanced around the room, looking for a place to hide. But she was safe here, right? With the door locked a million times?

"I'm sorry," came Clementine's voice through the crack in the door. "Leo made me do it. I was afraid if I didn't, he'd hurt me too. I'm so sorry."

So Clementine had sliced her throat . . .

"I came to see you at the hospital," she said. "But you were leaving with the detective, so I hid."

Iris and Clementine had met at the shelter. Iris had been playing homeless, but Clementine was the real deal.

"I have pizza," Clementine said. "Mushroom and pineapple, your favorite. Please let me in. I need to see you. I hope you're okay." She let out a sob.

Iris believed her about Leo. He was so charming and hot. He could convince anybody to do anything. She'd seen it. Even when she knew he was manipulating her, she'd allowed him to. And had even asked for more.

She uncurled herself from the sofa, checked the peephole, and unbolted the door, all but the chain lock.

Clementine was holding a pizza box with both hands. Dark floral dress and black sneakers, her hair braided and wrapped around her head, a colorful headband over that. She did "cute" so well. On the floor next to her feet was a six-pack of beer.

"I'm sorry," she repeated. There were tears on her cheeks, but Iris knew what an actress she was. Clementine was the worst of the bunch— or maybe it just seemed that way because she looked so innocent. The campers at the river. That had been so easy. She'd approached them and asked for help. And while they'd talked to her, comforted her, the rest of the gang had done their job in a few quick slices.

"I need to talk to you about Leo," Clementine said. "We need to do something. Stop him. Maybe go to the cops. I don't know how I got sucked into this, and I don't know how to get out of it."

Her words connected. "I know." Iris felt the same way, and once or twice she'd actually considered confessing to Jude. But she didn't unlock the door. "I can't let you in," she whispered. She didn't bother to tell her that she couldn't eat solid food.

"That's okay. I get it. I don't blame you. Look, I'll leave the pizza right here." She put it on the floor and backed away. "If you feel like talking, call me." She turned around, hand on the stair railing.

Iris felt so alone. She had nobody now. "Wait." She slid the chain free and opened the door.

CHAPTER 46

Jude came to a sharp halt in front of the downtown Saint Paul public-television building, where the telethon was being held. Behind her, the light-rail train chimed as it pulled to a stop. Doors opened and people exited to the sidewalk. Once the telethon was over, volunteers could either walk the half mile to the gala at Union Depot or take the train.

She set the kickstand and swung her leg free. Not bothering with the meter, she hurried through the glass doors of the broadcast center. The guard behind the check-in desk eyed her with suspicion.

"I'm here to answer calls for the telethon," she said. "Jude Fontaine."

Her words did nothing to alleviate his doubt. Maybe it was the leather jacket over the evening gown. Without waiting for an okay, Jude headed down the corridor that led to the studio. The hall was dim, and the light above one of the doors said *On Air*. A wall of glass revealed Uriah, dressed in a black tuxedo, sitting on a stool, heels of his shoes locked on a rung, hands clasped between his knees, sweating under the stage lights hanging from the black industrial ceiling. Next to him was the head of the Crisis Center. Her lips were moving with words Jude couldn't hear.

The stage where Uriah sat was to the left of two rows of tables and beige telephones. Only one seat at the back was empty.

Speaking into a receiver was the crime-scene-cleanup guy. One
of the many volunteers answering the pledge-drive calls. A man also
known as Leo Pisa.

He spotted her through the glass. His eyes widened in recognition, and he gave her a small wave. He wore a black jacket over a
black turtleneck, and his dark wavy hair looked like something from
a men's fashion magazine. Jude motioned for him to join her outside
the studio. He shook his head and pointed to the telephone receiver
in his hand. She'd hoped to coax him from the crowded room and
away from the others. Ignoring the *On Air* light, she eased the door
open and slipped inside. Ducking under a camera, she aimed for the
empty chair.

Uriah spotted her and did a double take, then watched her with a
slightly smitten expression. The interviewer repeated her question, and
Uriah pulled his eyes from Jude.

The conversation dealt with the suicide survivor's perspective. "I
don't know if it's anything you get over," he said. "We need to educate
families, but I also think we need to do something for the people left
behind. Because they have to live with the guilt every single day."

The room was cramped, and Jude squeezed and sidestepped behind
people to take the empty spot, placing her helmet and bag on the table,
leaving one person between her seat and Pisa's. She had to remind herself that she had no proof of his guilt. Right now he was only a person
of interest. *Great* interest. But if what the professor had related was
true—Pisa's connection to the blond girl, the essay, his infatuation with
the Fibonacci sequence, his name, the performance art—it made him
a prime suspect.

The incessantly ringing phones, the combined voices of the volunteers, the interview going on yards away were a sensory overload that
made it hard to focus, and Jude struggled to keep a subtle eye on Pisa.
Three calls and two hundred raised dollars later, she caught a shift of

movement as he got to his feet and began edging his way behind the occupied chairs. Now that Pisa was standing, she saw he was dressed in black from head to toe. Like the people in the murky security-camera footage from the house near the Roth crime scene.

Restroom, he mouthed, pointing to the exit door.

She'd blown it with her signal for him to meet her outside the studio. He knew she knew something, and he was getting ready to bolt.

CHAPTER 47

Clementine sneezed. "Is there a cat in here? I'm allergic to cats." Good thing the animal was hiding somewhere. "Don't hurt him," Iris said. Due to her liquid diet, she'd finished two bottles of beer while Clementine had eaten three pieces of pizza.

The blond girl prowled around, searching for the cat, but paused in front of the refrigerator and opened the door. "I always wondered what a detective's place would be like. Didn't imagine a dump like this." She swiveled on her heel. "We should look through all her shit."

"Detective Fontaine's?" Iris let out a snort, then put her hand to her throat. It hurt, and she hoped the pill she'd taken would kick in soon. "I don't think there's anything to see. She's like a monk or a nun or something," she whispered. "She doesn't even have a TV."

They both plopped back down on the couch. "You should let me braid your hair like mine," Clementine said.

Iris liked that idea, and slid to the floor between her friend's knees. Clementine finger-combed her hair, dividing it into three strands. "I could do a French braid."

Iris nodded and closed her eyes. The medication was hitting her. She hardly noticed when the braiding stopped. She didn't even open her eyes. Instead, she sat in a comfortable half doze. She was so sleepy that at first she didn't understand what was happening when she felt pressure against the gauze bandage. A sharp pain jerked her to full attention.

Too late.

The next sensation was one of warmth soaking into the neckline of her dress. She tried to speak, but no sound came out this time.

It had been easy to fall in with them, as her mother had always put such things. *"You're running with a bad crowd. You've fallen in with the wrong people."* *Wrong* usually meaning people who weren't rich, or people who might not always know the correct grammar. But Leo Pisa was well educated and one of the smartest people Iris had ever known.

Clementine leaned over her, a gentle smile on her pink lips while she held the bloody knife for Iris to see. It might have been the same knife Iris had used on the woman in the burned-out mansion. "You were never one of us," Clementine said. "You could never be one of us." She kissed Iris on the forehead and laughed.

CHAPTER 48

Bracing her gun with both hands, Jude said in a clear voice, "On the floor."

People gasped while Pisa slowly raised his arms in the air, an innocent look of surprise on his face. "What's going on?"

"Floor!" she repeated.

In her peripheral vision, she caught a movement, followed by the sound of Uriah speaking her name. He had left the interview platform and was standing a couple of feet behind her. She didn't waver and didn't take her eyes from the suspect.

"What's this about?" Pisa asked again. He looked so concerned she began to doubt herself. This all hinged on information garnered from a man who thought he taught at the University of Minnesota when he really didn't. A *very* unreliable witness.

"You're a suspect in the Fibonacci murders," she stated. *Go big or go home.*

"That's insane." He cast a look around the room, searching for a sympathetic face. He found several. "She's crazy."

"The floor."

He eased to his knees.

"Hands behind your head."

"He's a respected member of the community," the director shouted. Then, "Turn off the cameras! Turn off the cameras!"

"My father was a respected member of the community too," Jude said. "I didn't do anything," Pisa told her. "I'm here to help people."

Someone hiding nearby decided to play hero. He latched on to Jude's ankle and gave it a firm tug, knocking her off balance. She caught herself, but wasn't fast enough. Pisa jumped to his feet, pulling a handgun from his jacket.

Had this been his plan all along? Performance art, played out on live TV? And how had she missed the signs at the Roth crime scene? She'd talked to him face-to-face. But then, psychopaths didn't feel guilt, and guilt was the thing that gave people away.

With one hand, he seized a woman by the hair and pulled her close. A human shield. With the other hand and with no hesitation, he began firing his automatic pistol, spent shells flying.

People screamed, glass shattered, blood spattered against white walls. In the fresh chaos, he shoved the woman away, turned, and ran from the room. Jude moved through the scattered tables, leaping over bodies, never taking her eye off the exit door. Unattended cameras were still capturing the scene.

Uriah caught up with her. Blood trailed down the side of his face. "Call for ambulances and backup," he shouted. Someone scrambled and reached for a phone, but sirens were wailing in the distance. The police already knew. The madness had been witnessed on live television throughout the Twin Cities.

Jude and Uriah ran down the hall, past the guard, who was slumped over his desk, a pool of blood at his feet. With no hesitation, Jude burst outside, halting long enough to scan the area. The light-rail train was at the station, no sign of Pisa.

Jude took off again, arms pumping. She squeezed inside the last car as the door closed behind her, leaving Uriah on the sidewalk. With her gun held high and legs braced to steady herself against the shifting movement of the train, she ignored the frightened faces of people on each side and zeroed in on Pisa, who stood at the front of the car.

She could certainly read him now. He was trying to formulate an escape plan. A hostage was his only hope, and that hope was slim. The nearest possibilities were a frail-looking man, a child, or a young woman. None of them would put up a fight, but the child would be the easiest. He could carry her with one arm, use her for a shield. That's what Jude would do if she were him.

"Put the gun down," she said. "There's no way out. Transit police and Homeland Security have been alerted." Protocol. "A SWAT team will be waiting at the next stop."

Her focus was narrow, yet she noted a gradual increase in the train's speed until it was traveling much faster than normal. The speed didn't seem to register with Pisa. He looked at the child, then back at Jude. She wanted to tell the little girl to run, but her command could push Pisa too far and he might react the way he'd reacted back at the studio. "There's no death penalty in Minnesota," she told him, her voice level and clear. "Give yourself up. You can live out your life in relative comfort. It's not the end. You don't have to die. And if you confess, you'll be given privileges."

"I'd rather die than go to prison. Living my life in a cell. You should understand that." He was winding up, his voice rising, indicating that a total loss of control could be near.

"I do understand." She needed to calm him down, distract him, so she changed the narrative, deciding to flatter him. Performers loved applause. "I have to say, cleaning up your own crimes was genius. If any clues were left behind, you could make sure they were never reported. And arriving so early at the Roth house, before we were done. Smart too. But I'd like to know *why* you went into crime-scene cleanup in the first place. I'm guessing it started with a death." That comment registered with him. "A lot of major life changes are driven by triggers," she said. "Our desire to correct something. A do-over. Often the trigger is loss." Her tone was one of compassion. "Is that it? Did you lose somebody close to you?"

"My mother died at home," he told her. His voice trembled a little, but it wasn't as high as it had been. "It was an unattended death and I didn't discover her for almost a week."

He was lying about something, sharing a half truth. Had he killed her himself? That would fit. Was his mother the reason he'd dropped out of college and was unable to continue pursuing his degree?

"It was hard to find someone to come in and clean up, and when I did, they weren't very nice."

"Did you have to take care of her? Before her death?"

"Sometimes."

Even psychopaths could love, or at least had their own private and twisted version of love. And once they'd experienced the death of someone close to them, some tried to avoid reminders. Others welcomed and even created them.

His next words surprised her. "Kill me. It would be a great finish."

"I've killed enough people." It said a lot that she didn't want to end the life of someone as evil as he was.

"It would be an honor to be killed by you," he said. "I've admired you for a long time."

Was that what this was about? Had it been for her benefit? No, she couldn't think that. How could she live if she thought all those innocent victims were dead because of her?

"Kill me or more people will die."

The train's speed changed. Brakes were applied, the engagement so violent that screaming passengers were tossed out of seats. Backpacks and purses flew through the air and slammed against windows.

In the confusion, Jude rushed him. His gun discharged as she brought him to the ground while the train wheels screeched and the car continued to slow. She knocked the weapon from his hand and pinned him down, all the while hating that she had to touch him.

The car came to a halt; doors were pried open. The SWAT team rushed inside dressed in armor and carrying shields. They secured Pisa, two of them dragging him upright, his wrists cuffed behind his back. He didn't take his eyes off Jude, smiling at her as if he knew a secret.

Passengers slowly emerged from beneath seats. Thankfully, no one had been hit by the stray bullet from Pisa's gun. They gathered in the aisle, crying and hugging one another. Uriah burst into the car, his shoulders sagging in relief when he saw Jude. She asked him whose idea it was to slam on the brakes. He said it was his.

While the sky grew dark and lights strobed silently around them, someone took her statement. A medic bandaged Uriah's head, cut by shattering glass, and told him he'd need stitches. Then Jude and Uriah caught a ride back to the television station in a patrol car.

The wounded were already gone, but from where she stood on the sidewalk, she could see the guard still slumped over his desk.

"Detective Fontaine." Jude's messenger bag and helmet were handed to her by an officer attending the scene. He nodded and returned to the building.

Jude ducked under the strap of her bag. "I'm going home." She'd seen enough.

"I'll drive you," Uriah said.

"I prefer to ride my motorcycle." When she saw his expression, she added, "I'll be fine. I'll be careful."

"You did good tonight," he told her.

"Not good enough. People were shot. One person dead."

"It could have been much worse."

Someone called Uriah's name.

They looked up to see his father and a woman who must have been his mother striding down the sidewalk. Jude couldn't do this. Meet someone new.

"I can't talk to them now."

"That's okay."

"And I need to get home to break this new development to Iris. I want to see how she reacts to the news." She was hoping for a confession and an arrest, yet she still felt sympathy. There was no justification for murder, but the girl had suffered years of molestation that her parents had denied. That would warp any mind. Leo Pisa and his crew had given her what she needed. Family and what might have seemed like a way to correct the wrongs that had been dealt her for so long. "Then I'll meet you downtown and we can interrogate Pisa."

Uriah turned and walked up the sidewalk to meet his parents. They hugged, and Jude heard his mother's exclamation of joy at finding her son relatively unharmed. Were they just arriving, or had they been at the gala when they got news of the shooting?

Jude's motorcycle had a ticket on it. She pulled it off and tossed it in the street. Straddling the bike, she tugged on her helmet, tucked the tattered hem of her dress under her thighs, and roared away, past the flashing lights and police cars, media, and onlookers. Fifteen minutes later, she pulled into the parking garage of her building and brought the bike to an abrupt halt. Her phone vibrated. She pulled it from the pocket of her jacket and checked the screen. A text from Iris. It was composed of two words: Number eight.

CHAPTER 49

Jude raced for the interior parking-garage door, boots pounding up four flights of the stairwell, taking two steps at a time to burst into a corridor stained with red footprints. Her apartment door was ajar. She pulled her gun and pushed the door open the rest of the way. Iris was lying on the floor, surrounded by a pool of blood, a number eight carved in her forehead.

Breathing hard, legs threatening to buckle, ears roaring, Jude distantly noticed Iris's hair had been braided. Beside her on the couch was a purple hairbrush. The table was strewn with empty beer bottles, along with a partially eaten pizza. BCA might be able to lift prints from the bottles, and it would be easy to trace the pizza purchase. A glance at the side of the box told Jude it had come from a place not that far away. It had been delivered or picked up, either one traceable. All these thoughts collided in her head at roughly the same time, and were over and done in seconds.

She crouched beside Iris.

Dead bodies were vacant. It was the best way to describe them. The person was gone, leaving behind flesh and bones and blood.

Iris's throat had been cut right through the bandage. Sliced deep, adequately silenced, the killer making sure she wouldn't survive this time. Jude checked for a pulse anyway, then mentally reconstructed the timeline from the moment she'd left the apartment. How long was she at the professor's? Fifteen minutes? That made it highly unlikely Iris had been killed by Leo Pisa; he would already have been at the telethon.

She made a quick sweep of the apartment. Her closet and drawers had been ransacked, but there was nothing for anyone to steal or find. The killer was long gone, and Roof Cat was safe and hiding in the box spring.

She wasn't sure why it mattered that she change clothes, but she felt the urgent need to get out of the gown. She stripped it off and tossed it on the bed. Standing in her underwear, hands shaking, she called Uriah and broke the news.

"Are you okay?" He sounded unusually concerned. Had her voice been shaking too?

"Yes." She hung up, clenching and unclenching her fists to get herself under control.

She got dressed, putting on clothing that wasn't frivolous, that was more appropriate for death—jeans and a black T-shirt—and waited in the living room with Iris.

There was no need to let Uriah in when he arrived ten minutes later, out of breath and too tense for the calm sorrow of the room. She'd left the apartment door wide open. "BCA's on the way," he said.

While Jude stood and watched with her arms folded over her stomach, he snapped on a pair of disposable gloves from the evidence kit he kept in the trunk of his car. He was still wearing the tuxedo, and his white cuffs were stained with blood. "Because of the telethon shooting, crime techs are spread thin, so it might be a while. In the meantime, some of our people are coming to begin processing the scene." He handed her a pair of gloves, then began moving around the apartment. "Anything in the bathroom?" he asked. "Did the perpetrator shower?"

"Not sure. I didn't notice any attempt to hide anything or clean up anything." She slipped on the gloves.

"Flagrant, careless, or they had to leave in a hurry," Uriah said.

Jude picked up the purple brush and held it high. "Look." A long, light hair was trapped in the bristles.

"Our blond girl."

Jude could have gone on about how she shouldn't have left Iris alone, but that would be too easy, and it would direct attention to her rather than the victim. This moment was about Iris, so Jude said no more. Instead, she slid the brush with the single hair into an evidence bag, sealed and signed it.

Uriah tilted his head to one side as if listening to something beyond the room. "You hear a cat?"

Jude retuned her ears and heard it too. Pitiful meows, coming from somewhere deep in the building. It sounded too far away for Roof Cat. "I'll be back." She needed to talk to Elliot anyway, find out if he'd heard or seen anything.

On the way to the third floor, she paused long enough to take photos of the bloody footprints on the marble steps. At Elliot's door, she knocked, but there was no answer. Maybe she was stalling so she wouldn't have to go back upstairs, but this time, instead of breaking in, she retrieved the key from the caretaker. "I'm worried about him," she said.

The caretaker eyed her latex gloves and gave her a key. Checking on a neighbor was an acceptable excuse, while spying on him wasn't. When she got back to Elliot's apartment, Uriah was waiting outside the door.

"Could be connected to Iris's murder," he said, pulling his weapon. She turned the key in the lock and they slipped inside. Elliot's black cat came running, tail straight up, meowing loudly. His food dish was empty, and there was no sign of his owner.

Jude tried to remember when she'd last heard Elliot downstairs. "He can't have been gone long." The cat still had water. She banged around, searching kitchen cupboards, found a bag of cat food, and poured dry kibble while Uriah topped off the water dish. They put down the bowls at the same time. The cat went straight for the food.

"Poor thing," Uriah said.

Watching the animal, Jude pulled out her phone and called Elliot's number. It went to voicemail. "I'm going to see if his car's here."

She checked the garage, plus the street where he sometimes parked. No sign of his vehicle. Back in his apartment, she gave Uriah the news.

"What's the connection between his disappearance, the blond girl, and Iris?" Uriah asked aloud.

"That's what I'm wondering." She glanced around the space. "His laptop and camera are gone. I hate to say it, but I'm guessing he and the blond girl left together. It explains why she was in the building at all, and how she knew Iris was here."

"I'm not sure," Uriah said. "If he left today, the cat would have been fed."

"Not necessarily. Maybe he didn't care about the cat. Maybe he just got the cat as a conversation starter." She opened another cupboard. Cereal. Drinking glasses. A half-eaten bag of Oreo cookies. The cookies weren't charming and funny anymore. "Maybe he neglected him with no thought about the harm he was doing."

"Mass murderers sometimes love their pets."

"Mass murderers often start out by killing their pets."

"We know there were more than two people involved in at least one of the killings," Uriah said. "We saw video footage of four people walking down the sidewalk. And Elliot was at every crime scene. Killers love to watch the aftermath."

Jude wanted to keep searching the apartment, but Uriah stopped her. "Let's go. If he's a suspect, we can't be here without a warrant. Nothing we find can be used against him in court. In the meantime, we'll try to find friends or relatives who might have a clue to his whereabouts. Or maybe we'll get the information from Pisa."

She opened a drawer.

Uriah slammed it shut. "I'm serious. We have to go." He motioned for her to leave.

From outside came the wail of sirens. Then someone was pounding on the foyer door. They left the apartment, locking it behind them. In the lobby, Uriah apprised officers and crime-scene specialists of the situation. Evidence cards were set up on the steps. BCA agents, with their heavy black cases, squeezed past.

"There's a cat up there," Jude shouted after them. "In the bedroom. Don't bother him."

Yellow crime-scene tape was strung, and people inside the building and out began to gather, hands to mouths, eyes worried. "Go back to your apartments," Jude told them. "Please."

Beside her, Uriah issued a BOLO on Elliot.

"We need to get that search warrant ASAP," Jude said.

Her phone rang. *Unknown Number.* She answered. "Detective Fontaine."

"This is Ruthie Logan. We met outside the house where you were held captive. You told me to call you if I had any information."

"That's right."

"You might want to come to the shelter I stay in sometimes."

"Can it wait?"

"I think you'll want to see this."

"What's it about?"

"A blond girl named Clementine." She gave Jude the address. It was Light in the Darkness, the same shelter where Clementine and Blaine Michaels had stayed.

CHAPTER 50

Jude and Uriah arrived at the shelter fifteen minutes later. Ruthie, the woman who'd called, was waiting for them. She pulled Jude aside and glanced over her shoulder. Behind her, lights were dim and people were milling around, some clutching clothes, others a blanket and pillow, ready to stake out their cot.

"This way." Ruthie crooked her finger and led them to a bathroom with a row of shower stalls on one side, sinks on the other. Stuffed under a sink were a floral dress, bloody towels, and black tennis shoes. Above the sink was a framed affirmation.

ALL I SEEK IS ALREADY WITHIN ME.

"At first I thought abortion or miscarriage," Ruthie said. "Something like that, but Clementine was grabbing her stuff like the devil was after her, and I started wondering if this might be connected to the murders."

Using a paper towel, Jude leaned under the sink and rolled one of the sneakers over. Then she pulled up a photo taken on the stairs of her apartment building. The tread pattern matched.

"What can you tell us about Clementine?" Uriah asked.

"A lot of these youngsters are rail kids." The woman looked from one detective to the other. "They ride for free all over the country, and this is just one of the places they stop, usually in the summer. I'm gonna guess she's catching a train out of here."

"Do you know where she might be going?" Jude asked.

"Clementine and her boyfriend came here from California. Maybe she's going back there. They usually hop the train downtown where the tracks cross the river. You know what I mean? Near the Gold Medal sign and Saint Anthony Falls. You better hurry if you want to catch her."

It was the place where Michaels had died. Jude and Uriah were already moving.

CHAPTER 51

Instead of parking near the spot where Michaels's severed body had been found, Jude and Uriah opted for the stealth approach. It would allow them better control of the situation. Backup would be notified if and when it was needed.

Car doors were gently closed, and the detectives moved to a small overlook that afforded an expansive view of the tracks below.

Most Minnesotans could tell you the Mississippi River started at Lake Itasca, over two hundred miles north of Minneapolis. Jude had once gone on a school field trip to the headwaters. Before that disappointing day, she'd always pictured the beginning of the river as a small trickle, maybe something bubbling up from a field, or running softly from a crack in a slab of granite. No. The Mighty Mississippi started in a nondescript lake that looked like any of the other ten thousand lakes in Minnesota. But due to the restrictive terrain of the area known as the Iron Range, the river became powerful very quickly. Unlike the more placid Mississippi River of Iowa and Missouri, this one raged red through narrow gorges, and slipped beneath sheer black cliff faces topped with towering evergreens. The violence of the water sculpted the landscape in a breathless and beautiful way. It carved deep chasms and rushed through rugged valleys until the water lost the red of the Iron Range to finally reach downtown Minneapolis and Saint Anthony Falls. It was here, along the gorge carved by the raging river, that train tracks ran parallel to the water, then turned to cross. This was the place where the train hoppers boarded.

"Access to the tracks is almost impossible from this outlook." Uriah scanned the area for a better plan.

The city was never dark, and the night was cloudy. Light reflected off the water and bounced off clouds. Jude strained her eyes and caught a movement. "I think I see something." A dark shape appeared, then vanished behind a wall of steel held together with rivets the size of fists. She pointed. "Someone's on the bridge." She braced her hands on the metal railing, prepared to swing a leg over. "I'm going down."

"Too steep," Uriah said.

"I can do it."

"I'll circle around to the Third Avenue Bridge. We can come at her from both directions." He turned and ran for the car.

The darkness added another layer of complexity, but hopefully it would also keep Jude hidden from the person below. The terrain was steep, almost straight down in places, but she spotted a faint trail. She wasn't the first to go this way.

It was treacherous, but not impossible. A couple of times she slid and caught herself, once by digging in the heel of her boot, another time by grabbing a branch that luckily remained embedded in rocks and soil as she skidded to a stop.

Descending, she shifted her gaze from the ground to the place where she'd spotted the movement on the bridge. With a few feet of incline left, she dropped with soft knees. Head down, she ran for the tracks, then followed the curved, parallel metal rails to the bridge. A few yards from the joist where she'd spotted the shadow of movement, she pulled her gun. Without waiting for Uriah, who might or might not get there before the train, she quietly spoke Clementine's name. No response or appearance, so Jude got serious.

"Step out with your hands up."

"Oh my God." A girl with long blond hair appeared from behind the slanted metal beam, hands in the air. "Are you punking me? I didn't think anybody really said that."

Was she alone? "You're under arrest for the murder of Iris Roth." Was Elliot with her?

"You thought Iris was such an angel," the girl said, "but she wasn't." Past tense. "I'm listening."

"Iris killed just as many people as I did, but you were protecting her."

"Even bad people need protecting from bad people."

She let out a loud snort. "Iris even came up with the idea of killing her family so it would look like another piece of performance art."

Jude suspected the first killings hadn't been Iris's idea. But when they needed higher numbers, she'd sacrificed her family, something she later regretted, like most people with a conscience would, even when dealing with relatives who'd hurt her deeply.

From off in the distance a train sounded its horn. They both heard it. "I knew she was guilty," Jude said. "I just didn't know how guilty."

"She squealed, didn't she? She told you about me."

"She never said a word."

"I don't believe you."

"It's true. You killed her for no reason."

"Doesn't matter. The performance is over. By now thirteen people have been killed on live TV, and my boyfriend is on his way out of town. We'll meet in a couple of weeks and spend the rest of our lives together."

Boyfriend. "If you're talking about Leo Pisa, he's locked up downtown, soon to tell us everything he knows about you."

"You're lying!" It took Clementine a little while, but she finally started wailing. It almost drowned out the sound of the train.

CHAPTER 52

The drive from the bluff to the traffic bridge would have taken ten minutes at a normal pace. Uriah made it in five, easing through red lights, keeping his eyes open for pedestrians and bikers. As he drove, he put in a call to Molly, their information expert and all-around miracle worker. He told her where they were. "We need all train traffic stopped."

"I'm on it." Keys clicked.

"Contact Dispatch. We're going to need backup."

"Got that too."

"What about Blaine Michaels?" Jude asked when Clementine finally stopped screaming to stand hunched over, hands on knees, sobbing. "He died on these tracks. I heard *he* was your boyfriend. I suspect it was murder. If so, we'll prove it, along with everything else."

"It doesn't matter!" Clementine glanced over her shoulder at the water below. Was she thinking of jumping?

"Where's Elliot Kaplan?" Jude asked. "What does he have to do with this?"

She became aware of the sound of the approaching train. Clementine heard it too. Without answering Jude's question, she turned and ran.

Uriah pulled to a sharp stop at the foot of the bridge, dust flying. He jumped from the car and ran up the incline, slipping on loose gravel. Once the rails were no longer over solid ground, walking grew treacherous and the glimmer of water below his feet was dizzying. Out in the open, the wind kicked up, maybe as strong as twenty miles per hour. His jacket flapped and his hair snapped against his forehead.

The train was getting closer. The engine labored across the bridge, pulling an expanse of coal cars behind it. Keeping an eye on his feet and on his target—the running girl with a waving flag of blond hair—he moved forward.

Jude slipped her gun into the holster and ran after Clementine. The cry of a police siren drifted across the water. Train cars flew past, metal wheels clacking rhythmically, the iron rails bouncing, the close rush of movement disorienting.

Someone shouted from a boxcar. "Come on!" Hands were extended to both her and Clementine.

Uriah appeared on the other side of the bridge, running straight for the girl. She was trapped. Shouts from inside the car increased.

"Halt!" Uriah commanded.

Jude saw a glint of gunmetal. "Don't shoot!"

Maybe the shout startled her. Maybe Clementine stepped into a hole, or tripped over something in the dark. What followed that shout happened so fast Jude wasn't exactly sure of the cause.

Clementine was almost to the open door. People on the train were cheering her on, ready to grab her hand. Some held up phone lights meant to help, but maybe the lights themselves blinded her. She stumbled. She tried to correct, and then she vanished.

The shouting inside the car turned to screams.

The train's brakes engaged and metal shrieked against metal until the giant beast came to a complete stop. Jude pulled out her phone and ran, shining the flashlight beam until she spotted what she was looking for. She crawled under the train, the heat of the wheels and rails hot against her face.

Clementine was still alive, but her injuries . . .

"I must be okay," she mumbled. "It doesn't hurt."

Jude grasped her hand. "Look at me. Don't look anywhere but at me."

The girl's head shifted slightly and her eyes locked with Jude's. She was an evil person, a heartless person, but right now Jude only saw her as a frightened, dying child.

And she smelled like cookies.

It was over quickly. In a matter of seconds she quit breathing and her eyes went blank. Jude waited a moment, then crawled from under the train to join Uriah on the embankment.

Sirens and patrol lights were upon them. Kids jumped from boxcars and scrambled up the bluff, scattering like mice, loose rocks skittering to the ground behind them.

"Not how I wanted this to end," Jude said.

Uriah put a reassuring arm around her. She didn't recoil. "There was nothing else you could have done."

There was always a better way. "I don't like killing people. I don't want to kill people."

"You didn't kill her."

Two breathless cops appeared. "Holy hell," one of them said, spotting the body on the ground. His face blanched.

More cops were swarming now, setting up a perimeter. A few train kids who hadn't run off were giving statements, one girl wrapped in a blanket even though the temperature wasn't much below sixty. Shock did that. Sucked all the heat from your body. The conductor was gesturing, and a few of his words drifted Jude's way. "Not my fault."

No, not his fault, but he would live with this the rest of his life. And then Jude had another thought. Had he been driving the night Michaels had been killed?

Clementine's backpack was nearby, the contents scattered near the tracks. Clothing, along with a camera. Jude aimed her light at it. An expensive Canon model, with white peace signs on the wide black strap. "That's Elliot's." She walked over and picked it up even though it was part of a crime scene. It was smashed and broken, the SD card mangled. Elliot had mentioned using cloud storage, but that would take a subpoena to access, and the most recent photos might not have been uploaded yet, so it was possible some had been lost for good.

Also on the ground was a phone with a pink case. Iris's. It still worked. While Uriah watched over her shoulder, Jude scrolled through the images. The most recent were of Iris, dead on the floor in Jude's apartment.

"Trophy shots, taken with the victim's own phone," Jude said.

The biggest question: Where was Elliot? Was he part of Pisa's crew and was he now on the run?

"We need to talk to Leo Pisa," Uriah said.

CHAPTER 53

It hadn't ended the way Leo had planned, but he was still pleased with the results. As he sat cuffed, ankles chained to a chair that was bolted to the concrete floor, a camera recording the interrogation by Detectives Fontaine and Ashby, Leo felt good. The thirteen kills on camera hadn't happened, but the performance had been fed into living rooms around the Twin Cities. And now it was probably on YouTube with millions of views. That counted for something. He hoped he'd be able to watch the footage for himself one day. He planned to disclose a lot, but not everything. And he would include embellishments and lies to keep things interesting.

"What can you tell us about Elliot Kaplan?" Fontaine pushed a photo of Kaplan across the table.

Leo leaned back as much as he could. It was hard to look casual when your ankles were strapped to a chair. "I can tell you he's dead."

Fontaine was good at hiding reactions, but he caught a flinch. Next to her, Ashby was sitting with bloodshot eyes and a bandage on his temple. He looked like hell, so at least that was something.

"He took photos of someone in my group at the Roth funeral," Leo said. "Maybe he planned to give them to you. Not cool."

"Would that someone be Clementine?" Jude asked.

No sense in keeping her name out of it. They obviously knew she was connected somehow. "Yeah." And she had more blood on her hands than anybody else. A lot more. "She followed him and killed him. Nothing to do with me. I mean, that didn't fit anything I was doing. A kill of one was way out of sequence." Even now, thinking about numbers being out of sequence bothered him so much he started jiggling his leg like an addict in need of a fix.

Both detectives noticed. He stopped briefly before starting again.

"So, where's Kaplan's body?" Ashby asked. "The more you cooperate, the better off things will be for you."

"I don't know. She never told me. Clementine came back with his camera and said she'd killed him. You need to ask her."

"That could be a problem," Ashby said. "She's dead too."

After a stunned moment, Leo threw back his head and laughed so hard tears streamed down his face. Not what they were expecting, or what he was expecting either. "I'm not surprised," he finally said. "That crazy bitch was out of control. Biting people, gutting them. Eating pieces of them raw. Isn't that some sick stuff? She turned it into horror when it was supposed to be art. When it was supposed to be a thing of beauty." He attempted to wipe the wetness from a cheek with one shoulder. "But she really loved to kill people. And she really loved her affirmations."

"The coroner will be able to match the bite marks to Clementine if what you say is true," Fontaine said. "So if you're lying . . ."

"Oh, they'll match."

Fontaine leaned forward. "What about the numbers?"

"You want to talk about numbers?" He would talk numbers to anybody who'd listen. "It was so beautiful when everything was working perfectly. But we messed up. It was supposed to be random people. That was the plan, but then Iris told us about her family, and how mistreated she'd been. They obviously didn't deserve to be alive, but that's where things went wrong. Never kill an acquaintance. It brings the investigation too close to home. I'm sure you know that. We could have kept going for a long time if we hadn't involved Iris's family. And then, when the numbers weren't right and Iris didn't die? I knew she'd talk."

"She didn't," Fontaine said.

"She would have. She was slumming. She wasn't really one of us."

"And the telethon?" Ashby asked.

"I decided to wrap things up with a live finale. With all the phone-bank volunteers, I knew the room would have more than my required thirteen. I didn't want a repeat of the Roth house."

"Not sure I'm following this," Fontaine said. "You basically had the spotlight, but you were trying to get away. That doesn't sound like a finale to me."

He didn't respond.

"He chickened out," Ashby said with a laugh.

"Ah." Fontaine nodded. "You didn't have your crew with you. You couldn't pull it off by yourself. Especially without Clementine." She tapped the table and leaned closer. "You know what? I think Clementine was your muse. She was the person who pushed you to up your game. She was the person who dared you to escalate. Without her, you were a coward, afraid to go through with anything. Am I right?" Fontaine had always looked so removed and shut off. Not now. Now she was plugged in, her eyes intense. "Here's an affirmation for you," she said. "Behind every great man is a great woman."

That wasn't even an affirmation.

"It's close enough," Fontaine said.

She'd read his fucking mind. "What's going on? I heard you were always nice, even to criminals."

"Incorrect."

"I wonder if you killed anybody at all other than the guard," Ashby said. "And he was an accident, really. Not part of the show. Your solo performance was a disaster."

Pisa pulled against his restraints. They were baiting him. But were they right about Clementine? God, maybe. All of this started when they met. Had she planted everything in his head? The telethon shoot-out had definitely been her idea. It hadn't even involved knives.

"You asked me to kill you," Fontaine said. "You couldn't even do that yourself."

"I'm not a coward! I've killed people."

"Who?" Ashby asked. "Who have you killed?"

"My mother," he whispered in horror. Then louder: "I killed my mother!"

CHAPTER 54

Four days after the arrest of Leo Pisa, Jude and Uriah stood in the middle of the street with a mob of onlookers, waiting for her house to be razed. In all that had happened, she'd forgotten about her order for demolition. When the company called, telling her everything was ready, she'd decided to go forward.

Would she regret destroying it?

Yes.

But the regret and loss wouldn't mean she'd made a mistake. You could make the right choice while still feeling regret.

Some of the crowd were press, but many were people who just wanted to see something torn down. Phones were already held high. The destruction would be captured on video, music would be added, and everybody would count their "likes" after the footage went live.

The case was probably as wrapped up as it was going to get. Pisa had given them the names of his remaining accomplices, all homeless kids, one with long gouges on his face from Iris's nails. DNA from the semen taken from the Lake of the Isles body was a match too. They were all in jail now, Leo and his team of terrors, awaiting trial. Clementine's autopsy had revealed she was left-handed. That was backed up by the girl's mother, whom Jude managed to track down with a photo of Clementine that had gone viral. The woman cried while admitting that her daughter—real name Mary—had done some terrible things to animals and later to children, beginning when she was very young. The bite marks were also a match, as Pisa had said they'd be.

Jude had been right about him. He'd quit college to take care of his ailing mother, in the process losing a full-ride math scholarship. The woman had died under circumstances that hadn't seemed suspicious due to her poor health. Pisa had killed her, and the overwhelming guilt of matricide, combined with a decrease in the popularity of his street performances, had been a trigger. And then he'd met Clementine . . .

Jude was relieved to find that Professor Masucci hadn't been involved. She liked him. And she'd already picked up some special tea to deliver to his apartment while he awkwardly basked in the media attention his role in solving the crime had brought him. The one thing that still haunted her: they hadn't found Elliot's body. She thought maybe Leo had been lying, but Elliot's credit cards hadn't been used, and they couldn't get a signal off his phone, and no one had spotted his car. Jude was feeding Elliot's cat, trying to talk Uriah into taking him. The apartment would have to be vacated soon, and she'd offered to pack up the few things that were left. She hadn't given up on him. Maybe that was delusional of her, but she wanted a body.

She was sorry Elliot couldn't be here to document the demolition and add it to his photo collection. She'd almost postponed the event in hopes they'd find him, but things didn't look good. His return would more than likely be in the form of his body being found in the woods or in a lake. It didn't seem he had any siblings or a father, but they'd been able to locate his mother. Uriah had spoken to her a couple of times. She was in poor health and currently bedridden, and a trip from Texas to Minneapolis was more than she could handle right now. A sad situation all the way around.

Today, before leaving the pet-friendly hotel where she and Roof Cat were staying while her apartment was cleaned and painted after being the scene of a murder, Jude had put on a black knit cap to cover her white hair, hoping her presence would go unnoticed. It didn't seem to help. People still did double takes, then quickly glanced away. The foreman spotted her, approached, and handed her a clipboard with a checklist attached. Every little box, from the permit to the environmental-hazard inspection, had been marked. The signature line was empty. "Gas and water have been disconnected and capped," he said. "We made a final examination of every room, so we're good to go. Just need you to date and sign off on it."

She signed the form and passed the clipboard back.

"That's all I need." His voice was jolly. "It's a small house, so it'll take about an hour, maybe a little more." He tucked the clipboard under his arm, strode away, and gave the man in the demolition excavator the signal to begin.

"It'll make a nice garden spot for the neighborhood," Uriah said, squinting and shading his eyes with his hand.

Jude had decided on the public garden, and she felt good about that. Something positive and beneficial. Studies had proven that green space reduced crime, and public gardens built community.

The operator in the cab of the excavator put the machine in gear and accelerated. Jude had expected a bulldozer, but the equipment was something used exclusively for demolition. Strange to think a company could sell enough of the things that demolished buildings to stay in business.

The engine revved, and the machine began to crawl forward on rubber tracks. With a whine and a shudder of metal, the bucket on the end of a hinged hydraulic arm moved into place, hovered spastically, then dropped to the roof. Looking like the jaws of a flesh-eating dinosaur, the metal teeth bit out a hole, exposing trusses and pink insulation. The arm shuddered and bobbed as it moved to take another bite.

Jude's phone vibrated. With scant attention, she pulled it from her pocket and glanced at the screen. The message was from Molly, their information specialist.

Elliot Kaplan's car is in the Minneapolis impound lot. His laptop was still inside when they processed the vehicle.

The machine continued to whine and the roof continued to collapse. Jude sent a reply.

Where was the car found?

Abandoned in an alley. The report is a bit unclear, but it seems power-line workers reported it when they disconnected the electricity to a house.

That information was followed by an address.

Jude wasn't sure if she responded before running straight for the demolition excavator, waving her arms and shouting. The foreman stepped in front of her with a *What the hell* look on his face.

"Stop!" she said. "Now!"

With a scowl, the foreman pulled out a walkie-talkie. He passed instructions to the man in the cab, and the diesel engine idled.

"You gave us permission to proceed," the foreman told Jude. His voice wasn't jolly now.

"I need to go inside the building."

He shook his head. "Too late. The structure's been compromised. That's why we have you sign off on it. It's a done deal."

"Are you sure you checked the entire house?" she asked.

"Yep."

"The basement?"

"Yep."

"The cell in the basement?"

"Yep."

"You personally?"

"No. One of my crew—"

She strode past him. He made the mistake of snatching her wrist. In one swift motion and without conscious thought, she put her self-defense classes into play, seized his hand, pulled, and twisted, bringing him to his knees. She let go as a cheer went up behind her.

The foreman pushed himself off the ground. He wasn't hurt, just humiliated.

"I don't like to be touched," she said in a half apology, picking up her dropped phone as Uriah appeared next to her.

"He had it coming," he said.

She had to give Uriah credit for no longer jumping to the reasonable conclusion of her shaky mental health. "Elliot might be in the house," she told him.

"That seems unlikely."

"Only if you trust someone to do their job in a competent and professional way." She ran for the back steps, Uriah beside her. "His car was impounded in the alley behind this property," she explained. "And I'm not confident someone checked the building thoroughly."

She kicked the door open with a crash. They both recoiled at the odor, then ducked inside. In unison, they activated flashlight apps, the beams reflecting off floating demolition dust. Above their heads, sunlight poured through the roof, and compromised beams creaked. The path to the basement was clear. Before Jude reached the concrete floor, she noted that the cell door was locked with the set of three deadbolts. She pounded down the steps, slid the bolts free, and pulled the door open. And discovered the source of the odor.

A man tumbled out.

Elliot.

While Uriah made gagging noises, Jude dragged Elliot's body from the cell. "It's too dark."

A beam of light wobbled closer. She glanced over her shoulder. Uriah was turned away, the back of his hand against his face as he held the light in Jude's general direction. She pressed two fingers to an ice-cold neck, felt a faint flutter, then looked up. "Call an ambulance."

The light vanished and Uriah made the call.

Jude pieced together the simple events that had led to this. Clementine had followed Elliot from the funeral to the house, where he'd come to take photos. She took his camera, locked him inside the cell, and left him to die. Like Jude, he'd used the corner for a toilet. Then, later, when he was delirious from dehydration, he'd slept in his own excrement.

"You're going to be okay," Jude told him, unsure if he was aware of anything.

"Ambulance is on the way," Uriah said.

Elliot's lips moved slightly and Jude leaned closer.

It seemed like a superhuman feat, but he managed to whisper two words through cracked lips. "My . . . cat?"

CHAPTER 55

Elliot lay in bed, petting the purring cat on his stomach. A week had passed since he'd almost gotten buried in the demolition of Jude's house, longer since the girl named Clementine had left him to die. Turned out, she'd been squatting there sometimes. He'd walked right into her lair. Now he was back in his apartment, and Jude was upstairs after her stint in a hotel. It was late, a little after one a.m., and he was talking to his mother on the phone.

"How are you doing?" she asked. "Are you okay?"

"I'm fine now." He'd come around pretty quickly after the fluid IV. It had taken less time to feel humiliated by the way Jude and her partner had found him, lying in his own shit. He couldn't face her. He tried to avoid the public spaces of their building, and if he did run into her, he mumbled hello and kept his eyes averted.

"Honey, you scared me to death," his mother said. "But I didn't give up hope, and I never thought you were dead."

No, she wouldn't have.

"Do you feel well enough to talk about it? About her?"

"She's not as bad as you think."

"Don't let her find out who you really are, or your life could be in danger again."

"She *saved* my life." He patted the cat on the head. "I like her."

"You've been brainwashed."

There would be no winning the argument, so he didn't try. "I need more time to figure things out. I'm thinking of sticking around and maybe opening a private-investigator service."

"Your father sent you to college to study journalism and photography."

"Both of those helped with the case. My photos were instrumental in solving it. You could move here. Minneapolis isn't a bad town." He didn't mention the high crime. "You can stay with me. We'll get home health care just like you have in Texas."

"And live in the same building with that woman? Not going to happen."

"I think you'd like her."

"I'll never like the person who shot your father dead in the middle of the interstate."

Elliot had believed his mother's theory for a while, that Jude was evil and had framed and killed both his father and half brother so she could inherit millions. But Elliot didn't think that anymore. Jude was a puzzle, she was messed up, but she was a good person. And now Elliot wondered about his mother's story. Worse, was it possible she'd been abducted by Jude's father, Phillip Schilling, like he'd abducted so many other women, and he'd let her go for some reason? Maybe after she found out she was pregnant. Maybe Elliot himself had been some form of leverage. He didn't know if he wanted to discover that he was the result of rape, and that his benefactor was every bit as evil as Jude believed him to be.

He'd been in touch with the person handling his father's estate. Through the attorney's urging, Elliot had taken a DNA test. When a recent email confirmed the match, he'd requested that the results be kept a secret for now. He didn't care about an inheritance, but his mother was getting older, and she'd had a tough life. Money could help. She deserved something.

"What's that?" she asked. "It sounds like someone screaming."

"Just the TV. Bye, Mom. I love you."

"Bye."

They disconnected. With a sigh, Elliot grabbed the broom and banged the handle against the ceiling.

ABOUT THE AUTHOR

Anne Frasier is a *New York Times* and *USA Today* bestselling author. Her award-winning books span the genres of suspense, mystery, thriller, romantic suspense, paranormal, and memoir. *The Body Reader* received the 2017 Thriller Award for Best Paperback Original Novel from International Thriller Writers. Other honors include a RITA for romantic suspense and a Daphne du Maurier Award for paranormal romance. Her thrillers have hit the *USA Today* bestseller list and have been featured in Mystery Guild, Literary Guild, and Book of the Month Club. Her memoir *The Orchard* was an *O, The Oprah Magazine* Fall Pick; a One Book, One Community read; a B+ review in *Entertainment Weekly*; and one of the Librarians' Best Books of 2011. She divides her time between the city of Saint Paul, Minnesota, and her writing studio in rural Wisconsin.